BLURRED VISION

A Polly Hart Chronicle

Also by Steve Harrison

TimeStorm

Earthsale
in **Existence is Elsewhen**

BLURRED VISION

A Polly Hart Chronicle

Steve Harrison

Elsewhen Press

Blurred Vision

First published in Great Britain by Elsewhen Press, 2019
An imprint of Alnpete Limited

Elsewhen Press, PO Box 757, Dartford, Kent DA2 7TQ
www.elsewhen.press

British Library Cataloguing in Publication Data.
A catalogue record for this book is available from the British Library.

ISBN 978-1-911409-46-5 Print edition
ISBN 978-1-911409-56-4 eBook edition

Designed and formatted by Elsewhen Press

For Sophia

And for all those lovely memories of us reading together

LATER

You know when you come up with a course of action, but suspect it's a bad idea? Or, more likely, you *know* for certain that it's a bad idea, but you go ahead anyway?

The rational, intelligent part of your mind is fully aware of the dangers and tells you, *if you do this it will end badly. Everything that can go wrong, will go wrong. You could be seriously injured or even die.*

You accept without doubt that this is sound advice and, in addition to your conscious thoughts, every instinct agrees. You know in your bones it is true. But the remaining half percent of uncertainty – the irrational, stupid mind – says, *Bah! Stop exaggerating. If everyone had this negative approach to life, we'd still be living in caves.*

Yeah! you agree, as rationality and intelligence shake their metaphorical heads, *that's right.* You are not going to wimp out.

And stupid wins.

As Kylie crouched behind a tree, breathing heavily after her long sprint and facing imminent death, she took a moment to reflect. All of this could have been avoided. She could have remained where she was. She should have stayed for a short visit, just to have a quick look around, and then returned. Even until a couple of hours ago it would have been easy to fly away and no one would ever have known. Coulda, woulda, shoulda. Didn't.

Maybe her mother was right: "One day, you will go too far." *Or in this case, not far enough.*

Kylie's rational, intelligent mind was now in a huff, as though looking at her with arched eyebrows. *Oh, so now you want my help? Sorry, I don't do escape, I only do common sense and considered avoidance. Why don't you ask Ms Half Percent? I'm sure she has it all worked out.*

But Ms Half Percent was nowhere to be found in the conscious recesses of Kylie's mind and was probably hiding behind a different tree.

Kylie cautiously peered out from behind *her* tree. It was dark under the leafy canopy, only a little moonlight filtering through to the forest floor. Not that it mattered. Her four pursuers were equipped with lightflexers and to them the forest was lit up like a shopping centre. Kylie's only defence was her hologram projection refractor, a device that sent out multiple images of herself each time she made a dash, filling the forest with running Kylies. The real Kylie had so far avoided the blasts from their vaporons. So far.

Kylie could see the group now, the unarmed leader and the three armed girls, standing two hundred yards away in the open field that had been a heavily wooded part of the forest only seconds earlier. One of them was pointing away to the right and the others turned their weapons in that direction, allowing Kylie a few more welcome seconds of rest. Their silent vaporons opened up and she felt the concussion from the ground-shaking WHUMP! as a dozen trees were atomised. So much for English forest conservation orders. More open field.

Not looking good, said Kylie's rational, intelligent mind rather superfluously.

If I go, you go, thought Kylie in response, which finally reunited her and all parts of her mind on the same page. Unfortunately, focussed though they were, none of them knew what to do.

But the only course of action was to run again. She stood up against the tree. The pointing man and his female companions now turned back in her direction. Kylie steeled herself and made a final – she hoped not too final – apology to herself. *I'm sorry for getting us into this mess, but hey, I'm only human.*

She bolted away further into the forest at speed, replica hologram Kylies darting in all directions. WHUMP!

EARLIER

ONE

The bell. *At last!* Polly Hart slammed her textbook closed, jumped up and pushed through her classmates and out into the hall. It had been the longest day ever, possibly in the history of the world. So slow, in fact, that unless she was mistaken, this time last week it was tomorrow. But tomorrow last week was in the past and... *stop doing that, Polly*! Whatever the time and date, now she could go home and get to work.

Polly felt a tugging at her sleeve and knew before she turned around that it was Josh Steele. They had known each other since they were three – their families were very good friends – and in the twelve years since, he had never outgrown the irritating habit. Polly stopped and turned. Josh had recently begun standing too close and staring at her, and it made her uncomfortable. Particularly when he didn't speak. Like now.

"Is there some particular reason you stopped me? I'm in a hurry."

"Kate is missing."

Polly grabbed Josh's fingers, prised them from her sleeve and rubbed the pinch marks on her shirt. She frowned. She'd have to get dad to iron them out. "No she isn't. I saw her during lunch."

"But she wasn't in class."

"Lucky her."

Josh glared at her and stomped off, but before she could resume her exit, another voice called her to a halt. Polly sighed.

"Ms Hart!" It was Mr Oberon, the science teacher, a large and imposing man in his fifties, very intimidating in his 1950s three-piece tweed suit with leather elbow patches, bow tie and watch chain hanging out of his waistcoat. He also had an unfortunate twitch in his left eye. Unfortunate mainly because when you looked at him it was hard not to develop your own twitch, which Mr Oberon always took as being mocked, whether that was the intention or not.

Polly turned and Mr Oberon smiled and twitched, which was not pleasant. The smile was such a rare expression, the rest of his face seemed confused.

"Did you speak to your mother?"

"Not yet. She's been working nights and we keep missing each other." Polly looked at the time on her phone, hoping the teacher would get the hint. "I should catch her now before she goes to work."

"Hmm," said Mr Oberon, taking a puff on his pipe, which never held any tobacco. "Well, don't let me hold you up. Please give her my regards and I look forward to hearing what she has to say."

Polly nodded and managed to stop her eye from twitching just long enough to turn her back on the teacher and dash for the main door.

"No running in the corridor, Ms Hart," called Mr Oberon.

Polly burst from the building, free at last, and was about to bound down the stairs three, perhaps even four, at a time, when she felt the familiar tugging at her sleeve. More creases!

Polly turned to find Josh standing even closer this time, so close she could clearly see her reflection in his eyes. A nose in each.

"What now?"

"You going home?" Josh asked hopefully.

Polly frowned. "I'd be there already if you didn't keep grabbing my shirt."

Josh looked at his hand, surprised, and released his grip. Then his face contorted into that familiar cheeky, embarrassed expression. Polly couldn't frown for long when he did that.

"Mind if I tag along?"

Polly shrugged. "Please yourself." She felt glad, but couldn't quite understand why. "Kate's supposed to be coming, too, but I can't wait." Polly set off down the steps.

"There she is," said Josh, pointing across the yard.

Kate Andrews walked briskly towards them, almost jogging, her cheeks flushed. She was a tiny girl and looked even smaller with three much bigger girls hard on her heels.

Polly felt her anger rising. 'Evil' Gwen Hooper was right behind Kate, taunting her all the way. Her only-slightly-less-evil followers, Helen Kerslake and Maddy Summers, laughed and heckled.

Kate saw Polly and Josh and ran the last few yards to join them, gratitude and relief on her face.

The three girls stopped nearby, not as threatening now the odds had evened.

"Look at this," said Gwen. "A nerd convention."

"And what are you," responded Polly, "a reunion of Macbeth's witches?"

Polly's blood boiled. She hated being called a nerd, even though she did sometimes have slight nerd-like tendencies. Occasionally. *OK, more than occasionally, but not mostly. Maybe sixty percent of the time at school, give or take, and maybe thirty percent outside, unless a problem...*

Gwen laughed. "Look at her. She's drifted into nerdland, probably thinking about Eisenstein's theory of relatives or something."

"Why are you always picking on Kate?" asked Josh, with just the right amount of feigned interest.

Gwen summoned up her most innocent expression, which, frankly, wasn't worth the effort. "We were just having a chat, weren't we, Kate?"

Polly and Josh turned to Kate. "That's right," she agreed. "Gwen was threatening me, while I was analysing the root cause of the insecurity which manifests itself in her compulsion to bully people. It's actually fascinating, Gwen. Let's talk again tomorrow." Kate had no problems with being a nerd, Polly knew, and often described herself as 'nerdacious'.

Polly and Josh burst out laughing, while Gwen struggled for a response. Her face reddened, but that was about it. She turned on her heel and stormed off. Helen and Maddy gave them a nasty look, which, frankly, was pathetic, and hurried off after Gwen.

"Nice one," said Josh.

"Well, I'll probably pay for it tomorrow," said Kate ruefully.

Polly watched Gwen cross the yard to meet her boyfriend, Eddie Burke. How someone like Gwen could snag the most handsome boy in school was beyond her, she thought jealously. Maybe she's holding his mother hostage or something. Eddie was far too nice for her, though to be fair he was not the sharpest knife in the block. But they'd been going out for at least six weeks, so maybe it was the real thing. *Shame*.

"Didn't you want to get home?" said Josh, following her gaze and looking annoyed.

Polly looked at her watch. "Oh, yes," said Polly. "Let's go." She hurried away, Kate and Josh in hot pursuit.

TWO

Josh followed closely behind Polly and Kate, who were deep in conversation, speaking some strange language involving satellites, orbit trajectories and probability theories. The drawback of having nerd friends, he supposed. He also supposed he should find out what they were on about.

"What are you both on about?"

They stopped and turned, surprised he was still there, which was extremely irritating. *And rude*.

"The satellites," said Polly.

Josh looked at her, completely blank.

"The satellites," repeated Kate, louder, as though talking to an elderly uncle who had lost both his hearing and his marbles. "It's all over the news."

Resisting the urge to finish the job started by Gwen, Josh leant closer. "I don't follow nerd news."

Polly laughed, which was nice, and Kate frowned. But then she grinned.

"Come on," said Polly. "I have to get home."

They set off again at pace, this time all three of them side by side.

"You've heard about the unexplained damage to satellites over the last couple of weeks, haven't you?" asked Polly.

Josh had no idea what she was talking about. It was the football season, after all. "Oh, those satellites? Yes, of course."

Polly looked at him and he knew she knew he didn't know.

They stopped at the corner of Waterloo Street, where they usually parted ways.

"See you tomorrow," said Kate.

"You're not coming back to my place?" said Polly, surprised.

"No. It's been a big day. I need a large glass of milk to settle my nerves."

"We have milk," said Polly.

"Soy milk?"

"Ah, no."

"Maybe I can come over later."

"OK," said Polly. She looked disappointed. *I'm still here*, thought Josh.

"Thanks for helping me," said Kate. She walked away down the street.

Polly watched her for a while and turned to Josh. "Do you want to come back?"

Josh could feel his blood begin to boil. It had been happening a lot lately, particularly around Polly. He found himself analysing every comment, each look and her tone of voice. Trouble was, she hadn't changed at all, she was still as horrible to him as always. He was the one who had changed. But he didn't have to put up with being a poor second choice, though. *It was just plain rude*.

He stared at her, all hopeful expression and that cute dimple in her cheek, while he assembled a clever sentence in his head telling her where she could stick her satellites.

"OK," said Josh.

"Great," said Polly, setting off again without looking back. Josh had to hurry to keep up.

"Now," she continued, "I'll give you the dummy's version."

Josh learned that in the last fortnight a dozen satellites had suffered unexplained damage, some of it serious, most of it superficial. The space agencies were baffled and the internet was filled with speculation and conspiracy theories. "It's a real mystery!" exclaimed Polly.

Polly's mum worked for NASReC, the North Atlantic Space Research Centre, and was a key member of the team conducting the European investigation, hence science head Mr Oberon's interest. Polly followed events closely and had been doing her own research. She was in a hurry to see if her mum had any news to tell her before she left for work. "Then I need to follow my own lead."

Josh smiled and nodded. This promised to be as exciting as a school assembly.

Polly was jogging by the time she turned into Edgehill Road, Josh running alongside. "Why can't you just ring your mum?"

"She keeps her phone on silent and never listens to her messages."

"Oh," said Josh.

Polly looked a little embarrassed. "She's quite mad, you know," she said. "And dad's worse." She started to get that faraway look on her face again, but quickly snapped out of it. "There she is!"

She sprinted the last fifty yards as Marianne Hart backed her car out onto the street. Josh struggled to keep up. Polly had won the girls' one hundred metres earlier in the year with a time faster than all but two of the boys in their own race. Josh was neither of them.

Marianne saw them and stopped.

"Hey mum!" called Polly.

Marianne lowered the window. "Sorry, Polly, I have to dash. Hi Josh."

"Hi, Mrs Hart."

"Your dinner's in the fridge. Throw it in the oven for half an hour, OK?"

Josh joined Polly at the car window. "Oh, Mrs Hart, mum asked if you all want to come over for dinner on Sunday."

"We'd love to, but with this work stuff going on, I'm not sure. Tell your mum I'll ring her."

"Don't hold your breath," said Polly quietly out of the corner of her mouth.

With a wave, Marianne backed out of the driveway.

"Mum! The satellite last night…"

"I wrote the details down on the pad in the kitchen."

She drove away and Polly turned to Josh, suddenly animated. "Come on."

This actually was genuinely exciting to her, Josh realised. *Perhaps I should take more interest.*

THREE

Josh followed Polly inside. She and her parents often went round to Josh's place for dinner, but it was a while since he had been inside their house.

Not that it made much difference to Josh. Treating the place like his own home, he headed straight for the fridge, opened the door and broke off a large piece of chocolate from the bar Polly had hidden behind a jar of gherkins. "You're so predictable," he said, wedging the whole thing in his mouth.

"You'll have to replace that," she said absently as she grabbed the scribbled note from the kitchen bench and read the long number. "That looks familiar," she said, looking back at Josh with excitement in her eyes.

Good for you, thought Josh absently as he turned to look at the photos on the fridge. He touched the one of Polly and her parents to straighten it, but it slipped from the magnet, danced in the breeze and wafted under the fridge. He knelt down but couldn't reach it.

"I'll get it later." Polly shook her head at the sheepish Josh and waved the paper. "Come on."

They stopped in the corridor at a door studded from top to bottom with a dozen locks of all styles and sizes, some for keys, others with tumblers and a couple with digital touch pads. Polly took a key from her pocket, opened one lock and paused, pretending she had forgotten the other keys. But Josh pushed open the door and walked in. "It wasn't funny the first five thousand times, either."

Polly grinned and followed him inside.

Both she and her parents used the office. It had three large mismatched desks, all covered with computer equipment, two a complete mess, the other very tidy.

Josh lifted a pile of documents from a chair next to an untidy desk and rolled it to the neat one, next to Polly.

She sat down and switched the computer on, placed the note on the empty desk and smoothed it out while she waited. She saw Josh looking at the giant space-related posters on the wall, particularly the huge signed photo of her grinning mum being carried like a plank by four fully suited NASA astronauts. "I've always loved that photo," he said.

"Yep. It's pretty cool." Polly's mum and her dad, a mathematician, worked at NASA for a year on an exchange program when Polly was nine and the family lived in Houston.

Polly smiled at the memory; but there was work to do! She turned to find Josh sitting so close their knees almost touched. Polly swung her legs away and her cheeks reddened.

"What are you doing?" asked Josh, pretending not to notice. He nodded towards the computer.

Polly grabbed the note and waved it. "I'll tell you in a sec." The screen lit up and she attacked the keyboard until the screen showed a list of ten numbers. She scanned them and looked at the number written on the paper. "Yes!" she exclaimed, pumping her fist and making Josh jump. "I'm a genius!" she declared, then reddened again, remembering she was not alone.

Josh raised his eyebrows.

Polly spun around in her chair and waved the paper, too excited to even notice their knees touching. Josh felt his cheeks burn this time, which for some reason made Polly lose her train of thought.

"It's…it's…um…er…"

"Slow down," said Josh. "Take a few deep breaths." He took a few himself.

"OK." Polly forced herself to breathe. "OK," she said again as Josh imagined the jumble of thoughts in her head disentangling. "I've been tracking the satellite incidents and came up with this model." She hit the keys again and the screen was filled with a mathematical formula. She leant back proudly so Josh could see her genius in all its glory.

"Very impressive. What is it?"

"It's a mathematical formula. It's the sum of all the satellite information I could get hold of, some 73% of all satellites orbiting the earth, the precise trajectories of all the damaged satellites and, here's where it gets interesting, it predicts the location of future incidents."

"Are you serious? How can you know all that?"

"I'll come to that. Anyway, I came up with ten likely satellites…" – she flicked back to the first screen – "…and this is one of them!" She waved her mum's note, proud of herself.

"That's really clever, Polly. Should we grab something to eat?"

"No, no! You don't understand. I activated the maintenance cameras on four of these satellites last night. I couldn't access the others, but this..."

"Isn't that against the law?" asked Josh.

Polly shrugged. "I suppose. In a strictly legal sense, maybe. But that doesn't matter. I..."

"Stop!" said Josh. "Polly, what are you doing? It may be cool, but you could go to jail."

Polly was getting frustrated. "No way. I'm very careful. I hacked into the main computer system of the Chinese space agency and routed all my commands via an Indian space agency mainframe which in turn has been hacked by the Chinese secret service."

Josh's mouth hung open.

"If NASA or the CIA tries to trace me, they'll assume it's the Chinese."

Josh rubbed his temples. "Have you gone nuts? Chinese spies, the CIA, NASA! What have you done?"

"It's science, Josh. This is bigger than mere countries. I'm doing this for the world."

"That's what all the movie villains say."

Polly laughed. "It's very safe. I'm untraceable."

"Hmm." Josh wasn't convinced.

"You don't want to see the footage?"

He looked at her hard. "No. Well, yes. A little bit, then. Maybe."

"Great." Polly attacked her keyboard like a deranged concert pianist and Josh tried to follow the succession of pages flashing across the screen, as they filled in turn with Chinese and Indian characters, then a long list of cascading numbers before the screen froze on the NASA internal access page. There were four boxes to complete, none of them marked with instructions.

Polly grinned at Josh and began filling them in with numbers and letters.

"How do you know those?" asked Josh.

"Dad."

"He gave them to you?"

"Not exactly. They change every day and dad uses a formula based on family birthdays, the names of his cousins and the number of letters in the names of the Grand National winners in odd years, counting backwards from 1997."

Josh opened his mouth, but closed it again.

"I found it taped under his desk. He can remember blackboard length strings of formulae, but passwords – forget it."

"Oh," said Josh.

"Here we go." The screen went black, then red, then yellow. Red writing flashed:

UNAUTHORIZED ENTRY
WILL RESULT IN PROSECUTION AND
IMPRISONMENT OF UP TO 300 YEARS

"Americans are very dramatic," said Polly.

"Still..."

"It's no different to those piracy warnings on DVDs." She had the grace to look embarrassed and avoided looking at Josh.

A menu appeared, Polly clicked, another menu, click, menu, click, click click click.

"Here we are." The screen displayed

Satellite type: E6750DCB
Purpose: Classified
Clearance: A1
Designation: Top Secret
Reference: ....

Polly copied the number from the slip of paper and hit 'Enter'. She sat back triumphant with her arms folded and smiled at Josh.

He smiled back, but he looked worried. "If they put you in an English prison, I'll visit you."

Polly looked troubled and Josh felt a little sorry for her. She clearly hadn't considered the legal ramifications. But suddenly she brightened again as the maintenance camera on the US military spy satellite sparked into life on the screen.

"Here we go," she said, her voice a strangled squeak. She coughed and continued in a deeper voice. "This was last night."

Josh looked at her as though she was mad, then turned back to the screen.

The camera was angled to cover the side of the cylinder shaped satellite body, revealing a view similar to that from a car's wing mirror. Aerials bristled along the entire length, making the vehicle look like a shiny hedgehog, and the picture was remarkably clear. Distant stars twinkled beyond the satellite, but there was no sense of movement.

"It's travelling at fifteen thousand miles an hour and if that was on Earth you could go from New York to London in twelve and a quarter minutes!"

"Wow!" exclaimed Josh. "Have you got a pen, I'd like to write that down."

Polly actually reached for a pen before she realised he was being sarcastic. Josh grinned at her, though he didn't take his eyes off the screen for long.

"Well, I think it's interesting," said Polly, which sounded pathetic to Josh.

They watched for a couple of minutes and nothing happened.

"I'll move it forward," said Polly.

"Good idea."

She moved the time bar forward slowly until something caught her eye. "Whoa."

"What?"

She slid the bar back. "Watch…there in the background!"

Josh saw it straight away, something moved between the satellite and the stars. They were still visible, but it was like seeing them through a shimmering lace curtain. "What is it?"

Polly leant closer to the screen. "I have no idea."

A small hole appeared in the shimmering, revealing a reflected metallic glint. Something black moved toward the camera. Polly and Josh exchanged a glance. The object flexed, snake-like, then changed direction and they saw it was a long, black extending arm, its movements fluid and snake-like, with what looked like pincers at the end. The pincers opened and pushed against the side of the satellite, making the camera shudder.

"This is it! Unbelievable!" shouted Polly.

The arm moved on, scratching marks along the metal side. The camera vibrated with each movement.

"That's not very nice," said Josh. "That's vandalism, that is." *I sound like my dad!*

Suddenly, the arm reared up, like a cobra, and the pincers turned towards the camera. It moved a little closer and small lights glowed on each pincer. They were like eyes and to Josh it felt as though they were boring into him. Then the arm flew toward the camera and the screen seemed to explode with a deafening bang and blinding light. Josh yelped in shock and Polly fell off her chair. They were unable to see or hear for a moment as hundreds of flashbulbs seemed to explode all around them.

Finally, the room came back into focus and she saw that Josh was glaring down at her, his cheeks bright red. "You did that on purpose!" He felt incredibly embarrassed.

"No," protested Polly. "I had no idea that was…"

"Oh, shut up," said Josh and ran out of the room.

He could hear Polly behind him as he stomped angrily down the hall. He slammed the door hard behind him as he left the house, his cheeks so red they felt hot to the touch.

FOUR

Dinner was tasteless – *it must have been cooked by mum* – and lonely. Polly picked at her food, but didn't eat much. She tried to call Josh, but he didn't answer. And when she called his house, Mr Steele said Josh "has a mood on," whatever that meant. *Josh was spooked by what happened, that's all. He'll be fine when she explained.* But she didn't like him being angry with her, which was odd. It had never bothered her before.

She flicked through the channels on the TV, but nothing interested her. She knew she was avoiding the computer. In truth, she was spooked, too. Whatever that thing was, it had only attacked the camera, so why did she feel it was looking directly at her?

Polly edged back into the office. The circuit breaker on the power board had been triggered by the flash, so she flicked it back on and turned on her computer. Then she retreated to the hall and watched from the doorway. The screen took longer than usual to fire up and then bright, indecipherable full-screen images flashed rapidly. Polly edged away further into the hall, hardly daring to watch.

The screen finally settled on a bright image of the earth from space, which looked suspiciously like live footage. *Not good*, thought Polly. A cold sweat broke out on her face. *This could mean serious trouble.* She dropped to the ground, crawled across the room and underneath her desk. She pulled the power plug from the socket and slid back out to look tentatively up at the screen. It was black.

Urgent, decisive action was clearly called for.

I'll worry about it in the morning, she decided. *Maybe it will have fixed itself by then.*

For once, she left the hall light on and climbed the stairs to her bedroom. The hairs on the back of her neck were standing on end and she felt strongly that she was not alone. But there was nobody there. The house was empty. *Wasn't it?*

She decided to check. Her parents' bedroom was its usual

mess, but empty. She wished her dad was home, but like mum he was mostly working night shifts at the moment. The wardrobe and en suite were also deserted, as was the spare room and main bathroom. She felt she should check downstairs again, but decided there was no way she was going back down there. She left all the upstairs lights on and went back into her bedroom and locked the door.

This is nuts, she thought, sitting on the edge of her bed. *Settle down*. But Josh was right. She could go to jail. Forever. Or maybe they wouldn't bother prosecuting her. A joint Indian, Chinese, American hit squad would snatch her and she would be pushed out of an aircraft without a parachute high over the mid-Atlantic, never to be seen again. Or she could be rendered to an unnamed Middle Eastern country for a spot of torture. Or given a choice between execution or a suicide mission behind enemy lines, where there really was a fate worse than death…

Polly did not feel settled down at all and when she heard the sudden tap on her bedroom window she screamed, leapt from the bed and tugged desperately at the door handle, momentarily at a complete loss as to how to unlock it.

The second tap made her freeze. She slowly turned and flattened herself against the door. The curtains were drawn and she wondered how many were outside and what weapons they had and if they would open fire as soon as she opened them and how much of the house would be left standing afterwards and what they would say at the funeral of an enemy of the state. If she was allowed a funeral, that was.

A strange calmness came over her. There was no escape. The house must be surrounded, or they wouldn't have alerted her by tapping on the window. *I'm resigned to my fate*, thought Polly, dramatically, *and this is my last moment of freedom and maybe even life itself.*

She calmly walked to the window, raised her arms and slowly opened the curtains. She closed her eyes and clenched her teeth for the expected floodlights and volley of gunfire and held her hands high above her head. Nothing happened and after a very long moment, she opened one eye. All she could see was her ridiculous reflection in the window. No lights. No SWAT team. No tanks. It could be a trick, though, so she stood there, hands aloft, for another two minutes, opening her other eye to confirm the evidence of the first. Then her arms got tired and she let them slowly fall to her sides. After another minute, she started to edge backwards across the bedroom, her eyes fixed on the window, and when she backed into the door, she reached behind to flick the light switch off, plunging the room into darkness.

She stood, frozen. The street lights were unchanged and the flicker from Mr Granger's old square TV three doors away deceptively indicated all was normal. But she could see nothing else. *What were they playing at?*

Gingerly, Polly edged back to the window. Nothing appeared amiss, *and yet…*

It was a still night, not a breath of wind. She opened the window and slowly leant out. Paranoid Mr Granger's TV blared, the coloured light from the screen clearly visible through the uncurtained window, which was framed by the red glow from the two security cameras trained on his garden. The old man didn't own anything less than forty years old, so Polly didn't know why he bothered, unless he was scared of antique thieves. Everything appeared to be as it always was. *But it wasn't.*

When she looked up from the garden, level with her bedroom window, she saw it. Or, more accurately, she didn't see what she saw, because she could see through it. A seemingly very thin, shimmering lace curtain hung between her house and next door. *Just like the one between the satellite and the stars!*

Polly's legs buckled and she had to grab the windowsill to stop herself falling over. The 'curtain' appeared to be circular and roughly ten yards wide. It made the house next door ripple beyond it like a wave and Mr Granger's TV sound became distorted and seemed to echo around the gardens. Polly tried to move, but couldn't. None of her limbs worked, though her eyes were blinking rapidly and she could feel sweat trickling down her back. *Yuck! Where's the SWAT team when you want one?*

A gap appeared in the curtain and widened into a door-sized shape. More curtain material flowed from the base of the opening, a kind of platform walkway, unravelling quickly to reach the window. Polly would have swallowed, but it felt like she had a golf ball lodged in her throat.

A dull light could be seen through the opening, but this was replaced by a figure. The shape and size looked human and when it walked along the curtain platform, it walked like a human, too. Polly stopped blinking and stared as the figure got closer, but she couldn't make out any details, despite the close proximity.

The figure ducked down and stepped through the window onto the sill and looked around the room. At least that's what it looked like it was doing. The figure was literally a blur. A three dimensional grey, human-shaped smudge.

Polly finally regained control of her legs and backed away. The smudge didn't seem too interested in her, turning its fuzzy head this way and that to look at Polly's posters and interesting nick-nacks, like the rock with the fossilised insect she picked up on a geography field trip.

But Polly could not make sense of what she saw. The figure was not just blurred, it was out of focus. But however hard she squinted, it didn't make any difference. She backed into the door and hit her head. The unfocussed head angled towards her and stood there, presumably staring. The figure was a little taller than Polly and its blurred outline pulsated lightly, the edges swirling softly like contained smoke.

The figure took a step toward her and Polly was stunned when it spoke in a very deep, yet female voice. "Take me to your leader, Earth creature."

Polly's mouth dropped open, but no sound escaped.

Blur-woman raised her hands in a conciliatory gesture. "Sorry," she said, "but I've always wanted to say that." This time the voice was higher, younger – sounding a similar age to Polly – and the accent was a very odd mix of English, American, French and…something else. Bizarre.

Polly still had her mouth open and although she tried to speak, nothing came out. She closed it again and squinted at the figure.

"Your face will stay like that," it warned, "and I won't look any different."

The blur sat down on the bed. "This is where you can ask questions."

But Polly was speechless. It was like she had a mouthful of wool. This couldn't be real. "Who are you," she tried to say, but the noise that seeped from her mouth sounded like a resigned sigh. "Whooooo…"

"Who am I?" said the blur, inclining her head. Polly imagined she had an unfocussed look of amusement on her face. "I'm Kylie."

The spell was instantly broken. "Kylie!" Polly blurted. *This had to be a joke. Some kind of prank. One of those TV shows, maybe. I'm going to look a right idiot when this goes to air.*

The blurred figure laughed, a rich sound. "That's not my real name."

OK, thought Polly, *this is surreal, but hang in there and go with it. You must have dozed off and when you wake up you will have a good laugh about it.* "What is your real name?"

The blurred woman made a short sound like a chicken being strangled by an angry gorilla.

Polly let the sound hang in the air for a few seconds. "I'll call you Kylie."

"Good idea."

Polly felt behind her for the door handle.

"Take it easy," said Kylie, still with a hint of amusement. "You're perfectly safe. Think of me as a tourist."

Polly squinted back at her. She couldn't help herself. "Are you invading earth?"

"Are you kidding? Do you know how much that would cost?"

"Then what are you doing here?"

"We found you after you activated the camera on the satellite and were impressed by the other stuff you did to hide your tracks. Easy for us, but we all thought it was very cool. For an Earth human, anyway."

"You don't talk like an alien."

"How many do you know?" asked Kylie.

Polly couldn't argue with that. "Good point."

Even a vivid imagination had not prepared Polly for anything like this. *Here I am, having a perfectly ordinary conversation for the first time in human history with this, this thing – no offense – from outer space! Shouldn't it be more, well, historic?*

Kylie was silent and after a minute Polly couldn't stand it any longer. "We must be very primitive to you."

"Yep."

Polly started to relax. If Kylie was going to kill her, surely she would have done it by now. "What's with your…blurred appearance?"

Kylie shrugged. "Fuzzy logic? But seriously, are you prejudiced against blurred people? Because on some planets my people are treated like freaks. Go figure."

Polly rubbed her eyes. They were getting sore. "I have no problem with it." *Some of my best friends are blurred,* she wanted to joke, but didn't dare. "What happens now?"

Kylie suddenly stood, and Polly crashed back against the door.

"Now," said Kylie, "I'd like to invite you to come back with me."

Polly swallowed. "You're kidnapping me!"

"Look," Kylie sighed, "we checked up on you. You're an intelligent, nerdy person. It's true alien kidnappings took place for a while some years ago, but it was badly handled and failed because the removal team kept grabbing incredibly dumb people and no useful data was obtained. And no one got hurt, despite all the talk about bodies being probed. Honest. In this case, we just thought you might like to check out our ship and some other cool stuff and we'll drop you back later."

Polly looked at Kylie with a suspicious squint.

"But it's not compulsory and I understand if you have other plans for the evening," said Kylie, turning towards the window. "Maybe next time." She walked away.

"Wait!" yelled Polly.

Kylie turned back. "Come on, then."

This dream gets more and more interesting, thought Polly. There was something about Kylie that was reassuring. Her face, if she actually had one under that swirling mask, could not be read. *Maybe I'm just gullible, but she sounds like a regular girl. Alien. Whatever. Hopefully, she won't turn out to be a flesh eating monster*. Polly took another hard squint at Kylie and nodded. *There is no way on earth I'm going to refuse an offer like this.*

Polly watched from the windowsill as Kylie walked back to her…*pod*? She paused in the doorway and turned to look back. Polly looked down at the shimmering curtain walkway, the only thing between her and the ground twelve feet below. Then she turned back to take a long and hopefully not final look at her bedroom.

With a deep breath she stepped out. The platform was firm but spongy, like the safety matting in playgrounds, and felt safe. She held her breath and walked quickly across to the pod and stepped inside. A strange ripple of air briefly caressed her entire body, underneath her clothes, from the top of her head to the underneath of her feet. It was like she had been coated in something, but touching her hands and arms, she felt the same.

The door sealed behind her – at least that was what the 'whoosh' sounded like – and she suddenly felt nauseous. She was standing in mid-air.

Polly could not see how big the pod was, maybe ten feet across, maybe more. With nothing to see, there was no way to tell. The curtain had disappeared and she and Kylie stood, floating above the garden. There was no movement, but Polly put her hands out to stop the disorientating spinning sensation.

"You'd better sit down," said Kylie.

Polly's head spun. There were no seats or anything else. "Where?"

"Just sit. Let the seat find you."

It was ridiculous, but Polly really did need to sit down, so she bent her knees and immediately felt something envelop her bottom. "Whoa!"

"Relax," said Kylie.

Polly floated into a sitting position. It was the most comfortable chair she had ever experienced. It felt like it was moulded to her shape, snug at first, but as she relaxed it released its grip and, with each movement, the invisible 'chair' adapted to accommodate her.

"Cool!" said Polly.

"Watch this," said Kylie. She suddenly flung herself sideways, but only moved a couple of inches before her body was cushioned by an invisible force. It lowered her to a sitting position, but she stood again and this time tried to do a somersault. She was caught again and lowered to a sitting position next to Polly.

"It's like an airbag," said Polly.

"Hmm," said Kylie. "Not quite, but for want of a better explanation…"

This was the closest Polly had been to Kylie, and close up she could see the alien did have facial features. She was still very blurred, like a rough pencil sketch, and her outline swirled and shifted, but there were eyes in there and a mouth. Maybe a nose, but it wasn't clear.

"Now," said Kylie. "Can you feel any movement?"

"No. It feels like I could be sitting in a chair in my own house."

"OK, that's good," said Kylie. "However, while you are aboard this, er,..."

"Space pod?" offered Polly.

Kylie nodded. "Yeah, sure. Pod. Whatever. Anyway, this is how you will feel whenever you are aboard a pod or on one of our ships. It's the same whether you're in flight or stationary. You will have no sense of movement."

"Really? But that's good, isn't it?"

"Well..."

The earth suddenly dropped away from the pod as though it fell off a cliff at their feet and Polly felt her stomach lurch.

"Pretty cool, huh?" said Kylie.

But Polly felt very strange even though there was no sense of movement. It was disconcerting to see the earth leave without her. She felt alone and insignificant sitting in an invisible pod, watching the world go bye-bye.

Kylie laughed. "You will adjust in a few seconds. Just focus on a country."

Polly did so and suddenly felt a sense of elation. Britain appeared beneath her, its edges identified by the lights of cities, and as they flew higher – or the earth moved further away – the great European cities became visible, shining like jewels on this dark side of the world.

Then the sun became visible and the blinding light raced around the edge of the earth, forming a stunning halo. Polly looked at Kylie, seemingly sitting in space, her swirling outline dancing like fire in the sunlight.

"Ohhhhh," said Polly, which was as profound as she could manage. Her stomach had settled and she felt a kind of intense joy unlike anything she had ever experienced. The view was breathtaking, wondrous. Incredible.

"Something special, huh?" said Kylie. "But just wait until you see the double dawn of Rygol or the vapour fall between two planets in…I've forgotten the name. Anyway, there's a lot of neat stuff."

"Neat stuff," repeated Polly, entranced by the view. She took a deep breath and shook her head. "This is surreal."

Kylie nodded.

Polly turned to look at her. "Who are you?"

Kylie shrugged. "Believe it or not, Polly, in a universal context, I'm just a regular gal like you."

It was Polly's turn to laugh. Earth fell further away, but Polly was now used to the high speed non-movement of the pod and was prepared for the approach of Kylie's mother ship. At least that was what she assumed the shadow that fell across the pod was. The now familiar curtain appeared to envelop the pod, though she knew the pod had actually flown into the curtain. Earth and the surrounding stars faded from view and blackness descended on them. Polly felt a very brief flash of panic, but then the pod was sitting at one end of a brightly lit room the size and shape of a railway carriage.

"This is it," said Kylie.

Polly was disappointed. The spaceship looked too familiar and too ordinary, the walls were smooth and bare – devoid of screens or flashing controls – but there were tables and chairs, admittedly oddly designed, and a general air of…untidiness. Half a dozen blurred figures were in the room, a couple of them waving their fuzzy arms like orchestra conductors, the others draped lazily over the furniture, one with out-of-focus feet up on a table. Music was playing in the background. Polly vaguely recognised it and assumed they were tuned in to a radio station on Earth.

"We're not weightless," said Polly.

"There's no fooling you," said Kylie.

This is very weird, decided Polly, in what she reckoned was her biggest ever understatement. Maybe this was a dream, after all. But then she decided she had to go with the flow. "Very nice."

Kylie laughed again. "It's a dump, I know, but it does the job. Let me do the intros."

Kylie walked from the pod, or through the pod. Polly could no longer see it and had no idea if it was still there. She wondered if she should stand and was immediately lifted back to her feet. She followed Kylie to the others, gingerly feeling for the pod doorway. There was nothing there.

The other six aliens approached and Polly saw they were different heights, most shorter than Kylie, but two of them taller. Each was also a slightly different muted colour; yellows, reds and greens, possibly their uniforms under the fuzziness. Polly squinted hard, but they were no clearer than Kylie.

"This is Larry," said Kylie, nodding at the tallest alien.

"Howdy," said Larry, in an accent that sounded like a Russian making a poor attempt at an American accent.

Polly held out her hand and Larry turned to Kylie, who shrugged. "Why not."

Larry gripped Polly's hand and they shook. It was like being enveloped in a warm, firm sponge. Polly felt a wave of electricity pulse through her fingers and then up her arm and through her body. It didn't hurt, but when Larry let go, her whole body tingled. It felt, well, nice. She grinned.

Kylie introduced the rest of her shipmates. The other tall alien was Roger, who said 'Wassup?" in a high pitched boyish voice. Three of the remaining four were female and everyone sounded young, like Polly. At least Polly assumed they were female and made a mental note to ask Kylie later.

The first was Jenny, who asked her, "How's it hangin'?"

Betty: "Pleased to meet you."

Lateesha: "Hi, gorgeous."

The last was a boy called Rafael, who stood very close to Kylie. So close he reminded her of Josh. *He would love this,* she suddenly thought.

"You look taller in real life," said Rafael.

Like the others, they all appeared to have attended Bad Accent classes.

"Hi guys," said Polly, more than a little disorientated. This was not how she imagined something as historic as the first ever human contact with an alien race would transpire. She felt numb, wedged between the exciting and the underwhelming.

They were all looking at her. *I think they are all looking at me*. "Why are you here?" she asked.

"We had nothing better to do, "said Rafael.

Kylie and the others laughed, but to Polly it sounded forced, which made her uneasy. It was frustrating that she couldn't make out their faces. She squinted again, just in case. *No good.*

"No, seriously," said Polly, becoming concerned. "What's going on? I'm assuming you didn't come here for my amusement."

Polly also assumed the subsequent turning of the alien heads meant they were glancing furtively at each other. More squinting couldn't confirm this, but Polly was becoming irritated.

There comes a point when excitement or wonder or fear or disbelief can no longer be maintained and your mind says, *OK, what's next?*

"Well?" said Polly, feeling uncomfortably like a teacher asking a child to explain herself.

Kylie shrugged and opened her arms in a *you-can-trust-me* gesture. Polly still didn't trust her. The alien put a tingly arm around Polly's shoulders and guided her across the spaceship while the other aliens went back to whatever they had been doing.

How patronising, thought Polly, but she kept her mouth closed

"OK," began Kylie, "I'll be straight with you. Look at this."

The wall in front of them faded away and became the view of a planet, as though they were standing in space. There was no way of knowing its size, but it was blue, like earth. The land masses were different; lots of small islands and no – on this side of the planet at least – large continents.

Two moons and several other planets were visible, but the most striking features were the two suns illuminating the view, a sight that took Polly's breath away.

"That's home, Polly. Our planet. Our earth. It's called Syssine and is located in the Gynol bi-solar system, not that far from here, one of only four inhabited planets in the known universe with twin suns." Kylie opened her arms. "That's why we Syssinian humans evolved like this. Pretty cool, huh?"

Polly could only nod. *Humans!*

"Notice anything familiar about those moons?"

Polly turned to them and the image zoomed in. She shivered in surprise. "They look like the Death Star in Star Wars!"

"That's no coincidence," said Kylie. "They are actually space ships. They're used to transport colonists, for building projects, sometimes emergency evacuation; they're terrific utility vessels. The one on the right can hold four million people. There are interstellar cruise ships even bigger than that. And one is being built that can generate a gravity vortex to bump planets into a different orbit, making them habitable. Should solve the refugee problem. Progress, huh?"

It was difficult to take this in and Polly felt strangely disorientated. "You said it was no coincidence…"

The image disappeared. "You had better sit down. You look like you are going to throw up."

Kylie escorted Polly to the table and she sat down on a chair that moulded around her. Kylie walked away and returned with a bottle of water. Polly stared at it and the fuzzy alien and laughed manically. *I've gone mad.*

"We can go into detail later," said Kylie, dropping into the chair across the table. "You asked why we are here."

Polly was no longer sure she wanted to know, as the words 'colonists' and 'refugee problem' sank in.

But Kylie's next words surprised her. "We're students, like you."

"You're kidding!"

Kylie ran a fuzzy finger back and forth across her chest. "It's true. Cross my hearts."

Hearts!

"We're studying earth. Your earth. This is a field trip, that's all."

"Where are your teachers, then?" There was something about this whole situation that didn't add up. *OK, nothing added up.*

Kylie nodded and Polly could tell she was smiling. She was starting to understand fuzzy body language. She couldn't tell, however, if the smile was genuine or mocking. "We're on an orienteering trip. We're here to study your earth and devise our own special project to enhance our cultural knowledge of your customs and practises."

"That sounds really boring," said Polly.

"Actually, we've come up with something cool," replied Kylie. "Our teachers are nearby and monitoring everything, so there's no need for concern."

Polly felt concerned. “Can I meet them?”

“Not yet. We are not allowed to contact them until the conclusion of the mission or in an emergency.”

“And you expect me to believe all this?”

Kylie shrugged. “Say the word and I’ll take you back, Polly. We’ll just have to find someone else.”

Ouch! Trapped. Go back down to earth and let someone else do this? Polly decided that would happen over her dead body. But she hoped it didn’t come to that. “OK, tell me how I can help.”

Speaking to a ‘person’ without being able to see a face was very difficult, but Polly could sense the relief when Kylie spoke again, which only reinforced her unease. “It’s more about how we can help you.”

FIVE

Polly remained silent and braced herself for what was coming. Clearly, all of this was a calculated plan and she was the victim. Perhaps they were going to implant her with some weird mind controlling technology or turn her into a rampaging robotic weapon or make her spy for them while they plotted the invasion. She would have to decide on which side of the universe she sat. *How can they expect me to turn against my own planet?*

Kylie leant across the table. *Here it comes*, thought Polly.

"I want to swap places with you for a day or two," said Kylie.

"What!" exclaimed Polly, feeling strangely relieved, yet disappointed by the mundane request.

"It's part of our project. If you agree, I'll take your place to experience what it's like to be a student on Earth. Think of it as an exchange program."

Polly squinted at her blankly.

"And the guys here will help you understand how we, this ship and the universe operate. I'm sure you'll find it interesting."

Polly rubbed her eyes. This was insane. And very exciting. "How is this going to work? You're not exactly inconspicuous."

"Aha!" said Kylie. Polly could 'hear' the smirk, even if she couldn't see it. "Come over here."

Polly followed Kylie into the middle of the craft. She reached out and held Polly's head lightly between her hands and started to pulsate. As Polly watched, she felt a very odd pulling sensation in her insides, not altogether unpleasant, a bit like when you put your hand against the suction pipe of a vacuum cleaner. Her organs felt like they were being sucked against her stomach and chest.

Kylie let go and Polly staggered back, her organs sloshing back into place making her feel queasy for a moment. She would have fallen if the invisible force hadn't intervened to keep her upright. Kylie began to spin, the swirls of her outline whipping around at ever increasing speed until she looked like a miniature tornado. Polly was vaguely aware of the others gathering behind her to watch.

The spinning slowed. Colours became visible and suddenly Polly stood face to face with…herself! An exact replica of Polly stood grinning at the stunned original.

"How do I look?" asked Kylie, her voice sounding vaguely familiar. Polly rarely heard herself speak, just the occasional video or voice mail recording, but Kylie had it down pat. Kylie grinned more broadly than Polly usually did. "What do you think?"

Polly swallowed. "Invasion of the Body Snatchers."

They all had a good laugh at that. Probably too much of a laugh, in Polly's uncomfortable opinion. "How do you do that?" asked Polly.

Kylie shrugged. "I'd explain, but you wouldn't understand.

But Polly now had a face to study. "You don't know!"

Kylie had the decency to look embarrassed. Then she shrugged sheepishly. Polly experienced relief. She hadn't realised how much she missed normal human interaction after such a short time. "Look, I'm sure there are lots of things you use, but don't know how they work," said Kylie.

"Sure," replied Polly, "but if I was able to duplicate the appearance of someone, I'd definitely find out."

Kylie became irritated briefly. "I'll find you the instruction manual later," she said, forcing a smile. "Science is boring."

Polly hid her alarm. *Science is boring!* They couldn't be more different, she thought, but there was no point arguing. It was disconcerting to see 'herself' like this. It was like watching your image in a mirror suddenly take on a life of its own.

Polly studied her double. *So that's what I look like to other people.* She looked pretty good, truth be told. Kylie had the same air of confidence as the real Polly, but there was also a touch of arrogance. *Is that how I come across?* wondered Polly. *I think I'm pretty wonderful – doesn't everyone secretly think that about themselves? – but I hope it's not visible like this.*

She made a decision. "If I agree to this, you have to tone it down a bit. You have to stay in contact with me, do what I tell you and we have to swap back the minute I say so." She liked the way she sounded.

"Sure, no probs," grinned Kylie, far too quickly. 'Whatever you say. All I want is a little taster of life on Earth." She pinched the air to emphasise how little she meant.

"You're not going to change into anyone else down there, are you?" Polly asked. It occurred to her there might be a more sinister reason for her visit.

"Are you kidding?" replied Kylie. "The strain this puts on my body means I'll be aching from head to toe and covered in green and white bruises when I change back. And I'd have to do that before changing into someone else, so forget it!"

Polly didn't believe her, but she experienced a growing sense of excitement. She knew there was danger, but she realised, with some surprise, she didn't care. Every instinct told her Kylie couldn't be trusted, but that didn't concern her either.

What was the worst that could happen? Kylie might piss a few people off, but Polly had never been interested in being popular and certainly wasn't influenced by peer pressure. And school might even benefit from being stirred up. Yet Kylie was more than your usual wild card. What if she destroyed the school and everyone in it? Nah, that was ridiculous. *Wasn't it?*

Polly sensed that she stood on the edge of a chasm and was poised to jump into it. She took a deep breath, ignored her nagging worst-case-scenario fears and crossed her fingers. "OK, let's do it."

"Yes!" Kylie was triumphant and she tried to perform some weird American handshake, high-five, fist bump thing with Polly, which failed miserably because Polly had no idea what she was doing. *There's no going back now*, thought Polly, as she took a gigantic mental leap of faith.

Kylie clapped Polly on the shoulder and walked away to where the pod had arrived. "Rafael will look after you." And then she was gone. *Like she was never there*.

"Great!" said Rafael without any enthusiasm. He clearly was not in a good mood and even his swirling edges pulsated angrily.

Polly suddenly felt alone. It was all a bit quick. "I thought we were going to discuss what to do down there..."

"Don't worry," said Rafael, "you will be in contact the

whole time."

He gestured towards the blank wall of the spacecraft, which dissolved into an image of Kylie sitting in the invisible pod dropping towards Earth. Or rather, Earth was rushing up at her. The 'camera' angle changed half a dozen times, but she looked directly at each one in turn and winked.

"Whoa!" said Polly.

"We will be in constant visual and voice contact while Kylie is down there," explained Rafael. Polly looked at him blankly and Rafael sighed, resigned to having to explain. "She's surrounded by hundreds of micro imagers. Like a swarm of mosquitos. It will be like being there with her."

Polly tried to think of an intelligent response. "Cool," she said.

Southern England was rising to meet the pod and Kylie grinned broadly. Polly was not sure she could produce such a wide smile on her own face, but she started to feel happier about the situation. There was something reassuring about seeing 'herself' like this. Sometimes you just had to step outside yourself to really see. It was a pleasant glimpse of the possible. Or, in this case, the impossible.

Polly turned to squint at Rafael, but she had no more luck than when she stared at Kylie. She smiled at him. She felt happy and although she normally, all things considered, felt reasonably happy, she had never felt this happy. Or alive.

"Are you OK?" asked Rafael. "Your face looks weird."

"Is there too much or too little oxygen in here?" she asked. "I'm not light headed or anything, I just feel…nice."

"I'm sorry," laughed Rafael, a light, breathless sound that Polly liked very much. She could sense him relax. "Want me to adjust the balance to make you miserable?"

"No, no," protested Polly. "This level is just fine."

She looked back towards the wall as the pod descended into her garden. The curtain platform extended to the bedroom window and Polly watched from a succession of angles as Kylie jogged to the window and dived through it to land on the bed. "Neato!" said Kylie, lying down with her hands behind her head.

So far so good. Polly turned back to Rafael. "How is this ship powered?"

"You've heard of matter and anti-matter?" he asked.

"Yeah."

"Well, this craft flies on wassamatter."

"Wassamatter?"

"Nothing. Wassamatter with you?"

Rafael and his shipmates howled with laughter and Polly thought she could hear Kylie chuckling in the background.

Polly grinned. She would get her mum and dad with that one. "Can you show me around?"

Rafael raised his blurred arms. "No need. This is it."

Polly glanced around the empty chamber. "That's a joke, right?" Rafael didn't respond. "Really?"

He nodded.

"No," said Polly. "Where's the bridge? Your cabins? Toilets?"

Kylie, who was busy wandering around Polly's house, looked up. "You got a lot to learn, Polly."

"Am I showing her around, or are you?" asked Rafael testily.

'Well, you haven't exactly been Mister Wikipedia so far," said Kylie. "Just sayin'"

"This isn't about you, Kylie. I won't interfere with your little indulgence as long as you butt out and leave the running of the ship to me. I told you I'm not going to put up with any more of your crap," he said.

Kylie looked annoyed, then embarrassed. "OK," she said, reluctantly.

"Good," Rafael snapped back.

Polly stepped away slightly and looked at the other crew members, who appeared to be wandering idly here and there, pointing and gesticulating. Pretending to be busy. Alien body language wasn't that different. She felt uncomfortable, not sure if she was in an alien spaceship or on the set of a soap opera. She found the domestic dispute both reassuring and concerning.

Kylie wandered off into the rest of the house, her dignity in shreds and Rafael turned back to Polly. "Well, what do you want to know?" He didn't sound angry any more.

Polly didn't quite know where to start. There was so little to see, but so much to ask. "Tell me everything."

Rafael laughed. "Could you be a touch more specific."

"OK. What's with the weird accents? You all speak perfect

English, but you could be from anywhere and everywhere."

"We don't speak English at all. We speak our own language and you are hearing an instant translation." Rafael gestured towards a chair and they both sat down.

"How does that work?"

"I don't know," said Rafael, "but it's kinda cool. It's just standard around the universe these days. They just scan planets and hey presto, everyone can speak to everyone else. There are billions of languages and the system is constantly being updated."

"They?"

"The confederation department that comes in when an inhabited planet is discovered. They pick up all the languages, culture, history, art, religion and, well, everything else. They soak up the whole shebang, you know, including all recorded knowledge, secret information and stuff."

Polly let this sink in. "Like Google?"

"No, not like Google. You have some seriously deranged leaders down there," said Rafael.

Polly felt him looking at her. "Hmm," he said. "Tell you what, I'll hook you up to Vryl's Galmanac – The Gal. It's the go-to guide to the universe and it covers everything you can think of. It tailors the explanations to the receiver, so it will do a much better job than me. Let me know when you connect."

"How will I know?"

"You will think you've gone insane."

Great! "Is it dangerous for me to know all this stuff about the universe?"

Rafael gave a fuzzy shake of the head. "Who are you going to tell when you get back?"

He has a point. Polly glanced across and saw Kylie was back in her bedroom and looking under the bed. "What are you doing?"

Kylie eased back out and grinned. "I'm searching for your secrets."

"I don't have any," replied Polly, becoming uneasy.

"Then what's this?"

Feeling her cheeks redden, Polly watched as Kylie held up a small photo of Eddie Burke. She had torn it from a class photo and neatly trimmed the edges.

"Is this your boyfriend?" asked Kylie, clearly enjoying herself.

"No," said Polly.

"Ah," said Rafael, "but you'd like him to be."

Kylie stood up and placed the photo on the pillow. "I'll see what I can do."

Polly also stood, enraged. "No way! That's none of your business. He goes out with Gwen, anyway."

Kylie raised her hands. "Jeez, OK. Don't blow a blood vessel."

"Next question," said Rafael, changing the subject.

Polly looked back at him, acutely embarrassed, but grateful. She quickly glanced at Kylie, who was now lying on the bed and whistling out of tune. Outside the bedroom window, it was starting to get light.

"Is she always this irritating?" she asked Rafael.

"Don't get me started."

Polly sat down again. Rafael sat across the table from her. "This isn't what I expected," said Polly. She gestured around the room. "We could be in a shipping container."

"The boring reality of space travel, huh?" replied Rafael.

"Where are all the controls? The flashing lights? Consoles? Beeping noises."

Rafael pointed a fuzzy finger at his head. "They're ancient history. The controls are in here. Everyone has a Cortex Implant. The ship is controlled by thought impulses. I have full control of this vehicle – unless I try to command something beyond the parameters of my level of authority – and the others are authorised for their own tasks."

A good recipe for mind control, thought Polly. "Do you also have women captains?"

"Earth really needs to get over this whole gender thing. It's holding you back!"

Polly didn't know what to say. "Sorry," she decided.

Rafael relaxed. "There is no discrimination. It's a thing of the past out here in the wider universe."

"Really?

"Officially, yes, but no, not completely. We are still human."

Polly wondered if she should be reassured or more worried. "How does the Cortex Implant work?'

Rafael was silent for a moment. Then he shrugged.

"You don't know?"

"We don't need to know. There's too much stuff out there, Polly. Most people just enjoy using technology. There really is too much to know without driving yourself nuts trying to find out."

Polly thought about this. It wasn't very satisfying. She had been exposed to something incredible, unbelievable, but in some ways she was none the wiser. Perhaps it was a dream, after all. It felt frustrating, just like a dream. She wondered if that was really herself down there, lying on her bed. Whistling and dreaming.

Kylie looked back at her – *can she read my thoughts?* – and winked. Now there was someone enjoying herself.

"Want to go for a spacewalk?" asked Rafael.

Polly was taken aback, but she quickly recovered and grinned. "Yeah!"

Rafael stood and walked through the hologram image of Kylie. Polly followed and suddenly found there was nothing between her and the Earth. "I don't have a space suit!" she cried.

"Yes, you do," Rafael replied, floating away from the ship. "You have been enveloped in a bio-suit since you boarded the pod. It supplies your air, controls your temperature, modulates the pressure, simulates gravity, controls communication and even feeds you and eliminates any waste. It also stops you falling over, as you would have noticed on the trip here. In fact, none of the furniture is real. It's just a bunch of images we set up to make you feel more at home. You've been sitting on your suit."

Polly began to float. She stared at her hands, felt them. She couldn't detect any covering at all. She was in space wearing sneakers, jeans and a Tshirt! She must look completely ridiculous. *Did I tie my shoelaces tight?* she wondered idly.

"We all wear them," continued Rafael. "We're all human, but every planet has subtle differences in atmosphere and climate and a million other little things. With this," he held his arms wide apart, "you can take your own planet with you wherever you go."

Polly realised she was holding her breath. She breathed out, then in, great gulps of air. In space. She laughed, tingling with excitement. Rafael held out his hand and she took it. He spun and flipped her over his head with a flick of his fuzzy wrist. Polly twisted and turned, weightless, Earth whipping in and out of her view. There was no nausea, only an immense feeling of exhilaration.

She stabilised and looked down. Up? And felt completely overwhelmed. The Earth, giant, blue and beautiful lay just beyond her feet, one foot seemingly standing on the alps, the other over the Atlantic. Morning sunlight drenched Britain for a change, though Ireland still lay mostly in darkness, the outline of the country's west coast barely visible.

Polly turned and looked back at Rafael, who drifted still and fuzzy a few yards away. Beyond him was the curtain-like outline of the spaceship. "It's wonderful!"

Rafael nodded. A vision of Kylie 'bloomed' next to her. She was sitting on Polly's bed, looking in the mirror while combing her hair into strange shapes. Polly laughed again. She felt euphoric and tears formed in her eyes. And she didn't care. She was free, but she wasn't alone. And neither was the world. She had always thought there was life 'out there'. Really, given the size of the universe, how could there not be? She hadn't expected confirmation in her lifetime, but if what Kylie and Rafael told her was true, the extent of life was staggering. *Maybe I could stay up here a little longer...*

"What do you think?" asked Kylie. She had teased her hair into a spiky Mohawk that Polly thought looked quite cool. "It looks goo…wait a minute, you're not thinking about going to school like that?"

Kylie had a twinkle in her eye. "Well…"

Polly waved her hands and started to spin. "No, no. That's not the deal here. You're an observer, remember? I don't want you to attract attention. I have to go back there and I don't want to have to explain any strange stuff. OK?"

Combing her hair back down, Kylie shrugged her OK in return. But unless Polly was mistaken, Kylie had thicker hair than before. However, she was floating upside down above the Earth and more than a little distracted, so she could be wrong. And nothing was going to spoil this wonderful moment.

Rafael spun around so that they were the same way up, eye to blur. "Had enough?"

"No," replied Polly. "Never. It's amazing. You see photos and film of this view, but it's completely different. The scale is so enormous, and yet it's so small in the vast realms of space."

"You sound like a documentary," said Kylie, back on the bed.

Polly laughed. *Have I ever felt this happy?* she wondered.

"I can hear someone downstairs, Polly," said Kylie.

Polly turned and saw excitement on the alien's – her – face.

"That will be mum. Dad's away."

"What do you call your mum?"

"Mum."

"Good. I'll try to remember." Kylie jumped up from the bed and ran her hands through her hair at superhuman speed. The Mohawk reappeared on her head, only this time it was bright blue. "Let's get this show on the road!"

Polly didn't know whether to laugh or cry as she watched Kylie leave the room and head for the stairs. "No!" she shouted.

Kylie smiled at Polly. "Don't sweat it, huh. Rafael, I'm switching to audio. The visuals are too distracting."

"OK," replied Rafael. "Don't worry," he said to Polly, "we'll still be able to see her."

Polly watched Kylie jog down the stairs. She put her hands to her face, but snuck a look through her fingers. Her horror was tempered by curiosity. How would mum react? It was like seeing an impending car crash. You know it will be horrible, but you can't take your eyes away.

In the kitchen, Polly's mum had her back to the door, making a cup of tea. Kylie looked around. Polly didn't like the almost manic look on her face. Her calm control was gone and she looked nervous. *What have I done?* thought Polly.

"I just got in," said Marianne Hart without turning around. "Want a cuppa?"

"Yo, mum," said Kylie. "Nope."

Polly cringed at the words she would never say. The movement of her face muscles was enough to make her weightless body turn a forty-five degree angle.

Marianne's head jerked sideways slightly, like in movies when the star hears a gun being cocked behind her. *Bad analogy*, decided Polly.

Marianne turned slowly – she looked very tired – and Polly again stopped breathing.

"Are you…" began Marianne, then, after a huge double-take, "…what have you done to your hair?"

"I felt like a change."

"Really?" said Marianne, her eyebrows disappearing under her hairline.

Kylie shrugged.

"Are you OK?" Marianne looked a little alarmed.

"Yeah, sure," said Kylie.

"Sit down."

Kylie sat at the table. She was looking more confident now, cocky even, and Polly felt sorry for her mum.

Marianne sat opposite. "I'm sorry me and dad haven't been around much. We've both been so busy with this satellite thingy…"

One of Kylie's eyebrows raised in expectation, a little too high in Polly's estimation.

Marianne cleared her throat. "You're not taking anything, are you?"

Kylie laughed. "Of course not!"

"Good," said Marianne, relieved. "It's just that you're a little…" she struggled for the right words, "…more animated than usual."

Thanks a lot, mum! thought Polly.

"I'm just happy being human, mum," said Kylie.

Marianne relaxed, a little, but didn't look convinced. She couldn't stop herself yawning. "I'm going to get some sleep. I have to go back in late this afternoon, but I'll be home when you get back from school. Let's catch up then, eh?"

"Sure."

Marianne stood and looked closely at Kylie. Polly thought she was going to say something, but after hesitating, she walked out of the kitchen shaking her head.

Kylie sat still as Marianne's footsteps thudded up the stairs. "That went really well."

"What the hell are you doing?" shouted Polly. "That's my mum you're messing with!"

"She's cool," shrugged Kylie. "She just thinks you've gone a little nuts."

"Well, thanks for that."

Kylie sighed. "Polly, if changing your hair is such a big deal, you must be the most boring teenager on the planet. I'm trying to make you cool. Lighten up!"

Polly didn't like the sound of that. "Let's call it quits. Making me cool isn't part of the deal."

"OK, it's an added bonus, then. My gift to you."

Polly rotated back to face Rafael. "Can't you control her?"

Rafael laughed at such a ridiculous suggestion. "You did agree to swap."

"By the way," said Kylie, "you can speak to me any time. No one but me can hear you."

Kylie left the house and started walking down the street.

"Where are you going?" asked Polly, nervous.

"School. You don't want to be late."

Kylie almost skipped along the street, taking long, loping strides. She did look pretty cool, Polly conceded. And, though she would never admit it out loud, blue hair suited her.

They were silent for a few moments before Kylie spoke. "What do your parents do?"

"They both work for the space agency," said Polly. "Mum is an astrophysicist and dad's a mathematician."

Another long silence. "So you're an hereditary nerd."

Ouch! Painful, but true.

Soon, Kylie turned into Balaclava Street and the school was visible up ahead.

"Is that it?" asked Kylie.

"Yep."

It wasn't very impressive, Polly had to admit, feeling a little embarrassed. A series of squat, two storey 1970s brick buildings with absolutely no aesthetic value or presenting anything remotely pleasing to the eye. Designed, her friend Josh once theorised, by someone who hated architecture.

Kylie stopped at the gate. "Well, Hogwarts it ain't."

Bunches of kids arrived at school and they all stared at Kylie's hair. She seemed to enjoy the attention, thought Polly. Kylie moved away from the crowd and strolled to one of the two trees on the school grounds.

"OK," she said. "Fill me in."

Polly could see the school and the whole yard and she

noticed that when she looked at anything specific, like Mrs Elswick unloading her car, the vision zoomed in. A little too close to Mrs Elswick, Polly thought. The Headmistress was scary enough from a distance.

"That's the headmistress, Mrs Elswick, next to her car. Those girls over there are the cool group. The bald guy is the English teacher, Mr French."

"Mr French! You're kidding, right?"

"No."

"Is the French teacher called Mr English?"

"No, the French teacher is called Miss Cutler. That's her just going into school." Polly liked Miss Cutler, who seemed more sophisticated than anyone she knew. Shame Polly hated French. The language, certainly, though she wasn't keen on the English teacher, Mr French, either. She could see why Kylie was confused!

Kylie took it all in. "Who are they?" She pointed at a group of boys playing football.

"Just some boys playing football. The girl behind them, on the steps reading a book, that's my best friend Kate."

"Hmm," said Kylie. "Now I know why you're such a wild and crazy girl."

Josh stepped into view. "Who are you talking to?" he asked Kylie. He was shielding his eyes from the sun. Then he saw Kylie's hair and his mouth dropped open.

"That's Josh," Polly said hurriedly. "My friend. Apologise for last night. Quick."

"I'm sorry about last night," said Kylie.

Josh's head jerked as he did a double take, just like Polly's mum. "What did you do to your hair?"

"Good looking guy," said Rafael.

"You think?" said Polly, looking at Josh a little more closely than usual.

"I needed a change," said Kylie, patting her hair.

Josh's eyebrows rose. "Are you OK?" he asked.

"Jeez, can't a girl dye her hair without causing universal suffering?"

"You're talking weird."

"Yeah," agreed Polly, becoming alarmed, "tone it down."

Kylie grinned and Josh visibly relaxed a little. Polly felt a pang of something. Jealousy? Surely not.

"I didn't sleep last night," said Kylie. "I'm a bit zonked."

Josh smiled. "I'm sorry I ran off. I know you wouldn't do that deliberately. I got freaked out. Did you find anything else?"

"It was just a bunch of aliens messing around," said Kylie. "Nothing to worry about."

Polly sighed.

"I have to go. I need to see Mr Mountford about my chemistry assignment before class." Josh looked closely at Kylie for a few seconds, then turned and hurried off towards the main school building. "See ya."

"Bye," said Kylie. She watched him. "Nice."

Polly and Rafael looked at each other. At least she looked at the blurred Rafael; she wasn't sure if he was looking back at her.

"What do you think you're doing?" she said.

"I'm being Polly," said Kylie.

"No you are not," replied Polly.

Kylie was unconcerned. "Call it an artistic interpretation, then."

Rafael was silent and Polly thought she could see him darken with anger.

It's going to be a long day, thought Polly.

But then something happened inside her head. Random words, strange images cascaded and her mind whirled. Panic threatened to overwhelm her. "What's happening to me?"

Rafael moved closer and put his hand on her arm.

"Ah," he said, "The Gal has arrived."

EXTRACT FROM VRYL'S GALMANAC

Vryl's Galmanac – An excerpt from the Introduction by Hrew Mjeds Rpiuseq, Professor of Literature (Interstellar Guides), Bgstul University

Vryl's Galmanac, or 'The Gal,' began some twenty thousand years ago when Adystal Vryl, an explorer from the planet Fruayar in the Star Fountain Sector, found herself marooned on a barren planet called Desfol 4. She was there for eighteen years and passed the time by compiling a list of everything she knew, or thought she knew, about the universe.

When rescued she had amassed a vast collection of facts and figures, history, legends, myths and stories from across the entire universe, and although most of the information was incorrect or misinterpreted, Vryl was obsessed – some say deranged – and decided the Gal would be her new career.

There were many other Galmanacs in existence at the time, but what made Vryl's stand out was her conversational style, irreverence and sloppiness of research. She made a token effort at accuracy, but with one thousand new planets – sometimes more – entering the confederation every year, it was difficult to keep up. Vryl and her team simply made things up to fill in gaps. The resulting Galmanac, growing by a million entries every hour is now a mish-mash of fact and fiction presenting an approximation (at best) or an opinion (at worst) of the universe rather than a factual record.

The Gal, despite this, is the preferred reference guide used throughout the entire universe. The general consensus is that the fact that everything is covered is more important than the accuracy of the information. And as there is a hefty fee to correct an entry, people are reluctant to make changes and much of the real history of the universe remains shrouded in mystery.

Though most incorrect entries are benign, a wrongly

attributed negative comment regarding the planet Lkroh upset the sensitive inhabitants so much that they went to war against a neighbour and four planets were destroyed before The Gal was updated.

Vryl died a very wealthy woman and her family still own The Gal to this day. They bought and refurbished Desfol 4 seven thousand years ago and the planet is now the Galmanac Headquarters and employs approximately five hundred million people. The figure may be higher as birth rates ebb and flow, so new employee numbers fluctuate widely and, as with the Gal itself, company records cannot be trusted.

The future of The Gal became assured four hundred years ago when all new Cortex Implants were given access to the work, allowing everyone to instantly reference the contents, which are now broadcast throughout the known universe and beyond.

Unfortunately, a significant number of planets consider sections of the contents to be politically or culturally unacceptable and offensive and have blocked, omitted or edited the work to suit their own sensibilities. The result, frankly, is a mess, and it has not been possible for the Gal to be adopted universally in any official capacity.

Despite this, it is agreed that nothing can match The Gal for anyone seeking an overall picture of the universe. However, individual entries should be taken with a pinch of salt and checked against local records. Accurate entries are generally considered to be accidental.

Yet for all its failings – and they are literally countless – The Gal is a much loved and revered ancient reference guide to the universe. Just don't trust it.

SIX

Kylie was irritated and disappointed. And disappointed because she was irritated. She really wanted to be cheerful and was trying to stay upbeat. After all, she was finally here, on Earth, or, to be accurate – until it was accepted into the Confederation – Planet HZCX165349872/3542/9/3, a name that didn't quite have the same ring to it. She was going to an Earth school, posing as an Earth human. It may be mission accomplished, but it wasn't the way she had thought it would be.

First of all, her 'Polly costume' didn't fit properly. It might be a miracle of technology to change her appearance so radically, but the process still needed some refinement. *It was so damned itchy.* But she could tolerate some discomfort, as there was no choice if she wanted to complete this adventure. It was all the other stuff that was the bigger letdown.

The school itself was awful, quite possibly the ugliest building on a planet with more than its fair share of grotesque architecture. Schools should inspire, not drive students to contemplate suicide. Kylie's own school, for instance, was modelled on a Skyrolian epoch star ranger outstation. It not only looked really cool, it was airborne and fitted throughout with retro gadgets for teachers, such as their ability to render unruly students weightless. Kylie used to howl with laughter when it happened...until it happened to her. There was little to recommend floating with your arse stuck to the ceiling for six hours.

But it was way more fun than this place, she thought, taking another look at the collection of shoe boxes commonly known as Greatmont High School. *No offence to actual shoe boxes.* None of the Earth TV shows or movies portrayed schools like this. They were all bright and colourful and filled with misbehaving teenagers having fun and generally driving teachers and parents insane. *As they should.*

Which was another thing. The students here looked about as dangerous as hamsters. *No offence to real hamsters*. They were boring, well behaved – she could just tell – and, even worse, wholesome. This wasn't a school, it was a cornflake commercial. No wonder Earth humans were so far behind.

Unfortunately, Polly fitted right in here. She was nice, no doubt about that, and bright. But boring! Admittedly, she was filled with nerd genes, but really! Kylie had handed Polly the biggest adventure she would ever have in her life and all Polly was worried about was blue hair! *And having her jabbering in my ear the whole time! It was so counterproductive and would only make her worse...*

Kylie grinned. Maybe she could liven things up a little. Maybe resuscitate this terminally dull place. It looked like a hopeless cause, but there was no harm in trying and perhaps afterwards Polly would be one of the cool kids. Or expelled. *Oh well, what was life without risk?*

"There's Kate." Polly sounded excited, but to Kylie the kid heading her way across the yard looked anything but. However, she looked at Kate more approvingly when someone kicked a ball which cannoned off the back of the girl's head. Kate didn't seem to notice. *That's cool*, thought Kylie.

"Who is she again?" asked Kylie.

"My best friend."

"Figures."

"What have you done to your hair?" said Kate as she arrived, seemingly hypnotised by the sight.

"Good question," said Polly.

"Has this planet never had anyone with blue hair before?" said Kylie.

"I like it," said Kate. "Did you know blue hair was sacred in Ancient Egypt?"

Kylie just looked at her.

"She's full of fascinating stuff like that," said Polly.

But Kate had moved on. "What happened last night? Did you find anything out?"

"Aliens," said Kylie. "It's the only explanation."

"Excellent!" said Kate. "I didn't miss anything, then."

Now she's getting irritating, thought Kylie.

"We'd better go in." Kate took off again across the playground. Kylie sauntered after her.

Near the steps, Mrs Elswick was still unpacking the boot of her car, placing boxes on a trolley. She was reaching for the furthest box as they funnelled into the building entrance with a group of other kids, who were also fixated on Kylie's hair.

"Huge arse," said Kylie.

Polly's voice boomed out. "What the hell are you doing?"

Mrs Elswick's head shot up and hit the lid of the boot, but by the time she angrily looked around, they were inside the building.

Kylie was surrounded by gasps of disbelief and Kate stopped to stare at her. "What are you doing?"

Having fun, thought Kylie. She grinned and shrugged. Clearly this was not the behaviour expected of the real Polly. *Good.*

"Kylie!" exclaimed Rafael. "Polly has to go back there, remember."

"Just a bit of fun. This school seems to be lacking in it," said Kylie.

"You're right, there," admitted Kate. "It would be really interesting to compare the statistics against other schools, though it would be difficult to assess the parameters and…"

But Kylie was not listening. The kids around her were dispersing in all directions to their classes. She grinned. She was here. She'd done it.

"Why's she grinning?" she heard Polly ask. Kylie heard the fear in her voice and while she could understand it, Kylie didn't care. Couldn't Polly see what a wonderful experience this was?

"Because she's an idiot," Rafael replied.

"…later," said Kate. She headed away down the corridor.

Kylie found herself alone in the corridor, but Mr Oberon bustled out of one door and across the hall to a classroom, performing a double take when he spotted Kylie's hair. "What!"

Kylie raised her eyebrows.

Mr Oberon was caught in two minds. He looked at his watch, then sharply back at Kylie. "We'll speak later. I want to hear what your mother said." He stepped into the classroom and slammed the door.

"Who was that?"

"Mr Oberon, the science teacher," replied Polly. "He's a bit weird."

"You don't say. What's he want?"

"He wants to know what's happening to the satellites."

Kylie felt both of her hearts miss a beat each. Her new face became clammy, which felt weird, and the itching increased all over. "Why?"

Polly's voice was reassuring. "He knows my mum is one of the investigators, that's all."

Kylie felt relieved. Then annoyed all over again. *Really, what do I care?* Problem was, she did care, which was completely out of character. Maybe the rumour was true that the transfiguration process incorporated more than the physical appearance of the subject. It had not been proved, but while the known universe was incredibly big, the unknown universe held the upper hand by an enormous margin. There were still forces at play that no one could understand. And she couldn't deny she was suddenly having unfamiliar feelings of Polly-like concern.

"You had better get to class. You're already late," said Polly

"I'm going to skip class and take a look around this…this…this place." *The school really was beyond description.*

"You can't!" said Polly. "You don't have a corridor pass."

'What's that?"

"It's a note. If you don't have one and you're caught between classes, it means big trouble."

"Let me guess," said Kylie. "Crucifixion."

"It's a secular school, not Catholic."

Kylie sighed. "Which class?"

"Maths. Room 106. It's down…"

Polly's voice was interrupted by Rafael's urgent shout. "We have to go…" and then the audio was cut.

"Polly? Rafael?" Kylie waited a moment. She called again. No reply.

Kylie laughed out loud. *Finally free!* The Polly part of her experienced a slight flutter, but she could feel her own persona surging back to life. She had no concern about the break in contact. It was most likely a passing zone sweeper and Rafael had followed procedure and shut down until it passed. *Peace in our time.*

Kylie pressed her nose against the window cut into the door of room 106. The class had started and – she stepped back to look at the sign below the window – Mr Peters was scribbling an absurdly primitive formula on the blackboard.

There were twenty or so students in various states of disengagement from proceedings already struggling to stay awake. *And the class couldn't have started more than two minutes ago*!

Kylie grinned and pushed through the door.

"...so that you can interpret and apply normal and binomial...," said Mr Peters, glancing at the door, "...probability distributions and..." He abruptly stopped as he took in Kylie's pallid green and sweaty face.

Kylie sauntered over to the teacher's desk, her face becoming more green and her throat contracting as though she was about to throw up.

Mr Peters shrank away in his chair and some students made disgusted noises.

"I don't feel well, sir. Can I have a corridor pass to see the nurse?"

Mr Peters finished writing the note seconds after Kylie finished speaking and dropped it on his desk, horrified.

Kylie convulsed in his direction and belched a "Thank you," before picking up the note and leaving the class.

She emerged into the corridor, face back to normal. *I wish Polly could have seen that!*

Walking through the deserted corridors, Kylie checked out the various classrooms and confirmed that the school was the most tedious place on Earth. What was she doing here...but then, through the main doors, she saw a sports car pull up in the car park. She pushed open the door and walked down the steps, feeling sad that this constituted something of interest.

She watched as two people climbed out of the car, one an attractive girl with a downturned mouth, the other a familiar good looking boy. *Of course!* The boy in the photo under Polly's bed. Eddie. Her secret love. And his girlfriend, Gwen. *Here's a chance for some fun*, thought Kylie.

When Gwen saw Kylie, she marched up to her. "Hey, Hart, are you looking for a fat lip?"

"What, to match your head?"

Eddie grabbed Gwen's arm and pulled. "Gwen. Later, eh?"

Kylie saw anger surge on Gwen's face. *Now it's getting really interesting.*

She heard footsteps coming down the steps behind her. "Gwen Hooper AND Edward Burke, you are late! Come here." It was Mrs Elswick, the Headmistress.

Gwen eyeballed Kylie for another second, then brushed past her as she approached Mrs Elswick, who began a long tirade. Apparently, this was not the first time.

Eddie came closer. "You're not scared?"

"Of her? You're joking."

He raised his eyebrows.

"Ditch her," whispered Kylie, "and meet me at lunchtime."

A hint of a smile. "Where?"

"…and you, Ms Hart," said Mrs Elswick.

As Eddie walked past, Kylie said, "Find me."

She waited while Mrs Elswick shook her finger at Gwen and Eddie. "I will see you both outside my office at the end of school." They walked away. "And don't be late for that!"

"Now, Ms Hart. What are…"

Kylie turned to face the headmistress, her face only a little less green than earlier.

Mrs Elswick took a step back in shock, her eyes flicking between Polly's face and her hair.

Pretending to be confused, Kylie waived her corridor pass. "I was feeling sick and Mr Peters gave me this note so I could come out for some fresh air. I'm feeling much better now."

Mrs Elswick eyed her sceptically. "You could have fooled me," she said.

I did, thought Kylie.

"Go and see the nurse right now."

Kylie looked at her blankly and Mrs Elswick, now recovered, rolled her eyes. "The nurse. Down the corridor. The door marked 'nurse'."

"Oh, that nurse," said Kylie

"I can ring your parents to come and get you," suggested Mrs Elswick, hopefully.

"I really would like to stay. Let's see what the nurse says, shall we?"

Kylie hurried into the building without another word. Mrs Elswick was looking at her a little too closely and by the time she reached the nurse's room her face was merely a tinge of green. Just enough.

The nurse was a short, frowning man who sat at a desk drawing a picture of a set of football goals. Mr Blenkinsop, his name tag said. He flipped the paper over as Kylie entered and frowned slightly less when he saw her, then slightly more again when he noticed her green hue.

"Sit," he said. He took her temperature, felt her pulse, measured her blood pressure, all without a word. Kylie made all of the results register as Earth human normal. Then he made her lie down for about twenty-four hours, or maybe it was one hour. It certainly felt like twenty-four. Time is relative. *Well, this is fun.*

Mr Blenkinsop passed the time by finishing his doodle of the goals and a particularly awful drawing of a stick figure kicking a ball. He didn't know she was watching.

"You can go," he said finally, as the ball hit the net, with his lesser frown, *probably a smile*. Kylie suspected that if she had presented with a severed limb, Mr Blenkinsop would have given her a paper towel to stem the bleeding.

The corridor was again quiet, so Kylie decided to attend the next class, which was science, or, as Kylie knew it, primitive technology.

She knocked and entered. Mr Oberon was either teaching or trying to keep the students awake. From their faces, Kylie thought he had not been successful at either.

"You are very late, Ms Hart. The class is almost..." He glared at her hair again and his eye went into overdrive. W*hat was it about coloured hair?*

No kidding. "I was in the sick room."

Mr Oberon waved her to an empty desk.

There was something unsettling about Mr Oberon. It wasn't the fact that he looked like he'd stepped out of a 1950s movie. Or his formal way of speaking. Or even his twitching eye. There was something else about him. It was like he *knew*. But how could he? He was just a particularly boring teacher in the most boring school in the known, and, most likely unknown, universe.

Kylie sat and noticed Oberon was still looking at her strangely. She suspected he looked at everyone strangely, but...

"We were discussing particle physics, Ms Hart, a subject I know you are very familiar with."

The boy next to her coughed to cover the word, "Nerd." Other kids sniggered. Kylie grinned.

"Perhaps," continued Mr Oberon, "you can assist by telling

the class the definition of the word, quark."

"Sure. It's the sound a duck makes in space."

The pent-up classroom boredom erupted into loud laughter.

Mr Oberon was shocked – his eye twitched furiously – but quickly recovered. "That's enough!" he boomed, never taking his eyes from Kylie.

The bell rang and the noisy students crammed their books in their bags and got out of the classroom as fast as possible. Kylie almost reached the door.

"Not you, Ms Hart. Please wait behind."

The students all filtered out through the door and Kylie turned to face Mr Oberon, whose eye now seemed completely out of control. *He should get that fixed*, thought Kylie.

"What is going on with you?"

Kylie stared back, all innocence and disinterest. She raised an eyebrow, although she probably misjudged the movement, as Oberon's good eye fixed on it and the twitchy one came to a halt on the same spot. *I must practise in the mirror.*

"You are behaving very oddly. Your hair. Your attitude. Is something wrong?"

Kylie didn't like the way Mr Oberon looked at her – it was like an interrogation – particularly with both eyes looking in the same direction. *What can he see?* She decided she had to get out of there.

"I'm not myself, Mr Oberon," said Kylie with a sigh. "I've got a bug and I've been staying up too late following all this satellite stuff." She pointed to her hair and grinned. "A friend talked me into this while I was wasn't thinking straight."

Mr Oberon didn't look convinced, but he did not seem as suspicious. His eye started twitching again and his facial features rearranged themselves. *Good enough*, thought Kylie.

"Have your parents found out any more information?"

"Not as far as I know," shrugged Kylie, edging towards the door.

"Hmm. Keep me up to date."

Who is this guy? "Yeah, sure. Bye."

She walked away down the corridor, happy that Mr Oberon did not call her back. She decided to steer clear of him for the rest of her visit.

"Polly? Rafael? Where the hell are you?" she asked, quietly. It was rather annoying, but she had started to miss them.

SEVEN

"We have to go!" Rafael said suddenly.

Polly was almost in a trance as she floated above the Earth. Once Rafael explained The Gal, she couldn't get enough. By mentally forming a question in her mind, she was able to obtain information instantly, as though it was punched directly into her memory. It was hard to understand how it worked, but words and images blended seamlessly into her consciousness, anticipating her follow-up questions and 'speaking' to her in Earth terms and time periods. It was truly amazing. And confusing.

Rafael gripped her arm and shook her. "We have to go!"

"What…" began Polly, but the spaceship rushed up to meet them and they were back inside, where Rafael and his crewmates moved about in what suspiciously looked like panic. She had been absorbed in the history of the universe, but now it was gone. Switched off.

Communication was also cut off with Kylie, and only the interior cylinder of the craft was visible. Rafael huddled with his comrades, their blurred outlines swirling like fog in a wind machine, and Polly felt a sinking feeling. *What's happened?*

She fought her own rising panic, but calmed when she saw Rafael and the others disentangle and move around the ship.

"Sorry to alarm you," said Rafael as he joined her. There was still something in his voice Polly couldn't fathom.

"What happened?"

"Nothing major. Just some space debris. Evasive action, that's all"

"Really?"

Polly squinted hard at Rafael, which she could tell made him uncomfortable, she noted with interest.

"Part of our, er, exercise, is to remain undetected, so if anything happens that could draw attention…"

"Bullshit!" said Polly.

"I beg your pardon?" said Rafael, nervously.

Polly had mixed feelings about making an alien uncomfortable, but nothing added up.

"Tell me what's going on."

"I told you. We've just temporarily relocated."

"Where to?"

Rafael waved his arm and the view from the spaceship appeared. They were in the shadows behind a huge sphere, the upper edge silhouetted like a ring held up to the light.

Polly drew in a breath. "We're on the dark side of the moon?"

Rafael shifted from one fuzzy foot to the other and Polly's stomach lurched.

"Where? Tell me."

"We're not really very far. That's Mars and..."

"Mars?" spluttered Polly and, for no particular reason she repeated herself, louder this time. "MARS?"

Polly's head felt like it was going to explode. *What the... Mars! That's, what, forty million miles away from Earth! And that's on a good day. It can be over sixty million at times. We got here in the blink of an eye. What the...!*

She could only think of one more thing to say. "MARS!"

"The moon was a little too close."

Polly looked at Rafael as though he was mad. "How big was this 'space debris'?" She felt silly using air quotes in front of an alien.

Rafael bristled with fuzzy irritation, which Polly preferred to his discomfort. "That's not important. We'll go back soon."

"Great." Polly raised her voice. "Can someone please tell me what's going on! Please?"

Rafael turned back to the others, who kept their distance and withheld their assistance. He turned back and appeared to stare at her for an awfully long time. Then he seemed to relax. "We shouldn't have been anywhere near Earth. We're not authorised. And we almost got caught back there."

Polly rubbed her temples. "What about Kylie?"

"Well," said Rafael, "obviously, we'll have to go back to get her and drop you home..."

Obviously.

"Look, it's just one of those things. We'll fix it up."

"So," said Polly, "we've lost contact with Kylie..." – Rafael nodded – "...and I'm stuck in space on the wrong side of Mars, some forty million..."

"Forty-two million six hundred and eighty-three."

"...miles from Earth." *Now we're finishing each other's*

sentences, thought Polly absently.

"Correct," allowed Rafael.

Polly found herself sounding like her mother. "It's not very good, is it?"

Rafael swirled and squirmed fuzzily. "No," he said, quietly.

What would mum do? She would make a cup of tea and they'd discuss the problem. Didn't seem quite adequate in these particular circumstances. "So, what's the plan?"

Silence.

"I was afraid you'd say that," said Polly. Crazily, she felt a growing sense of excitement. Sure, she was trapped out in deep space with a bunch of aliens, but they seemed a nice bunch, even if they were a bit dim. And they were keeping stuff from her. But she had left earth willingly and, although the last few minutes were a little alarming, it didn't sound particularly serious. And if they could get here in seconds, they could return in the same time. It took longer to visit the local shop to buy a bottle of milk than this trip to Mars!

She gazed hopefully at Rafael, who finally spoke. "We'll wait here for a bit, then go back."

"Sounds like a plan," said Polly. "A bad plan. How will you know it's safe to go back, assuming there is danger, which there must be, as we wouldn't have left in such a hurry."

"We'll work it out."

"Well, it's nice to know I'm in the hands of an advanced civilization."

Polly took a very deep breath. She'd made her point and as much as she would like to stick the boot in further, a more conciliatory approach might yield better results.

Polly walked to the side of the ship and looked out at the planet. Rafael followed.

"Will you please tell me what this is all about?" asked Polly.

Rafael stepped up next to her, close enough for Polly to feel his electric charge. "OK," he said.

He was quiet for a moment, but Polly managed to stay silent, too. Finally, he spoke. "We were on a school field trip to a planet called Sury in a nearby galaxy to see the Surynnian Cannon. It's pretty spectacular. We went between eruptions but it's still impressive. This is from the last event."

Mars was replaced with the view of another planet, this

time from further out in space. It was covered in swirling gas, except for a single, colossal volcano poking through the cloud covering the surface.

"Wow!' said Polly. "How big is that planet?"

"About ten times the size of your earth. Watch."

The gas suddenly shuddered around the mountain and a cloud ripple set off across the planet, closely followed by an enormous volcanic eruption, which punched a jet of fire out into space, thousands of miles in length, then suddenly stopped as if a switch had been thrown. The clouds around the volcano churned wildly, but quickly settled down and all again was calm.

"Wow!" repeated Polly.

"It goes off every twelve and a half earth years," said Rafael, "regular as clockwork. It's a huge tourist attraction and there were more than four billion people there on the viewing platforms for the latest eruption."

The fire jet was still visible in distant space when the view returned to Mars.

Polly shook her head, trying to make sense of what she just saw. *Wow!* She thought.

"Anyway," continued Rafael, "a few of us got separated from our group in the crowds and Kylie thought it might be a good idea to take the ship out for a spin. We were fairly close to Earth and…"

Polly tried to think, without success, of a universe, real, parallel or multi, in which that would be a good idea.

"…here we are." Rafael shrugged his shoulders and a blurred ripple travelled down his body like the clouds on Sury.

"So this is just a joyride, and not a profound moment in the history of the Earth?"

"Er, no. Yes. I don't know."

Polly laughed. "What about the satellites? What was that all about."

Rafael shifted on his blurred feet. "We each wanted to sign one before going back and Kylie liked making shapes from aerials."

Oh. My. God! Polly shook her head in amazement, and a little admiration. It was not something she could ever do – those satellites were very important and valuable – but the thought of cutting loose like that… She laughed.

"What's so funny?"

"The world's governments, scientists and space agencies are working around the clock to investigate a graffiti incident! That's what's funny."

Rafael clearly didn't get the joke. "We only had one more to do when you detected us, and after we'd checked you out Kylie thought it would be fun to swap places."

"If Kylie told you to jump into the Surynnian Cannon would you do it?" Polly winced inside. *I must stop sounding like my mother.*

"Don't be ridiculous," snapped Rafael.

"You need to assert yourself more," said Polly. "Kylie clearly has a few issues and from the sounds of it, this adventure is not going to end well."

Rafael didn't respond. *He knows he's in deep shit*, thought Polly. *Trouble is, that means I am, too.* She gazed out at Mars, wondering what…

A giant shadow descended across the planet. Rafael's fuzziness swirled and eddied and Polly could feel electricity crackling between them. She turned back and saw the others were frozen to their places, their outlines also swirling violently.

Everything went black for a split second and then they were enveloped in light so bright Polly was momentarily blinded. Her vision slowly returned, though she couldn't quite make sense of it. It appeared they were inside some gigantic vessel, but surely she was mistaken. It was too vast.

Her eyes were sore from all the squinting and now they watered as two fuzzy figures approached. They were a foot taller than Rafael and the others, more solid. Their fuzzy outlines were somehow tighter, more contained, and there was more power there, too. They bristled. Polly shuddered.

"Get over here, all of you." Deep voice. Male. Very angry.

"Faster!" Female. Authoritarian. Even more angry.

"Oh, shit," muttered Rafael, his swirling slowed. There was genuine fear in his voice.

"Who are they? Teachers?" whispered Polly through gritted teeth from the corner of her mouth. "Space police?"

Rafael turned to her slightly. "Much worse," he said quietly, but the male alien raised a blurred hand to silence him.

"We're Kylie's parents."

EXTRACT FROM VRYL'S GALMANAC

The Universal Confederation of Human Planets (a brief guide)

The Confederation consists of approximately thirteen million inhabited planets. Many more are classed as pre-confederated, meaning they are not sufficiently advanced for membership. Membership consists of three member categories:

The Ancients

The Ancients comprise the 27,548 surviving planets (of the original 59,201) from the Founding Epoch, when humans from different planets first came into contact with each other. This Epoch occurred over a three thousand year period approximately 500,000 years ago.

To say that this period was turbulent is an understatement. War began as soon as technology developed and planets became aware of each other. More and more planets were drawn into the conflict, alliances formed, shifted and fractured. The First, Second and Third (which lasted 1,200 years) Formation Wars, often referred to as the Stellar Wars, resulted in the destruction of almost 30,000 planets. The Air Rebellion conducted by enslaved and subject planets finally brought peace to the universe, although another 2,000 planets are thought to have been annihilated during that conflict.

Fortunately, the leader of the Rebellion, Airtesto Oudjar, was a benevolent and far-sighted leader. She decreed that the warlike Ancients would be barred from any influence or authority in perpetuity. However, recognising that the human universe had got off on the wrong foot largely as a result of understandable human fear and stupidity, she spared the remaining Ancient planets and confined all inhabitants to their surfaces, where they have remained ever since.*

These days The Ancients' planets survive on tourism and have some of the best museums and early cultural centres in the universe. Their leaders perform non-essential ceremonial roles and some are allowed to travel to perform naming ceremonies for new Confederation planets and other significant, but boring events.

StarCore

StarCore runs the universe. Comprising approximately 500,000 planets, 'The Core' is split equally into Administration, Economic, Military, Exploration and Supervision divisions.

The 10,000 planet StarCore Council (operating under the Administration Division) controls entry to the Confederation and also resolves disputes among member planets. The average time from dispute application to resolution is 400 years, which has resulted in most planets finding their own solutions to issues, an outcome the system was designed to encourage. However, on many occasions disputes have gone through the entire process only for the council to discover the planets under dispute had already destroyed each other. In the words of legendary Yresly Councillor Barthdol Gwalpin, "shit happens".

Worldlings

The remaining 12.5 million member planets are known as Worldlings. They all joined in the last 5,000 years and are being groomed for possible StarCore membership.

---

* Airtesto Oudjar, incidentally, was ably assisted by Tysl Cvaz, leader of the Typuir Galazin Network during the Air Rebellion. Cvaz became Oudjar's lover, but they fell out when he tried to claim credit for the victory. This, together with his affair with the Kmjii sisters, rulers of Dfutre, sent Oudjar into a rage. Though she always denied responsibility, Cvaz was killed after he went into hiding – along with one hundred and thirty-five billion others – on Putker, one of eighteen planets simultaneously destroyed in what was officially described by Oudjar's chief minister as an 'unfortunate accident', the cause of which was never explained

Promotion is usually attained in under 5,000 years, but some planets struggle to make the grade. But, like children, planets progress at different rates and, being human, they tend to stumble over the line eventually.

When assessed as ready, a Worldling is assigned a supervisory role over a pre-confederation planet by their StarCore Supervision Mentor planet. If their performance is satisfactory after the probation period, they are assigned a further 10 planets and so on until they supervise 100 planets and qualify for senior StarCore membership. They are closely watched and serious errors are punished by the removal of supervision status, elongating the qualification period by up to several hundred years.

Pre-confederation membership planets

It is not known how many planets inhabited by humans are in this category, as StarCore Exploration is not required to officially report them until all the Civilisation Markers on the planet are met. Estimates put the number of Pre-Cons at between 40 and 50 million planets. And Gryszl Pkuy of the StarCore Administration Statistics Bureau claims the total Confederation and Pre-Con planets comprise less than 1% of the total number of planets in this universe. Opponents claim he is only trying to increase the Admin budget, but given the relatively tiny amount of the universe which has been explored, hey, who knows?

NOTE 1: There are approximately 110,000 non-Confederation human planets which have chosen not to join for various reasons. For security purposes, all of these planets are off limits and all inhabitants are confined to their own solar systems. See 'Jaytorian Uprising' for background information.

NOTE 2: Non-human life form planets mostly co-exist peacefully with Confederation members, but complacency is dangerous. For the history of these planets and their organisations, see 'The Alien Galmanac'.

EIGHT

Really, thought Kylie, *surely life on Earth can't possibly be this boring*. After the excitement of the last few days, this was a bitter disappointment. At least she was in good company. The English teacher, Mr French, looked close to unconsciousness as he listened to one of the boys, Dan Perkins, recite a passage from Henry V. It was such a lifeless rendition that Kylie wondered if she had stumbled on a cure for insomnia.

"Old men forget…," said Dan, beginning another verse.

I wish I could, thought Kylie.

"…yet all shall be forgot, but he'll remember with advantages, what feats he did that day. Then shall our names, familiar in his mouth as household words – Harry the King, Bedford and Exeter, Warwick and Talbot, Salisbury and Gloucester…"

Mr French had reached the limits of his endurance and raised a hand. "Who will rid me of this troublesome boy?" he asked of no one in particular, paraphrasing an earlier Henry, Kylie noted.

"If Henry V had your oratory skills, Perkins, Shakespeare would never have heard of him, never mind dedicated a play to his memory. You are reading one of the most wonderful plays in the history of the world, not the phone book." Mr French scanned the class. "Would anyone else like to destroy the work of our greatest poet?"

Kylie had absently memorised her copy of the entire play while listening to Dan Perkins drone on, so she raised her hand. "I'll do it!"

Mr French looked at her briefly, then at her hair, then looked away. "Anyone else?"

No one would meet his eye, so Mr French looked at his watch, sighed, and turned back to Kylie. "Very well, Hart. Break a leg. But don't break our hearts. Ha ha."

Beam me up, Rafael! thought Kylie, hopefully. *Time to liven things up.*

Kylie stood and walked to the front of the class. She didn't need the book, as it was on hand on her Cortex Implant.

Surprised, Mr French got up from his desk and moved across the classroom to lean against the window frame, his interest piqued and his arms folded.

Kylie climbed onto Mr French's desk and launched into the animated speech. The teacher automatically moved to protest, but then resisted the urge. "Be in their flowing cups freshly rememb'red. This story shall the good man teach his son; and Crispin Crispian shall ne'er go by…"

Her voice rose, her eyes blazed with emotion and she gestured with her arms, as her classmates sat back in their seats, wide-eyed.

"…from this day to the ending of the world, but we in it shall be remembered – We few, we happy few, we band of brothers; for he to-day that sheds his blood with me shall be my brother; be he ne'er so vile…"

Kylie's voice boomed and her fists clenched as she reached a riveting and brilliant conclusion.

"…this day shall gentle his condition; and gentlemen in England now-a-bed shall think themselves accurs'd they were not here, and hold their manhoods cheap whiles any speaks that fought with us upon Saint Crispin's day." Kylie's final words seemed to echo around the classroom. Actually, they did echo because she had added the effect to her voice.

There was deathly silence as the students stared at Kylie, open-mouthed. She glanced at Mr French, who was also stunned. But then he grinned and began to applaud. "Bravo!" he shouted, "Bravo!"

That's more like it, thought Kylie. *It was pretty good, but the word should be 'brava'.*

Mr French stopped clapping suddenly as the classroom door opened. Mrs Elswick and Mr Oberon stood in the doorway, looking at Kylie, who was still on the desk.

Mr Oberon turned to the Headmistress. "I rest my case."

A few minutes later, Kylie discovered, to her disappointment, that Mrs Elswick's office was just like the rest of the school, neat, tidy and predictably uninspiring. Her desk, spotlessly clean, held a computer, in and out baskets, a pot with pens and pencils and a coffee mug with the words, *One Head is Better than Two.* Kylie decided Mrs Elswick did not have a sense of humour and neither did the person who gave her the mug.

She sat on the other side of the desk while the Headmistress tapped on her keyboard and squinted at the screen. It was impossible to estimate Mrs Elswick's age as she was one of those people who remained unchanged in the looks department from fifteen to ninety. *I'll settle for half way*, thought Kylie. The tapping went on for quite some time while Kylie wondered if Mrs Elswick would notice if she got up and left.

But Mrs Elswick finished typing with a flourish and turned to Kylie with a fake concerned parental face. *At least she's making an effort.*

"What is going on, Polly?" she asked, tilting her head in faux sympathy. *This is clearly a trap.*

I'm not Polly. I'm actually from another planet and I swapped places with her. Polly is in my spaceship, but we've lost contact. "I'm overtired. I've been staying up too late," she replied.

"Hmm," said Mrs Elswick. "Your hair and the considerable energy you displayed while standing on Mr French's desk suggest that is not actually the case."

Mrs Elswick stood and walked over to a cabinet with frosted glass doors. She unlocked one of them and took out a small empty urine sample jar. She turned and held it up. "I want you to fill this."

Kylie had not expected that. "What, from here?"

"Don't be silly, Polly. Now tell me, what are you taking?"

"Taking?"

"You are acting very strangely. You are usually so, so... predictable."

Talk about a backhanded compliment. "Perhaps I'm just coming out of my shell."

Mrs Elswick shook her head sadly. "I don't think so. Come with me."

Kylie followed the Headmistress back into the corridor. It was tempting to turn away and just walk out of the main door, but Kylie felt she should stay for Polly's sake. She did not like this feeling, as her usual method of coping with a crisis was to run and leave them all to it. After all, there's nothing particularly serious about climbing onto a desk and reciting Shakespeare, and Polly would only get detention or a short suspension at worst. Or, at best, thought Kylie as she looked around, expulsion.

Kylie's parents were always telling her to think of others and not just herself. Normally, she would ignore such stupid advice, but now, here, it felt like the right thing to do. She hadn't felt the same since she assumed Polly's persona. *What's happening to me?*

"Right," said Mrs Elswick as she stopped outside the girls toilets. She handed the jar to Kylie. "I'll wait here. Don't take too long."

"I went a short time ago, so it may take a little while," replied Kylie. She had to stall for time. She entered the bathroom, closed the door and leant against it.

The main problem with this scenario was that Kylie was incapable of producing urine. Which was probably a good thing, given what a test would show. On Kylie's planet, as with the vast bulk of advanced humans throughout the universe, there was no longer any waste and everything the body discarded was converted into fuel. An ingenious piece of bio-engineering, it was both efficient and tidy, although she suspected Mrs Elswick would not be impressed if she tried to explain this fact.

What to do? She looked at the long, narrow room in front of her, a row of sinks to her left, eight toilet cubicles stretching away to her right. At the end there was a long radiator beneath a high window. She inspected each cubicle hopefully but, as she suspected at such a goody-goody-two-shoes school, everyone had flushed. *I should have run.*

"How are you going?"

"I'm not," Kylie replied to the muffled question from the hallway. "Can I have a few more minutes?"

"Alright, but not too long." Mrs Elswick sounded irritated. *Join the club*, thought Kylie.

There was only one thing to do. Kylie climbed on top of the radiator and pushed open the window. It was still head-high, so she had to scramble up to see outside. To her dismay, she saw the building was two storeys high on this side, due to the school being built on the side of a hill, and the bathroom faced out onto a u-shaped indent into the main building. The other walls had similar bathroom windows and a few vents, but no classroom windows, so at least no one could see her escape.

She scrambled a little higher and managed to get her head and shoulders outside. Below were the school bins and assorted football goalposts and basketball frames. There was also a drainpipe between this window and the next, but it was too far to reach. Resigned to telling Mrs Elswick she was unable to produce the required sample, Kylie started to push herself back into the bathroom. But as she did, she heard a sneeze from below.

She pushed her head out further and saw, directly below, a girl leaning back against the wall of the building. Mindful of the Headmistress close by, she leant out further. "Hey!" she called, not too loudly.

The girl straightened up and looked around. Kylie could see she was a year or two older than her.

"Up here!"

This time the girl looked up the opposite wall. Kylie sighed. "Right above you!"

The girl stepped away from the wall this time and looked up, but she didn't show much surprise at seeing Kylie hanging halfway out of the window. *Obviously a common occurrence.*

"What?" said the girl.

Kylie wasn't big on small talk. "Can you pee in this bottle?" she said, holding out the jar.

"What, from here?"

Smart-arse. "I'll pay you."

"How much?"

Kylie had not considered money. She reached down and felt in Polly's pockets, but there was no cash. But… "This is worth more than money," she said, holding up the corridor pass.

The girl recognised it immediately and Kylie saw with some relief she was interested.

"Throw it down."

"I'll throw it after you fill the bottle."

They eyeballed each other for a moment.

"OK," said the girl.

Kylie dropped the jar and the girl caught it easily and went behind one of the bins. Kylie twisted her head back inside and called out. "I think I'll be done soon, Mrs Elswick."

She heard a muttered response through the door and contorted her head and shoulder through the window once again. *Who knew providing a urine sample would be this convoluted.*

The girl had finished and held up the bottle as evidence. "Throw down the pass," she said.

"Bottle first," replied Kylie.

The girl stared back and didn't move. *How annoying*. Kylie dropped the pass and it fluttered slowly to the ground, where the girl picked it up and studied it closely. *Can she read?* wondered Kylie.

The girl finally appeared satisfied and without warning hurled the bottle skywards and walked away. Kylie lurched through the window and stretched out a hand, but the bottle flicked her fingers and spun up and out of view above the window. Now it was down to guesswork. She turned and thrust her head and both hands out of the window just as the bottle came down. It smacked her on the forehead and ricocheted into her left hand, catching firmly between her little and ring fingers. *How easy was that?*

She quickly wriggled inside and jumped to the floor and was washing the bottle and her hands as Mrs Elswick came through the door holding open a clip-lock plastic bag. Kylie dropped the sample bottle inside and smiled. The Headmistress looked at her and the entire bathroom suspiciously. "I'll see you when the results come back. Now, off to class."

It was nearly lunchtime, so instead Kylie went outside and hid behind a tree until the other kids started coming outside. The Shakespeare incident was a lot of fun, but the rest of the morning sucked big time. Still, she had negotiated a few tricky situations and could only have enhanced Polly's reputation. Maybe not to the extent she would be considered cool – she was not sure that was possible given the material to work with – but she was on the map, so to speak.

Which reminded her. "Polly? Rafael?" Nothing. Kylie still wasn't worried. A little concerned, maybe. But worried? Nah. If there was any kind of emergency, they'd find a way of getting her out. Wouldn't they? Of course. There really was nothing to worry about. But what say, for the sake of argument, the ship had been destroyed somehow, and Polly and Rafael and the rest were dead? There was definitely a worry-wart side to her she didn't know about. *Must be to do with the transformation into Polly*, she decided. *I don't usually give a shit about anything*. Worse case scenario? Life on Earth. *How depressing*.

Well, no use worrying, she decided. There's still work to do. More kids were out in the yard now and she spotted Eddie Burke in the distance. He was searching the yard for something. Someone. *Me*.

Kylie decided to string him along for a minute or two, but as she skirted the edge of the yard Josh and Kate ran up to her.

"We just heard!" shouted Kate.

"Yeah. What happened." Josh said to her hair.

He was standing very close. "Back off!" she barked and he jumped back in surprise. *Doesn't he know how much space is available in the universe?*

"Is it true you climbed on Mr French's desk?" Kate shouted louder this time.

They are so irritating, thought Kylie. She watched Eddie in the distance. He hadn't lost interest in searching for her yet, but it was only a matter of time.

"Yes, it's true," she replied. "I'll fill you in later, but I've got a hot date and have to…"

She noted a frown on Josh's face – *interesting* – but spotted urine girl walking towards her and she waved, but the girl walked straight past.

"Woah! Did you smell that?" said Kate

Josh waved his hand in front of his nose. "Yep."

"What?" asked Kylie. The whole planet smelled weird to her.

"Dope," said Kate.

"She's a dope?"

Josh laughed. "No. She's been smoking marijuana. She reeks of it."

Kylie blinked. And again. "Whoops."

"What's wrong?" asked Josh.

"Nothing. I have to go." Kylie hurried away, aware that Josh and Kate exchanged a glance. *Bully for them!*

She had almost reached Eddie when he noticed her, a look of relief, then worry on his face. He looked furtively around.

"Hi. I haven't got long..."

"Are you dying?"

"What? No. I just told, er... I have to get back in a minute. I shouldn't, er..."

What does Polly see in this babbling idiot? "Take me dancing. Tonight. Pick me up from my place at seven."

Eddie stared back. "I dunno. I had, er... Why...I'm not sure..."

Kylie rolled her eyes. She could feel the Polly side of her beginning to feel sorry for him, but common sense prevailed. "Don't blow this, Eddie. Stick with me and I'll show you the stars."

She turned and walked away without looking back. *If he turns up tonight*, she thought, *please let Polly be back.*

"Polly? Rafael?" *Where are you?*

NINE

Polly stood in silence with Rafael and the others. Kylie's parents had circled the group and presumably stood behind them. She could feel their fuzzy eyes on her back. Polly's eyes had not adjusted enough to the light to get a look at the ship, but it was there beyond the small pool of darkness enveloping them.

"We're in trouble, huh?" she whispered.

"Big time," agreed Rafael.

"Just so you know," said Polly, "I'm going to blame everything on you and Kylie."

"That figures."

"Taking advantage of me, a poor primitive Earthling."

"Cut the crap," said Kylie's mum from just behind. "You're more intelligent than Kylie and her crew combined."

Polly spun around and was enveloped in bright light as the blurred figure loomed over her.

"The rest of you go to Deck Four. Your teacher is waiting and would like a few words." Kylie's mum made a blurred shooing gesture and Rafael and the others began a forlorn out-of-focus procession across the deck.

Polly's mouth dropped open as her vision cleared. The spaceship was a vast dome, bigger than a sports stadium. Much bigger. She and Kylie's parents stood in the middle of the deck, while above them was a wide glass platform spiralling up to the transparent roof of the craft, the stars spread out beyond. She could also see through the platform where hundreds, perhaps thousands, of fuzzy crewmembers milled around, walking and gesturing. There were no controls visible, or furniture. It was a pristine crystal dome of breathtaking beauty.

"It's so vast!"

Kylie's mum pointed down. "The other half is down there."

Polly looked down and saw a mirror image of the ship beneath her feet and realised the ship was in fact a gigantic globe and not a dome. Beyond the outer walls below was Mars.

She suddenly didn't know which way was up and staggered. Kylie's mum caught her arm and held her up. "This ship has a very old design and can be disorientating. Wait until you see a new one."

"This is old?" Polly thought it looked brand new. She felt distinctly queasy.

"Well, not that old, I suppose." Kylie's mum tilted her fuzzy head and Polly imagined she was calculating. "It was built in 1928, going by your calendar. They completely revamped the design in 1957 and that model has been so successful they haven't done much more than tweak some of the features since then."

Polly opened her mouth, but decided not to ask any more questions for the moment. This was overwhelming. Kylie's mum didn't offer any further information and stood, waiting. Polly noticed her smoky outline was calm, which she found reassuring.

Kylie's dad turned to her mum. Polly couldn't hear them speak, but Kylie's dad nodded slightly, then they both looked at Polly. "I'm Clive," said Kylie's dad. "And this is Gemma."

Polly stared at them. "Clive. Gemma. Kylie. You're kidding!"

"We don't get a choice," said Gemma. "The translator converts our names into the closest match in your part of the world."

"It's still weird."

"You're probably wondering what is going on," said Clive.

It had crossed my mind, thought Polly, though she managed to stay quiet this time. Maybe all this is weird for them, too.

"Let's walk. You'll find it will help you get used to the motion."

Polly was not aware of any motion at all, but as she followed Kylie's parents to the transparent platform, she did feel better.

Gemma began. "You know that Kylie stole the school vessel?"

Polly nodded. "Rafael told me."

"She's been in trouble before," said Clive, "but nothing on this scale."

"I don't understand," said Polly. "Can't you just swap us back?"

"No," replied Gemma. "If we had arrived sooner it wouldn't be a problem, but now there's a complication."

"A big complication," added Clive.

They walked up the platform, Polly between them, although there was no sense of climbing. They passed other fuzzies, but no one seemed to take any notice. Hard to tell, though, as she couldn't make out any faces. "Complication?"

Gemma and Clive exchanged glances over Polly's head.

"What?" said Polly.

"Do you like history?" asked Clive.

"Of course," said Polly.

"Good," said Gemma. "There's a lot you need to know, so we will start by showing you the history of the Earth."

"I heard a little about Earth's history via The Gal, but it didn't make a lot of sense. It mentioned Hyweirdos or something running the planet… "

"We'll get to that. But look at this." Gemma gestured to the centre of the space ship where an image bloomed, not sharp this time, more like CCTV footage. They stopped walking.

"This," announced Clive, "is the first known footage we have of the Earth. The planet was discovered a long time before this, but it was so remote it took several hundred years until the first probes arrived."

The Earth revolved, day turning to night. The night was so dark, Polly thought the probe was too far out to pick up the lights from the cities.

As day returned the planet suddenly zoomed closer as the probe entered the atmosphere and dropped down to the Atlantic ocean. A storm was in progress as the vision skimmed the wild sea and approached land. The skies cleared and they were above lush forest and then harsh desert, travelling at speed. The picture crackled and distorted every few seconds, but there was no mistaking the pyramids. Polly marvelled at the first alien view of the Earth.

The probe veered north and followed the Nile. A city passed below very briefly as the probe approached the delta and shot out over the Mediterranean.

"You'll like this next bit," said Clive.

The probe crossed land again, this time following a dirt road along a ridge through green hills. Ahead Polly saw a long procession on the road. They looked like cattle, but as the probe passed over them, she saw they were a tightly packed group of men jogging quickly in formation. They looked vaguely familiar, but the vision moved on and the probe rose into the air, providing a better view ahead, where a sprawling city appeared.

It didn't look like a modern city, although there were large buildings, some of them several stories high. It was only when the Colosseum came into view that Polly twigged. This was not a ruined building; it looked intact! The probe came in low and Polly could see figures inside. Hordes of men and women were sweeping the seating areas, while others raked the sand in the arena.

The probe dipped beyond the Colosseum and into the Roman Forum, passing between vast marble buildings with brightly painted columns. Crowds surged between the buildings, which were lined with street vendors, jostling each other and gesticulating. Polly's mouth fell open.

On a platform before the largest building, a stocky man in a bright, purple-edged white toga raised his arms in the air, one hand outstretched, the other waving a rolled-up scroll. He must look more impressive from this distance, Polly thought, as only a handful of men had gathered to listen to him.

"When was this?" asked Polly, unable to look away.

"203AD, during the reign of the Roman Emperor Septimius Severus," replied Clive. "Rome was the dominant authority at the time, but after an inspection assessment the planet was classified primitive and placed on the planetary watch file, which meant a revisit every few hundred years."

"Are you OK?" asked Gemma. "You've gone white."

Polly turned to her. "I can't believe it! I'm the only human to ever see this vision first hand."

"Actually, you're not," said Clive.

The picture faded and only the spaceship and Mars were visible.

"I'm not?" asked Polly in wonder. There was so much to take in.

"No," answered Clive, "but we'll get to that later. Anyway, by the time of the next visit, Rome had collapsed and despite thriving civilizations in Asia and South America, the planet as a whole had not really advanced and observation was placed on low priority."

Gemma and Clive started walking again and Polly hurried to join them.

"Who sent that probe?"

Clive shrugged fuzzily. "Back then? Geez, it must have been Mirrillon or maybe Gwaal. They were the only Confederation members in this region at that time. This was at the outer edges of the known universe back then. In those days the Confederation was a pretty loose and fairly powerless collective, a bit like your European Union is now. On paper it was an organisation, but in reality, a mess. It didn't really get its administration act finally together until about a thousand years ago."

Polly's mind whirled. The Gal had said something about this, but she thought she had misheard the bit about aliens buzzing the Earth for close to two thousand years. *Amazing.*

Gemma and Clive stopped and Polly almost walked into them. "This must be overwhelming," said Gemma.

"No, no," said Polly. "Well, yes." She wanted to know everything, but it was hard to make sense of the little bit she had heard so far. "Rafael gave me access to The Gal, which helps, but there's so much it's hard to take in."

"The Gal is a good start," said Gemma, "but it's a bit dodgy in the accuracy department. Hopefully we can fill in the gaps for you."

"Sounds good."

"Let's walk to the top first."

Polly followed them up the ramp until they reached a platform jutting out over the void. Beneath her feet, Polly could see the entire ship spread out, a strange gigantic transparent sphere populated by thousands of blurred figures oddly jumbled amid the various glass decks. The dark side of Mars floated beneath the craft, its mass dominating the view.

Gemma pointed up into the blackness of space and the hologram image of another planet appeared. It was Earth-like, mostly consisting of blue ocean with large green continents. The shapes were strange to Polly, but also a little similar to those maps showing Earth millions of years ago before the continents assumed their current configuration.

"This is Rambolt One," said Gemma. "One of the original leading planets of the Ancients."

"Ah," said Polly. "I've heard about them."

"They ruled harshly," continued Gemma, "for a little longer than Rome, but as the Confederation grew, the new members resisted and rival organisations were formed."

"The good old days," laughed Clive. "The Ancients were finally overthrown after the Air Rebellion and the modern era began. I say modern, but this was around half a million Earth years ago. The surviving Ancient planets have no power these days. They are just trotted out for ceremonial occasions to add a bit of colour."

"Like the Royal family?" asked Polly.

"Pretty much," said Gemma. "Anyway, in keeping with human history everywhere, they got too big for their boots and lots of people and planets were destroyed."

"Sounds like Star Wars," said Polly.

Gemma and Clive exchanged a fuzzy glance, which reminded Polly of her exchange with Kylie about the 'Death Star'.

"Today there are close to thirteen million members of the Federation, but governance of the human universe is very different."

Polly was absolutely riveted. "So how does it work?"

Gemma pointed again at Rambolt One. "This is now the Main Universal Administration Centre for StarCore. It's like the United Nations, only it's a planet instead of a building. Teams from all the member planets live there and vote on any off-planet issues affecting other planets. One hundred thousand regional councils resolve smaller localised problems throughout the universe, while bigger issues are referred to Rambolt One for a vote."

"Vote?"

Clive turned to her. "It works like the Eurovision Song Contest. Proposals are like songs, and the members vote for them, often in groups with vested interests. But no one dominates and with a large majority required, it means radical proposals rarely succeed and marginal ones are often shelved and resubmitted."

Polly shook her head. "But that sounds completely unworkable."

Clive turned to Gemma. "I told you she was smart."

"It is," said Gemma. "Very little gets done, or if it does, it can take generations. The Centre is both the undisputed governing body of the universe and deliberately almost completely ineffectual. It's the perfect form of government."

"Then what's the point?"

"I said almost. The Centre is designed to stifle major disputes, which must be referred if local planetary systems can't do it themselves. That's a tremendous incentive to co-operate with your neighbours. And if things get out of hand, the Centre only needs a five percent quorum to impose sanctions on a planet or system."

"What sanctions?"

Clive counted them on blurred fingers. "Trade, travel, financial, expulsion or, in rare circumstances, destruction."

Polly was shocked. "They would destroy a planet."

"In the early days they blew up quite a few, and during the Kylingen Insurrection, fifteen planets were destroyed simultaneously."

"That's barbaric!"

"That was an extreme situation," said Gemma. "But yeah, it was a little harsh. But gee, if you knew those Kylingens…"

A little harsh.

"It's not quite so extreme these days," said Clive. "The last planet to be destroyed was Arconia, about three hundred years ago, after they invaded another planet. But first the population was removed to an uninhabited planet and all technology was withheld until recently. They are still rebuilding. It will be some time before…"

Clive and Gemma became suddenly still. "What is it?" asked Polly.

After what seemed an age, Gemma turned to her. "In a few minutes we can head back to Earth."

Polly felt deflated. The thought of going back to her old life was horrifying.

But suddenly the spacecraft was bathed in sunlight as the ship emerged from behind Mars, although it appeared that the planet rose over the top of the ship and dropped into position behind.

Polly sensed something else, but she couldn't ask as Clive and Gemma had their heads close together and were either conversing or receiving a message. They both turned to her at the same time and she swallowed nervously. *Here it comes.*

"There's something else you need to know," said Gemma.

"I thought so," said Polly.

"Our planet, Syssine is a StarCore member and oversees more than five thousand planets, including Earth. We appoint Supervisor planets for each world in our assigned area."

"So you appointed the Hywar-whatsits?"

"The Hywardathians, yes," said Clive. "We appointed them, but we can't actively interfere, unless…" He looked at Gemma, who sighed.

"We can interfere in an emergency, although we might choose not to," said Gemma.

Polly was puzzled. "I don't understand. If you are in charge, what's all the fuss about me and Kylie?"

Kylie's parents exchanged fuzzy glances again, causing Polly to become irritated. "Tell me!"

Gemma shrugged. "OK. The StarCore planet – us, in this case – appoint a Mentor Worldling – Hywardath for Earth – for individual responsibility of a planet. We have our own observers, and there are independent Confederation auditors who come and go from many other worlds, who operate a bit like secret shoppers, and we don't know who they are. But the Mentor handles security and polices pre-confederation planets like Earth."

"I see."

"Certain milestones must be reached by each planet before they receive an invitation to join the Confederation. Political and religious, mainly, so that they are not a threat to themselves or other planets."

Clive stepped in. "The current schedule is for Earth to be notified that it is not alone in the universe in about fifty years. Then, if the planet meets the correct criteria, it will be invited to join the confederation around another fifty to sixty years later."

"That's so long!" said Polly, disappointed.

"Well, it's not like joining a golf club," said Gemma, "and we have told you about the way administration works. It's quite fast, really."

"So," said Polly, getting back to the nitty-gritty, "I take it that the Mentor is an issue."

"THE issue. Hywardath was unfortunately chosen as Mentor for Earth. It's fairly new to the Confederation – less than five hundred years – and they had been pushing for more responsibility for some time. They were put in charge straight after World War II. The development of primitive nuclear weapons is generally the time active intervention kicks in."

Clive interjected. "They were not a great choice."

Polly felt strangely powerless, like a child again, as all her preconceptions of Earth crumbled around her. "Why?"

"The Hywardathians are too…try-hard, I guess. They think they know it all, they are incredibly rule-bound and they are terribly sensitive to criticism. Trouble is, they won't bend the rules and you can't negotiate anything they consider black and white."

Gemma laughed, but Polly thought there was little humour in the sound. "Everything to them is black and white."

"I think I'm getting the picture," said Polly. "Kylie will be in trouble if she's caught and you can't get her out?"

"On most other planets," said Clive, "this wouldn't be a problem. It would be treated like what it is. A childish prank. But on Earth? It's the Hywardathians' only planet and they are keen to make sure everything goes by the book. Everything."

Polly couldn't read Clive or Gemma's fuzzy faces, but their cloudy outlines surged tightly as though their bodies were covered in miniature storms. And their calm voices belied their fear. The hairs on the back of Polly's neck prickled and her throat became dry. "What happens if Kylie is caught?"

"It's not just Kylie," said Gemma. "According to the 'book' you are an accomplice."

"What?" Polly felt her stomach lurch.

She saw Clive and Gemma turn to each other. They were motionless in a swirling kind of way for a moment, then Gemma nodded.

Clive turned to Polly. "You are both safe for the moment. The Hywardathians are on high alert, but they are not sure why. They detected Kylie's ship, but fortunately, Rafael got you out of there before they could confirm its identity."

"Both? Please tell me what is going to happen."

Gemma reached out and took Polly's hands in hers. A warm electric current pulsed through Polly's body, but it didn't make her feel better.

"If Kylie is captured," began Gemma, "and the

Hywardathians discover what has happened…"

"Which they will," added Clive.

"… we will have to hand you over."

Polly felt ill. "We'll be jailed?"

That look between Clive and Gemma again. "No," said Clive. "The penalty under Confederation law is instant vaporisation."

EXTRACT FROM VRYL'S GALMANAC

Planet HZCX165349872/3542/9/3
(Local Name: Earth)

'Earth', the third planet in the Cziphyl solar system was officially discovered 10,000 years ago by a passing Wfrik expedition. A scan of the surface identified humans, but they were only at Level 16 in the evolutionary scale so an official inspection was not required at that time.

The first surface survey was conducted 2,000 years ago and by then the population had reached Level 39, very close to the average final development range of 41 to 45. Regular monitor assessments were made prior to the Starcore Mentor Tender. This was won by Syssine, which appointed Hywardath to its first Planet Supervisor role. There was some controversy regarding this appointment, as Syssine initially requested a more experienced supervisor, but suddenly had a change of hearts when an anonymous (yeah, right!) regulatory issue was reported to the Confederation authorities. The two planets are not on good terms and due to the rule-bound and obnoxious nature of the Hywardathians, progress on Earth has slowed.

A local war involving most of the planet and the simultaneous discovery of nuclear fusion triggered a more active intervention from the Hywardathians. Syssine stated for the record that the world war could and should have been prevented, but Hywardath pointed to Rule YHT2345P987Z relating to intervention trigger points and claimed they were powerless to intervene. It was pointed out to the Hywardathians that preventing the deaths of over 50 million people might be a common sense overrider to the rule, but clearly, to them, the rule was more important.

To their credit, the Hywardathians did prevent certain nuclear war on sixteen separate occasions during the 35 years after the war (there were no rules against those actions), though their methods were not ideal, mainly due to their insistence on using their own antiquated technology and their well-known lack of empathy and human insight.

There is little to distinguish Earth from other human planets at the same stage of development. Governance is fractured across the planet. Primitive religious beliefs remain widespread. And science is reasonably advanced, due to the Confederation Confidential Mentoring of a local genius called Einstein and other scientists during the last few hundred years, although it is unlikely the locals will discover The Source by themselves.

Financial exploitation rights to Earth culture, particularly their very popular music, has resulted in above average funds, so Earth will have considerable wealth when it joins the Confederation.

Long term, Earth's solar system will function for the foreseeable future and two other nearby planets are available for population expansion with only minor modifications once capacity is reached.*

---

* Additional note of interest: Evidence has been discovered that one of the two neighbouring planets mentioned above, locally known as Mars, once had an advanced human civilization. No human life exists there now due to an unspecified cataclysmic event about 500,000 years ago, but archaeologists found an ancient, but well preserved abandoned city buried deep below the surface and believe that survivors may have travelled to Earth. Tests on Earth humans indicate that not all of their DNA evolved locally, which supports the Martian theory.

TEN

Kylie lay on Polly's bed and stared at the ceiling. *So this is Earth. Not much here to impress a visitor.* Her "Polly outfit' itched, she was fed up and finally decided she should have waited for a better opportunity. Polly was OK, but this school. This town. This life!

But despite this, she tingled with apprehension. She was, though she hated to admit it, scared. There had been no contact for hours. She could imagine Rafael playing a joke for a little while – fair enough given the way she treated him, although he was very annoying and deserved it – but not for so long. Something had happened.

Kylie had calculated the odds of discovery and assessed them as slim to nil. The Hywardathians thought they knew better than everyone else and relied on their old technology, making it easy to cloak her ship and avoid detection. Sure, the Confederation had recently forced them to buy an Instell-sweeper craft, but she doubted they knew how to use it yet and only one to cover the whole planet? Well, really, what were the odds?

Not high enough.

What was it her dad always said? Trust the universe. That was wearing a bit thin now. Rafael clearly was not close by, otherwise he would have got word to her. This meant the ship had bolted and would return when it was safe. She didn't want to consider the possibility they had been captured. Surely Rafael's Cortex Implant would have been downloaded and Kylie would now be in custody, too.

But what if the Hywardathians were playing a game and watching her. She wouldn't put it past them. They were a nasty bunch. Mum said so, probably when she said you should never go near the Earth without permission because the Hywardathians are a nasty bunch.

Speaking of which, Kylie could hear Polly's parents crashing around downstairs as they prepared dinner. She supposed she should go down and interact, but gee, parents were so…so…parental.

It was still an hour until Eddie was due to pick her up. *If he shows, that is.*

A rap on the door. "Polly! Dad's defrosting dinner. It'll be ready in half an hour."

"Don't worry about me," Kylie called back. "I'm going out."

Pause. "OK." Another pause. "Can you come down. We want to have a chat."

"Sure. Give me a minute."

Kylie listened to Polly's mum's footsteps pad down the stairs. She rolled her eyes and sighed. She couldn't roll her eyes as herself, so it was still an enjoyable novelty. She did it again and slowly stood up. She wore a simple, comfortable dress taken from Polly's wardrobe, the only one she could find. Polly was clearly a jeans and T-shirt girl, but really if she wanted to attract Eddie – though goodness knows why – she should at least make an effort.

Kylie stared at her image in the mirror and wondered if she needed makeup. Earth women seemed to like smearing stuff on their faces for some insane reason. She shrugged and the image shrugged back. She looked fine and her blue hair really went well with the orange dress and green boots.

She opened the door and followed the stairs down to the kitchen. Dave and Marianne Hart sat at the table, each with a glass of wine. Behind them, on the stove, what looked like a block of ice sat steaming in a pan.

They stared at her as she came in. Kylie smiled. This was the first time she had seen Polly's dad, who had a kind face and a completely bald head except for a tuft of grey hair behind each ear which looked like small, hibernating mammals. Polly had his eyes and her mother's cute nose. Her mouth, obviously, had been donated by an ancestor.

"Are you going out like that?" asked Marianne, tentatively.

"Yeah. Why?"

"You're wearing your dressing gown and slippers."

Kylie blinked. "Only joking." *There really is no fashion sense on Earth.*

"Sit down," said Dave.

Kylie slid onto a chair across from them.

"Mr Oberon phoned me this afternoon," began Marianne. "It was mainly to check if there's any news on the satellites, but he also said you got in trouble at school."

Kylie shrugged. "I didn't do anything. It's my hair. They all treat me differently now. It must be hair-ism."

"I'm safe, then," laughed Dave. Marianne gave him a sharp look, but Kylie could see she was trying not to smile. She turned back to Kylie. "What's going on. It's like you've become a different person overnight."

Literally. Briefly, Kylie wondered if she should confide in them. They were nice and she was reasonably confident they wouldn't mind adopting an alien... *Maybe not.* "I am feeling a bit weird, like I'm from another planet or something. Must be hormones." She shrugged and attempted what she hoped was a helpless-little-girl expression.

Dave looked relieved, but Marianne was not totally convinced. *She's not even my mother, but I can feel her eyes boring through me*, thought Kylie. Instinctively, Kylie manipulated her features into a defiant what-are-you-going-to-do-about-it expression and glared back at Polly's mum. Now Marianne looked satisfied. *Manipulation is fun*, thought Kylie.

The inquisition continued. "Who are you going out with tonight? Josh?" asked Marianne.

There was hope in that question. Interesting! "No, Eddie."

"Who's he?" asked Dave.

"Just a boy from school."

"Where are you going?"

Kylie shrugged. "Hanging out."

"I want you home at nine," said Dave, quickly.

Both Kylie and Marianne looked at him as though he was mad. "Ten," he said in a futile attempt to save face.

"Ten-thirty," said Marianne. "You have school tomorrow. We're both working tonight, but dad will be home at ten-thirty."

Oh, yeah, thought Kylie. *Parents are the same the universe over. Nice try, but I know you are both working overnight.*

"OK?" Marianne looked at her closely.

"Sure."

Kylie waited to see if there was any more, but neither Marianne or Dave said anything. They looked like they wanted to and even glanced at each other, but Kylie had thrown them. More confirmation that the real Polly was seriously deficient in the rebellious teenager department.

"I might go and get changed."

"That's a very good idea."

Kylie trudged back up the stairs feeling a little humiliated. *Please let Eddie be early!*

She changed into a pair of jeans, sneakers and plain shirt; a Polly uniform. And what she was wearing, presumably, if she and the others were still alive.

Don't go there, Kylie told herself. *They are all fine and will be back in touch very soon.*

She spent the rest of her time listening to Polly's music on her smartphone. Kylie had very particular tastes in Earth music, but Polly didn't share them. It was all just noise. Shame she didn't have any of the cool Earth stuff Kylie liked.

A more welcome noise came in the form of the front doorbell. Kylie sprang to her feet and raced down the stairs. Dave was almost at the front door. "I'll get it!" shouted Kylie.

She rushed past Polly's dad and pulled open the door to find a nervous Eddie standing there holding a small and pathetic looking bunch of flowers. "These are for you," he said thrusting them in front of her.

"I'm not hungry," said Kylie.

Eddie blinked and looked at Dave, who stood behind Kylie, but he gave a welcome-to-the-club shrug.

"It's a joke, duh," added Kylie.

"Eddie, is it?" said Dave, stretching out a hand. He and Eddie shook.

"Mr Hart." Eddie saw Marianne approach and swallowed. "Mrs Hart."

"Hello, Eddie," she said.

Kylie turned and saw Polly's parents staring at Eddie. She almost felt sorry for him.

Marianne opened her mouth to speak again, so Kylie pushed Eddie hard in the chest, stepped outside and closed the door behind her. "See ya," she called. *This must be Polly's first date*, Kylie realised with some surprise.

She followed Eddie to his car, which, at closer inspection, was not that sporty. In fact, it looked like it would fall apart if you gave it a half-hearted shake. "Is this safe?" asked Kylie.

Eddie bristled. "Of course it is."

"Can I drive?"

"You're not old enough."

Handy to know. "How old are you?"

"Seventeen."

Eddie fastened his seatbelt – Kylie copied him – turned the key to start the car and pulled out into the street.

Kylie saw Polly's parents at the window and waved like a dutiful daughter should. *That's a relief*, she thought. *I couldn't stand much more in there.*

She turned to Eddie. He was good looking in an expected, conventional way. Black hair, even features, winning smile. She wasn't convinced he was terribly bright, though, but he would be a passable male model or toothpaste commercial actor. But maybe she was too harsh.

"So, Eddie," she said, seeing as he hadn't initiated any conversation, "how's it hangin'?"

"How's what hanging?" he asked, looking confused.

Too harsh? Nope.

"How are you?"

"Er, good." They stopped at traffic lights and Eddie looked across at her. "You're a bit weird."

Kylie grinned back. "Then why did you come out."

"Because you're a bit weird."

That's better, thought Kylie. "So, where are you taking me?"

The lights turned green and the car lurched forward. "Jackson's. You know, it's the only place in town with music. They've got a jukebox. You wanted to dance."

Where the hell have I ended up? thought Kylie. "Great."

Kylie decided she didn't inject enough sarcasm into the word, as Eddie looked relieved. *Polly owes me big time.*

Jackson's was so busy they managed to find a parking space directly in front of it. As she stepped out of the car, Kylie could see that the place was a large, brightly lit café with an open area surrounded by tables covered with plastic red and white chequered tablecloths. The chequered theme, this time black and white, extended to the floor, which was made from the finest linoleum money could buy. *Classy joint*, thought Kylie, with a distinct sinking feeling. It's going to be a long night.

Eddie pushed the door open for her and they entered. There were people here, maybe a dozen, mostly couples dotted around the tables. At least one of the couples was dancing, Kylie saw, but they were so old perhaps they were merely stopping each other from falling over. She didn't recognise the song coming from the antique jukebox, but most pop music on Earth sounded the same to her. Most.

"Grab a table," said Eddie. "What do you want to drink?"

"I'll have a martini."

His mouth dropped open – *not an attractive look* – and he shook his head. "They don't sell alcohol here! And you're too young to drink!"

It was worth a try, she decided. "What are you having?"

"Lemonade."

"Hmm," said Kylie, "and I had you pegged as a milkshake kind of guy. I'll have a lemonade, too."

"Anything to eat?"

"Are you kidding?"

Eddie shrugged and went to the counter, where a large, friendly looking man wearing a stained apron with KISS ME QUICK printed on it took his order. Kylie inspected the place more closely and, ten seconds later, knew everything there was to know about the café.

The music finished and the old couple staggered back to their table, smiling and laughing. *At least someone is having fun.* Eddie joined her carrying two glasses, then sat and sipped his lemonade through a straw. Kylie pretended to do the same, tempted to explain her digestive system to him.

Eddie smiled at her to hide the fact he didn't know what to say.

Kylie did. She had remembered she was actually here in a matchmaking role and any fun, however remote the possibility, would be a bonus. She lowered her expectations even further. "How come you're taking me out? Don't you have a girlfriend already?"

Eddie squirmed. "Er, Gwen. Yes. No. It's nothing. Just a friend thing."

"Does Gwen know it's nothing and just a friend thing?"

Eddie squirmed more and his face turned red. *Not a good look.* "Well… I've…we've never talked…it's just…"

"Gwen thinks she's your girlfriend." It wasn't a question.

"Maybe," offered Eddie, stretching the word out to a whine. "Er, she may have got that… well, as I said, we haven't really talked and… it's not that simple."

Kylie leant closer to him. "Do you think it's fair to take out another girl while you still have a girlfriend?" She raised her hand to stop Eddie's reply. "I haven't finished. The question is in several parts. Have you considered her feelings? What if she came here tonight and found you with another woman? Have you any idea how she would feel? What would you say to her? 'Sorry you got the wrong end of the stick, Gwen. It was just a friend thing.'"

Eddie just stared back at her now in horror, the wheels turning behind his eyes. Very slowly, Kylie saw, but there was definitely some primitive machinery whirring in there. *Really, what did he expect?*

Kylie smiled. She would now be able to report back to Polly and advise her to look elsewhere for the love of her life. "Why don't we dance," she said.

Eddie's mouth fell open again. *I wish he'd stop doing that*, thought Kylie. She was silent for a moment, then said. "Can you stop doing that."

His mouth snapped shut. *A much better look. For any girl shallow enough to base her choice purely on good looks, she could do worse.*

Kylie stood and walked to the now silent jukebox and Eddie followed her meekly. She looked at him and this time did feel a little sorry for him. It must be some Polly residue, as he didn't deserve sympathy. It was incredible, but she could see none of this had occurred to him. Well, with any luck, he would return to Gwen a changed man.

There were hundreds of songs on the jukebox and Kylie scanned them all in a few seconds. All the songs were rubbish, of course, so she selected one at random. "Got any coins?" she asked.

She couldn't fault Eddie's preparedness, as he pulled out a huge haul of silver from his pockets. "Break open the piggy bank?" she asked.

"Ha," replied Eddie, sarcastically and, she was glad to see, angrily. Much better.

But then he dropped most of the coins on the floor and scrambled to pick them up. Several rolled away and showed no sign of stopping any time soon.

There was one song Kylie would have loved to have

played, but there was no way it would be here at a café in England. Shame Rafael wasn't still up there. He could have loaded it onto the machine. Or dad. He and Kylie had similar tastes in music and he loved the song, too. Oh, well.

"Kylie." The voice was in her ear. It was her dad's voice.

"Hi dad, you remember that song… what the..!" She felt an enormous wave of relief, followed by the feeling that everything was now fine.

"We've come to get you off the planet." Her mum's voice this time. Gemma did not sound happy.

Kylie glanced at Eddie, who was on the other side of the room stretching an arm under the counter to recover a coin.

"Are you close by?" asked Kylie

"Yes," said Gemma. "We're behind the moon."

"Are Polly and Rafael OK?"

"Rafael is having a chat with your teacher…" – Kylie winced – "…and Polly is here with me."

"Hi," said Kylie.

"Hi," replied Polly, in a voice dripping with ice. "What are you do…bloody hell."

Eddie was back. "Who are you talking to?"

"What's going on?" shouted Polly.

"I was just humming a tune."

"What are you doing with him!" Polly had lost it.

"I have to go to the bathroom," she said to Eddie. "Don't play anything." Kylie hurried to a door at the back of the café and pushed into the thankfully empty Ladies bathroom."

"Didn't I tell you…"

"Shut up for a minute," shouted Kylie. "He's not for you, Polly. You'll thank me later."

Clive jumped in. "Shut up, both of you. Listen, Kylie, the Hywardathians detected your ship and know something is happening and they are on high alert. We need to get you out of there now and return Polly to Earth."

"They can't know I'm here, dad," argued Kylie. "This town is the last place on Earth they would suspect anything interesting going on."

"Thanks," said Polly.

"No offence," said Kylie.

"We can't take that chance," said Gemma. "They are doing another sweep over your location now, so we will get there in one hour. Go to Polly's house now."

Kylie thought for a moment. "An hour? No real hurry, then. I'll just have a dance with Eddie – might as well get something out of the evening – and get him to drop me off. There's plenty of time."

"Unbelievable," said Polly.

"I don't think so," added Gemma.

"Hmm," said Clive. "She won't draw attention if she does that. Just one dance and then she can head back."

Gemma drew out her reply. "I guess…"

"Unbelievable," said Polly. "I can't believe you went out with Eddie!"

Kylie sighed. "This is a town where you've got to make things happen, Polly."

"Yeah, well let's worry about that later," interrupted Gemma. "Go and have your dance and leave, OK?"

"Sure." Polly left the bathroom and suddenly remembered. "Dad! That Earth song I played you a few weeks ago. My favourite. Can you play it through the jukebox."

There was a short silence and Kylie imagined her mother shaking her head at her father and him giving his 'what-can-I-do' shrug. "Yeah, sure," he said.

Kylie emerged into the café. Eddie was standing by the jukebox and turned to her. "You OK?" he asked.

"Yep."

"What do you want to play?'

"Don't worry, It's all sorted."

Eddie raised his eyebrows, then frowned, then his head snapped back to the jukebox as the music started.

Kylie felt a shiver run through her. She couldn't remember the name of the song, but the Middle Eastern drums and pipes immediately grabbed her and she started moving. Eddie's eyes opened wider, though it was hardly surprising as he had never seen the Walpherian Stomp before. She leapt high and rhythmically in front of him, her feet crashing against the lino, her arms waving and her head snapping back and forth. Eddie backed away, frightened, appalled and fascinated. Kylie was impressed with herself. She knew she performed a mean stomp.

"Is she alright?" she heard Polly ask. "Is it a fit?"

"Wait until she starts properly," said Clive.

The music got louder and the singer issued an incredibly long note in Arabic. *Fantastic!* thought Kylie, as the tempo increased and her dance morphed into the Kalotian Vortex. She performed one, two, then three stomp-spins to transition into the Vortex, then grabbed Eddie's hands, just as he appeared to be about to turn and flee. She released one hand and flicked him around her so fast his feet left the floor.

"Oh my God!" exclaimed Polly.

Kylie was lost in the music now and she tossed and spun Eddie like a doll. "Don't hurt him," said Gemma. "I'm not sure he dances much."

But now Kylie was spinning like a top around Eddie, who was caught in, well, a vortex, as he stumbled and spun himself, Kylie's hands shooting out often to keep him upright.

Dancing to the best song on Earth, on Earth! Something memorable at last. Kylie was in raptures as the song built to the climax, instruments and voices soaring impossibly high. She was just a blur to Eddie now, who clearly had no idea what was going on. She pulled him close to her for the last few spins, then threw him in the air and caught him as the song ended and popped him back on his feet.

He wobbled as he faced her, his expression one of shock. He took three steps backwards and fell on his rear end. Everyone in the café was staring at her with pretty much the same expression. *I'd be impressed, too*, thought Kylie.

She helped Eddie back to his feet and guided him unsteadily to his chair. He was too stunned to speak and, as she'd hoped, in a bit of a trance. She had subjected him to more G forces than during Earth re-entry in one of their primitive rockets, which is hard enough to cope with when you are expecting it. She fished his car keys out of one of his pockets and turned to find herself face to face with Gwen Hooper.

"Oh, no!" said Polly in Kylie's ear.

"What have you done to him?" asked Gwen, her face a picture of rage.

"Eddie will be fine, Gwen," said Kylie casually. *This really wasn't her problem.* "He just needs a rest. I don't think he's used to dancing."

"I want to talk to you," said Gwen.

Kylie wasn't interested. "We can chat at school tomorrow.

I have to go. See ya."

"Oh, no, you don't," said Gwen, grabbing Kylie's arm.

She looked surprised, as Kylie's muscular structure was a lot different to anyone's on Earth and must have felt to Gwen like steel plate. But Gwen was too angry to care. "Come with me," she ordered, pulling Kylie towards the bathroom.

"Don't you dare hurt that girl," said Gemma.

Kylie looked around. Everyone was watching them, so hurling Gwen through the window might not be a good idea if she wanted to maintain a low profile.

"OK," said Kylie, loud enough for everyone to hear. "Let's have a chat outside and then I have to go home."

She allowed Gwen to guide her through the door at the back of the café, but Gwen kept going past the Ladies and pulled Kylie through the back door and into the lane behind the building.

"Oh, oh!" exclaimed Polly.

Gwen's two friends, Helen Kerslake and Maddy Summers, were waiting outside, arms folded and chewing gum. Kylie thought they must be very close to their multi-tasking capability limits.

Gwen grinned triumphantly as they surrounded Kylie. Pushing her face close to Kylie, Gwen snarled. *Not a good look*, thought Kylie. "What were you doing with my Eddie?"

"You're welcome to him, Gwen, with my pleasure. And commiserations."

"I don't like people taking what's mine."

"Just walk away," said Clive. "She's all talk."

Gwen suddenly whacked Kylie across the side of the head with her hand, squealed and jumped back nursing her arm.

The other two girls stared at her, surprised. And scared.

A look of realisation crossed Gwen's face. "What are you?"

"Your dad is right," said Gemma. "Walk away."

Kylie was in two minds. This could be a complication. But walking did make…

"Grab her!" yelled the furious Gwen.

The girls hesitated for a second, but then they ran at Kylie and grabbed her arms. Gwen slowly walked back, a little more wary this time and shaking her injured hand.

The scene would start to attract attention soon, thought

Kylie, so she reached across to Maddy, effortlessly dragging Helen, who clung to her arm. She quickly slid her hand under Maddy's jawbone, searching for the right spot, then pressed lightly. Maddy dropped to the ground like a sack of potatoes.

Helen only had time to raise her eyebrows before she met the same fate. Gwen's mouth fell open – *not a good look* again – and she turned on her heel and ran.

"You've killed them!" screamed Polly.

"No," said Gemma. "They're asleep."

"That's my girl," said Clive.

"Clive!" said Gemma.

Despite a thirty yard start, Kylie easily caught up with Gwen and dragged her sleeping body back to her friends. She propped them all sitting up against a wall and walked away.

"What are you doing?" asked Polly.

"I have to get to your house," she said, holding up Eddie's car keys and shaking them.

"Jeez!" exclaimed Polly. "You can't leave them there, unconscious in a dark alley."

Why not, thought Kylie. *They just tried to beat me up*. But Polly was right. "Where can I take them?"

"I don't know," said Polly. She sounded worried.

"Well, I can't take them to their homes. Their parents might want to ask why their daughters are unconscious."

"There must be somewhere," said Gemma.

"You could leave them in Eddie's car," suggested Clive. "He can drive them home when he recovers his wits."

"Assuming he had any in the first place. But good idea, dad," said Kylie. She set off at a run down the lane and round the building to the main street. She reached Eddie's car and saw him through the café window, sitting in exactly the same position as when she dumped him in the chair, staring vacantly towards her and seeing nothing.

"No good," she said. "He could be in that trance for hours."

"Where, then?" asked Gemma. "We don't have much time."

"Well, work it out while I get them in the car," said Kylie. She unlocked the door and jumped into the drivers' seat. It was so simplistic. *Like a toy*, she thought. She started the engine, shunted the gears and backed into the car behind with a crunch. "Whoops!" She swung the car out into the street, scraping the vehicle in front and wrestled the car into the alley at the side of the building, bumping over the corner of the pavement.

"Try not to run over the girls," said Clive. He wasn't joking.

Kylie became irritated. She hated being rushed, but there was an edge to her parents' voices, so maybe things were a little more serious than she thought. Apart from the problem of three unconscious girls, that is. But they'd figure that out and surely she had done nothing else to draw attention to herself, aside from the blue hair, strange behaviour at school and her dancing, which, on reflection, may have seemed a little odd to Earth folk. But all that was localised, surely.

She stopped the car next to the girls, jumped out and ran round to the passenger side. One of Gwen's feet was resting against the rear tyre. *Whoops!* She opened the rear door and tossed the girls onto the back seat one at a time and slammed the door shut.

"OK, what next?" she asked.

Silence.

"Hello! Have you gone again?"

"I'm thinking," said Polly, irritated.

"There's a first time for everything."

"Well, why don't you come up with something," said Gemma, "you got yourself into this mess."

"Yeah," agreed Polly. "What... wait a minute! I've got it!"

Kylie was relieved, though there was no way she would admit it. "Go on."

"School. Just break into a classroom with your, er, alien ways, and leave them there. Then they'll be safe and know where they are when they wake up."

"Good idea," said Clive.

"The only idea," said Gemma. "It will have to do."

Kylie hurried round to the drivers' door. "OK." She started the car and as it jerked forward she twisted to check Gwen and the other two girls were still out. Their heads lolled reassuringly. "Tell me the way."

The trip took ten minutes and Kylie managed to avoid hitting anything before she drove into the school car park. She killed the engine and lights and waited. "Any security, Polly?"

"I have no idea."

"No people detected," said Clive. "It's all clear."

Kylie jumped out of the car and ran around the side of the building to a classroom that could not be seen from the road. She looked through the windows and then up on the wall. "There's an alarm, dad."

"Neutralised," said Clive.

"How did you do that?" asked Polly.

"It's pretty simple for us, but may take a while to explain."

"You don't know, do you?"

"Quiet," snapped Kylie. "I need to concentrate." A long line of wooden framed windows ran the length of the classroom. She pushed against each and found one that was a little loose. With a sharp punch against the base of the window, the whole frame popped out and Kylie lowered it gently into the room.

"Wow!" said Polly.

Kylie ran back to the car and carried Maddy and Helen to the classroom, a girl under each arm. She lifted them through the window, then climbed inside the dark room and sat them against the wall under the white board. She climbed back out, fetched Gwen and soon all three girls were sitting in a line, their heads lolling against their chests in the gloom.

"Mission accomplished!" announced Kylie, feeling very pleased with herself.

"Never mind admiring your handiwork," said Gemma. "Get moving."

But Kylie had spotted a black marker pen on the teacher's desk and decided all three girls would look better with a moustache.

She popped the lid of the pen and suddenly had a much better view of the girls as all the lights in the room came on. She stared at the pen, idly wondering how opening it caused the lights to come on.

But she sensed someone else in the room and both of her hearts sank as she turned to the doorway, where the frame was filled by a very angry Mr Oberon, his hand still resting on the light switch.

"Oh, shit!" exclaimed Polly in Kylie's ear.

Kylie felt very sorry for Polly, who was going to be in big trouble over this particular escapade. *Oh, well, too late now.*

She glanced to the window and decided to dive through it. Oberon would hardly be likely to leave the girls and come after her.

But then he spoke. "Hacrgth i verlgmre trufsor walithe!"

The correct response by an Earth person to this statement, which was the formal Universal greeting, *Peace Be Upon Your Planet*, would be, "What?" or, "huh!" or, more politely, "I beg your pardon?"

But because the response had been drilled into her from an early age, Kylie replied, "Qra verlgmre trufsorii." *And upon yours.*

"Oh, shit!" said Gemma and Clive together. "That's a Hywardathian accent!"

Kylie spun around and leapt for the window, but Oberon, showing astounding speed threw himself over several desks and grabbed one of Kylie's ankles. Her stomach hit the windowsill and her upper body crashed against the outside wall beneath the window before Oberon dragged her back into the classroom.

"You have to get out of there!" yelled Gemma.

Thanks for the advice, mum! thought Kylie as her head slammed into a desk. She hit the floor and saw Oberon above her, his face bright red, as he leapt at her to pin her to the floor. He was alone, she was sure, and needed to control her before calling for reinforcements. This gave her hope and she kicked out against the wall and slid away as Oberon's large frame hit the floor next to her. She rolled to her feet, grabbed a chair and smashed it into Oberon's head. It shattered and he became even more angry, his dodgy eye going into overdrive.

They circled the desk now between them. "Can we talk about this?" said Kylie.

Oberon picked up the desk and used it to drive Kylie against the white board and pin her there. He had a wild look and Kylie could not be sure he heard her. She suddenly wondered if he had already called for help and was just intent on holding her there. He used all his weight to squash her against the wall.

"Can I take that as a no?"

"Listen Kylie," said Clive calmly. "We've detected a force of Hywardathian vessels heading your way, so he must have alerted them. We are going to have to disappear again in a minute. Your only chance is to take him out."

"How? I can't move."

"Don't be such a victim," snapped Gemma. "The Hywardathians have a physical weakness, a nerve under the left ear. You have to jab it hard."

"We have to go," said Clive.

Kylie heard Polly pleading before there was silence. "You can't leave her…"

Now she was immobile, Oberon grinned at her. *Not a good look.* "Who are you?"

"I'm Polly Hart, Mr Oberon. You just attacked me, so I think you must be unwell. How about you let me go and I can call someone to help."

Oberon looked confused for a moment, but then grinned again. "Nice try. But it won't save you."

"Save me?"

"You and Polly Hart have broken ordinance YW987TR243zx; Unauthorised incursion of a sovereign supervised planet. I assume you have swapped places with her?"

Kylie didn't reply. That sounded like a serious charge. She tried to look suitably confused. "But I'm Polly…

"No you're not," said Oberon coldly. "It's death for both of you."

"Death." *That's a bit more dramatic than I thought. He must be bluffing.*

But Oberon didn't look like he was bluffing. In fact, Kylie doubted he knew how to bluff. *Death? In this day and age? Surely not…*

Well, it did mean one positive thing: she had nothing to lose.

Kylie smiled at Oberon and lifted her feet off the ground. The desk against her chest still pinned her to the wall, but the movement shifted Oberon's balance and Kylie slid to the side, propelled by the teacher's weight. He tried to correct, but Kylie managed to squeeze free and scuttle across the floor under some other desks. Oberon threw his desk at her with force and it shattered against the others.

Kylie rolled clear and jumped back to her feet, two solid table legs in her hands, and came at Oberon swinging. He was more powerful, but she caught him on the back foot and rained blows at high speed about his head while trying the odd unsuccessful jab under his left ear. But Oberon grabbed another desk and hit back, destroying the classroom as they fought, and Kylie was forced backwards into the far corner of the room.

"You can't win," shouted Oberon, his face almost purple with rage. "Give up now."

Kylie fought back harder, but her desk legs bounced off Oberon's head as he advanced. He didn't even bother to protect himself. He just kept advancing as he juggled his desk in preparation for when he had her trapped. Now he raised it over his head and she felt the corner wall against her back. The final blow wouldn't cause any permanent damage, but if Oberon used all of his force, it would stun her enough for him to secure her until help arrived.

"OK," she said, smiling as she lowered her weapons. "You win."

In the split second between Oberon's look of disappointment and his decision to hit her anyway, Kylie ducked down and leapt forward. Oberon smashed the desk into the wall above her head as she swung one of the desk legs up under his chin. His head snapped back and she released the leg and drove the end of the other one two-handed just below his left ear.

Oberon's face froze, his hair stood on end and his body became briefly translucent – *again, not a good look* – and he went down like a felled tree, smashing one of the last intact desks to splinters.

Kylie didn't move for a moment, not quite believing she'd done it. She looked down at Oberon, who lay face up, his dodgy eye rolling like a golf ball around the edge of the cup. She vaulted out of the window, then looked back inside to make sure he was still out. He was. As were the three girls sitting under the far end of the white board, frighteningly close to where Oberon had had her trapped.

Kylie took off at a sprint around the building and headed for the gate. It was very dark and still. But for how long?

"Mum! Dad! Polly!"

No answer.

Here we go again, she thought. *But where to?*

EXTRACT FROM VRYL'S GALMANAC

Hywardath

The fifth planet in the Ywimzion solar system in the Yile District, Hywardath has very little to recommend it, both physically and culturally. The planet is generally featureless and because it is at what is normally ice planet distance from its star, it is habitable only due to being permanently enveloped in cloud. Hence its name, which in the local language means 'Rain Forever'.

As a result, the human population has always been miserable and had already developed an advanced space program – compared to similar stage worlds – when discovered by the Confederation. The advanced technology was the result of the collective eagerness of the population to find and move to another planet with a sunnier climate. (For local comparison, the climate of Earth's England would be viewed by a Hywardathian in the same way an English person would look at the Bahamas. Yes, the weather on Hywardath is that bad.)

This made Hywardath initially eager to join the Confederation, particularly when they discovered that almost every other human planet has a better climate. It still has the highest volunteer rate for dangerous humanitarian assignments in the universe – as residents would generally rather die than remain on their own planet – but this is combined with the highest rejection rate due to the temperament of Hywardathians.

On most human planets the population provides a varied mix of characteristics and temperaments due to environmental, geographical and evolutionary development, but on Hywardath, everyone, including happy, playful children, becomes grumpy, arrogant and dogmatic. On Hywardath, stereotype has been replaced by fact and it appears the only personal pleasure to be achieved is in making someone else more miserable than oneself. In a further irony, the average life expectancy of a

Hywardathian is close to one hundred and fifty, which makes them even more dissatisfied.

Another fact, although a sad one, is that Hywardathians believe they will be happy once they escape their planet. However, misery and discontent appears to be in their DNA and the many who have travelled to other worlds, due to their ability to put a dampener on any joyous or positive situation, have been ostracised. Hywardathians believe the universe is against them and dislikes them. They are right on both counts. Unfortunately, they believe this hostility is due to jealousy and in addition to all of their other unpleasant characteristics, they have now developed a strong and completely baseless sense of superiority. Of course, not all of their traits can be negative, so when any positive elements are reported, this description will be updated.

Their introduction to planetary supervision was, on the whole, competent, due to their dogged, rule bound nature, but the initial 'Flying Saucer' debacle caused by their insistence to use their own outdated technology and their dour, uninspired ways have hounded them ever since. Often derided throughout the universe, even the Hywardathians themselves regularly refer to the nickname given to their planet, 'Hywardeath'.

ELEVEN

Polly's mind was in turmoil. She and Kylie had been discovered. Kylie arrested. And Mr Oberon was an alien! She always thought he was weird, but…

She looked across at Kylie's parents, who had their heads close together as their fuzzy outlines swirled like storm clouds. Outside, the moon had disappeared and the spaceship could have been in another solar system for all she knew.

Everything had changed so quickly and the prospect that she would be handed over to Oberon and his fellow creatures sent shivers down her spine. But as she watched the fuzzy couple confer, she realised with a jolt that they were, for all their superior civilization and advanced technology, as clueless as she was. And, when push came to shove, what was Polly to them? A girl they didn't know who was at least partly responsible for their daughter being in peril. She suddenly felt very alone and a wave of panic ran through her entire body from head to toe. Then it came back up again.

Stop it! she said to herself. She remembered Gemma's last – hopefully not final – words to Kylie; *don't be such a victim.* There was only one thing to do when you have no control over your fate, and that's to take it back. Polly's dad always said that when you are stuck, you determine and analyse the problem to find the solution, because where there is a problem, there is always a solution. *What about the Middle East?* Polly asked him once, *they can't fix that.* Her dad smiled. *That's a bit different*, he said, *the solution is obvious and simple – shake hands, accept each other and live in peace – the real problem is that no one wants THAT solution.*

Is there a simple and obvious solution to our problem? she wondered. If Kylie had been captured, the solution would involve being blasted to atoms. *Where there is a problem, there is always a solution.*

She looked again at Gemma and Clive. They were arguing now, whether with each other or an unseen communicator she didn't know. *What a mess. If they didn't know what to do…* The feeling of panic solidified into fear, but Polly resisted. She was NOT going to fall apart. Her own mother's words came to her this time and she felt a surge of strength. *Fear is your armour. It's a positive form of self-protection. It keeps you focussed and alert. It keeps you alive. So be scared and do it anyway.*

She marched up to Gemma and Clive. "What's going on and what are we going to do about it?"

"We'll handle it," said Clive, testily.

"No," replied Polly. "Unless I'm no longer in danger. Then, it's all yours. Break a leg."

They were silent.

"OK," said Polly. "I'm now a big part of all forward planning. Any problem with that?"

Clive seemed to have a problem and appeared about to speak, but Gemma raised a hand to stop him. "No problem at all."

Polly gave Clive a triumphant look, though all she got in return was an angry swirl of his fuzzy outline. "So, bring me up to speed. Where are we and what's going on with Kylie?"

"We've popped out of your solar system briefly…"

Popped out!

"… to avoid a detection sweep. The Hywardathians are on high alert and pretty pissed off."

"And Kylie?" Polly gritted her teeth for the reply.

"We don't know," said Clive, "But there is reason for some hope."

Gemma took over. "There's a huge amount of frenzied communication between Earth and the Hywardathian orbital command ship. It's coded, so we have people working on it, but the volume and intensity seems to indicate, though we can't be sure, that Kylie might have escaped from Oberon."

Polly felt her hopes rise. "But you don't know for sure?"

"No."

"But how does that help?' asked Polly. "Oberon knows about us, so even if Kylie gets away and we swap back, he'll just grab me."

"He can't," said Gemma. "It doesn't work like that. If he has Kylie, he can prove she's not an Earth human. Without Kylie, he's not allowed to touch you. I'm sure he'll question you, but if you deny everything, he's screwed."

"You want me to lie?"

"Yes."

"OK."

No problem, there, thought Polly. "So, as long as Kylie gets away, we're both safe?"

There was a pause before Clive replied. "Yeeeees. In theory"

"Here we go again," said Polly, frustrated. "What's the catch?"

Gemma turned to her. "It's the Hywardathians. They're a little… unstable. Erratic."

"Unpredictable," added Clive.

"So, you put them in charge of Earth. Great!" Polly shook her head. "You're saying they will kill me anyway?"

"There's that possibility," admitted Gemma. "But we'll do our best to see it doesn't come to that."

Polly snorted. "Your best! I've seen your best. How could you let Kylie get us into this mess? How could she steal a spaceship without being stopped? Where was the security? The technology to track her and stop her? It's like all the adults in this confederation thingy have been sitting on their blurred arses twiddling their fuzzy thumbs while Kylie was allowed to visit earth without permission, draw me into her game, and most probably get us both killed by the unstable bunch of nutcase aliens you put in charge of the Earth in the first place! Unbelievable!"

"Sad, but true," said Gemma. "I understand you are annoyed…"

Annoyed!

"… but let's concentrate of resolving this issue…"

Issue!

"… and you can have your say after that."

Polly seethed. She had never had so strong an urge to punch an adult in the face before. "Well, as long as they let me say some final words before they zap me."

"There's no need for sarcasm," said Clive, sharply.

"You're not going to die, whatever the outcome, so you don't get to tell me not to be sarcastic."

Gemma reached out to touch Clive's fuzzy arm. "Polly's right." She turned to Polly. "It's a colossal balls-up from start to finish. It shouldn't have happened and we are truly sorry you have been caught up in the whole fiasco."

She reached out to Polly and placed a hand on her shoulder and Polly felt a warm, reassuring buzz through her body. "But it's happened and we're stuck with the situation. No use pussyfooting around. Things are desperate. You and Kylie are in deadly danger and time – at least here – is short. We all have to stick together, OK?"

Polly felt her eyes tear up and a lump came into her throat. It was much easier being angry, but Gemma was right. You couldn't do anything about an existing mess except tidy it up. She nodded, not trusting herself to speak.

"Good," said Gemma. She gave Polly a light stroke on the head before she dropped her arm. "While we've been talking I received an update."

Polly gritted her teeth.

EXTRACT FROM VRYL'S GALMANAC

Syssine

The fourth planet of the Yartga/Wryp solar systems in the Gyartga Nebula, which merged to form the two so-called Tango Suns should not, according to scientific research, be inhabitable.

And yet, it has a huge human population which has adapted to the extreme heat and radiation permeating the system. People from this planet have two of each internal organ and, the most striking feature, have evolved an outer gas shell which protects them from harm. It is the remarkable and unique feature responsible for their blurred, smoky, out-of-focus appearance. They are apparently capable of seeing each other as other humans see themselves, but have not allowed others in the universe the capability to do the same.

This has led to their reputation as a race of aloof people who consider themselves superior to everyone else. There is little actual evidence of this, although Syssinians do pride themselves on their mystery and do not seem perturbed at being referred to as 'fuzzheads' throughout the universe. They are also known as the best gamblers in the universe, no doubt due to their inscrutability.

Syssine is an A Grade StarCore Supervisor and administers a network of almost six hundred mentor planets. Known for its efficiency, rumoured to involve significant, but effective corner-cutting, the planet is often a go-to world when the Confederation needs a speedy response to an urgent issue involving other StarCore members. The planet is proud of this status, but hints at its methodology in its StarCore motto, 'We Blur the Lines'.

The planet's status has, however, come under threat in recent decades due to an incident with one of its early client planets, Hywardath. With everyone on Hywardath understandably eager to get off the planet (see **Hywardath**), their government felt Syssine was stalling their ambitions by preventing them from becoming a planetary supervisor. This feeling was correct, as leaked Syssine documentation reported that Hywardath was completely unsuitable for any role in the administration of the universe due to their complete unsuitability to mix with any other humans.

The Hywardathians were even more outraged than usual and their investigators reportedly uncovered a serious breach of protocol in the Syssine assessment and blackmailed the Syssinians into awarding them the administration of the planet Earth. This story has been categorically denied by Syssine, but as they say, 'where there's smoke, there's a Syssinian'.

TWELVE

The lights flashed overhead and the room appeared to spin. Then the spinning stopped, but only for a second before it started spinning in the other direction. The brief stillness revealed a number of fine cracks in the paintwork. Not surprising, really, as it must be what, fifteen years since the school was painted. He made a mental note to tell Mrs Elswick. She would tell him the budget cuts meant painting would have to wait, but she would see sense when he pointed out that flakes of paint falling like snow on the students' heads would have the parents up in arms.

The spinning diminished and the rest of his memory returned, bringing with it not only the humiliation of the last minutes of his consciousness, but the memories of decades of misery on this awful, stupid and… and… pointless planet! Brief triumph, followed by disgrace, banishment and a disastrous career.

Jasper Aloysius Oberon, the name he had carefully selected for himself when he first arrived on Earth in 1949, slowly woke. He experienced a very rare calmness before the familiar anger and resentment began to build to their normal levels and then tipped over into rage.

The open window yawned, the empty space silently mocking him. Polly had escaped. Not Polly, but whoever – whatever – had taken her place. He had been too willing to accept her strangeness, her hair, assuming something hormonal must have happened to turn her from a placid, intelligent and nice girl into a crazy person. Teenage boys were easy to handle; they were all consistently predictable, but the girls…

But it was obvious in hindsight that Polly was not herself – literally – and no doubt the Earth Council would point the finger at his failure. Another one. The promotion he had been working towards for two decades would now be gone. Unless…

Being beaten in combat by a teenage girl was disconcerting, but clearly whoever was disguised as Polly was a skilled fighter, so there was no shame in defeat, especially if it was only a battle and not the war.

He was fully alert now, but remained immobile. The weakness of the Hywardathian kalmic nerve was, unfortunately, well known and this was the third time in his life he had fallen foul of it. The numbness would wear off in a few minutes and once his dodgy eye started spinning, he would soon be good to go. His ocular discrepancy was the result of an early glitch in the transition-to-Earth-human-form process. He could have had it fixed years ago, but it was a handy distraction. He had never fully mastered his Earth human persona, so the eye became both a quirk and an explanation for his oddness.

Oberon was aware of the three unconscious girls sharing the classroom with him and wondered how it would look if someone came in and saw them propped sitting up against the wall and him flat on his back amid the rubble of the shattered furniture. He might have laughed at the thought, but unfortunately, he didn't have a sense of humour. It must have been lost in translation.

The Polly impersonator had knocked out Gwen, Helen and Maddy – not that Oberon thought this was a necessarily bad thing; he couldn't stand any of them – but why? Were they being kidnapped to be taken off-world? The thought triggered a very unpleasant memory. Or were they being dumped here in school? But again, why?

Well, whatever was going on, he had fortunately interrupted the plan and saved these girls from being transported into space, never to be seen again. Not an altogether negative prospect, thought Oberon, but what if more people – some perhaps less objectionable than Gwen and her hangers-on – were stashed away and ready to be taken?

He had spotted the car from his office window where he was working and despite the dark and distance, saw that the underage Polly was driving. He only had one good eye, but it was very good indeed. Oberon and every other Watcher on the planet had been put on high alert after the unknown craft sighting was confirmed, but he did not believe an insignificant little town in southern England would be anywhere near the action, more's the pity.

Yet the sight of blue-haired Polly cruising into the car park set off alarm bells in his head and sent his dodgy eye literally into a spin. Polly's parents were both involved in the investigation into the damaged satellites, particularly her mother. Polly herself – she had told him – was doing her own amateur sleuthing. The unknown craft was picked up very close to the time Polly's hair turned blue and she suddenly began acting strangely and with attitude. Even so, surely he could not be blamed for failing to connect the events at that point.

Oberon frowned, though no one but him would have been able to tell. While he was satisfied his face had regained movement, he knew with certainty that the Earth Council would blame him for everything that had and would happen. He would do the same. It was the Hywardathian way. The only hope of redemption or at least preventing a further demotion – how was that possible? – was to catch the imposter and uncover whatever plot was afoot.

He had some movement in his hands now and his legs tingled. It wouldn't be long before he could move properly. Help could arrive at any moment, but he hoped they would not arrive until he was fully functioning. The whole debacle was humiliating enough without them finding him sprawled on the floor. The girls were still out, but Gwen was now snoring softly, so they could wake up at any moment, too. Oberon sighed.

Polly couldn't be involved, could she? he wondered. While he hoped she had been kidnapped and was not party to what was going on, he was also aware it didn't really matter. The law was the law and she could well turn out to be collateral damage. Shame. She was one of the less objectionable children. *But who am I to defy the law?* thought Oberon. *I only follow orders. Sometimes a person just has to be vaporised.*

The atmosphere changed. The Source. He could smell it. They were almost here. He managed to sit up. His Earth body felt more like his real one after so many years and the joints ached. Rolling over slowly, he rested for a moment on his knees and righted one of the desks so he could pull himself to his feet. He wobbled and didn't dare let go of the desk, but at least he would be on his feet to greet his colleagues.

The three girls were still asleep as Oberon passed them, using the desk as a walking frame to get to the window. He leant outside and watched the red disker slowly descend. It was invisible to Earth humans, but he could see it clearly enough to make out the insignia of its mother ship. The diskers were laughed at around the Universe for being old fashioned, but they were very efficient and if it ain't broke...

They were an Hywardathian invention, proudly developed specifically for their first planetary administration role on Earth just after World War II. Unfortunately, the cloaking mechanism developed a glitch – a quirk caused by Earth's atmosphere – which made the craft occasionally visible to humans, who called them Flying Saucers. This was a great cause of mirth throughout the universe and Hywardath lost a great deal of face. It still rankled, even though it was more than fifty years since the cloaking issue was corrected, and the Council had been determined ever since to enforce every rule and regulation without variance. Not everything had gone smoothly on the planet since then – Oberon knew that only too well – but the name had stuck and now Hywardathians the universe over were known as 'Saucernauts'. It was mild compared to many of their nicknames, but the disrespect still grated.

Just the one disker? Oberon leant further out, but there were no more. Had they taken him seriously?

The disker hovered a few feet above the concrete area outside the window. It was four yards wide and half that in height. Very compact. But then again, Hywardathians were a very compact people. Oberon looked down at his stout body. *Usually*.

The hatch slid open and three men hopped out. Dressed in the grey and red overalls of Fleet Security Command, they filled Oberon briefly with homesickness as they formed a compact triangle, each holding a clunky lightflexer. They really were old-fashioned weapons, Oberon conceded, but the Council was consistent in its stubbornness and refused to update the equipment. If it ain't broke...

The tallest of the three, standing almost four feet tall, was the leader, Oberon saw by his badge. He was also more handsome than the other two, his green skin a darker shade than theirs and he had much finer features. Oberon decided he must be from Rayloth on the Hywardathian equator, while the other two had the flat, square jawed countenance and light lime-coloured skin of Oberon's own Joffilve continent in the north.

After a moment, the leader led the other two to the window and they all jumped inside. Oberon had to back up quickly and almost toppled over.

"You're late," he snapped looking down at the three green men. "And why are you alone?"

The leader eyed him coolly. "Do you know how many calls there are? More than a thousand. Every paranoid watcher on the planet has filed a report. You are just lucky yours was considered worthy to be followed up." Hywardathians had very deep voices at odds with their tiny, fragile-looking appearance.

"OK, what's happening?" The leader glanced at the three unconscious girls.

"The girl you want has escaped," Oberon said. "She knocked them out, but I have no idea why."

"You let her get away?"

Oberon felt his anger rise. He was on Earth when this idiot was still in his incubator. "The girl is not from Earth, and may not be female, for all I know. She is an expert fighter, though."

The leader didn't look very convinced, but he nodded slightly. "My name is Floothil and these…" he gestured to his men, who, Oberon thought, had expressions way over on the wrong side of intelligence, "… are Muoth and Thirt."

Oberon's opinion was confirmed, when Thirt turned his weapon towards the girls. "Want me to waste 'em?"

"Don't you dare," yelled Oberon. "I'm in charge here and…"

"No you're not," said Floothil.

"Yes I am."

"No, you're not. This is now a military operation and I say what happens."

"No, you don't," insisted Oberon. "I am the local authority here and until it's proven this is an organised incursion and not a solo incident, I'm the boss."

Floothil cocked his head to the side and the corners of his mouth slowly turned down as the situation was clarified by his commander. He turned back to Oberon. "Understood," he replied in a surly tone.

"Good," said Oberon, satisfied. He noticed he had stopped

leaning on the desk and felt his strength rapidly return.

"OK," said Floothil, reluctantly, "you established the girl was a non-Earth individual and tried to apprehend her. She easily beat you and escaped. Is that it?"

Oberon bristled. "In a coghudat shell, yes. Apart from the easy bit, which, if you looked around this room, you would notice."

"Any idea where she went?"

"Possibly the home of the girl whose identity she stole. The Earth girl has a couple of close friends, too, who she might go to. If she's still on the planet."

"She is," said Floothil, with far more confidence than Oberon felt. "Security is tighter than jiuloc's ghupot in a sun storm."

If security is being handled by numbskulls like these, thought Oberon, *the girl could be in Universe Central by now*.

"Then I suggest we head for the girl's house first."

The three little green men started for the window again.

"Stop," said Oberon, looking at them incredulously. "You can't go outside like that. Why aren't you in Earth human form, anyway?"

"It's chaos up there and everyone had to scramble immediately. It doesn't matter. It's still dark. We find the girl, put her permanently out of business and be gone in no time."

All three men cocked their weapons. Oberon sighed. "No. You are not leaving this classroom looking like that."

Floothil struggled to keep his temper. "Where are we going to find…"

Oberon was looking at the three unconscious girls.

"Oh, no, no," protested Floothil. His companions looked equally alarmed a few seconds later, when their wits caught up.

Muoth turned to his commander. "I'm not changing into a girl!"

"You will do as you're told," barked Oberon. He had enough. "So suck it up!"

None of them were happy, but they each dutifully sat at the feet of a girl. Oberon made Floothil swap with Muoth to ensure the leader took on Gwen's appearance, the closest Oberon would ever get to a humorous gesture.

They each took a shoe off their girl, sat down and grabbed a foot with both hands. Transurgification had become much smoother over the centuries, but Hywardath clung dutifully – and unnecessarily, thought Oberon – to their own method, which was convoluted and very painful.

The three green men began to convulse as their new shapes were gradually shaken out of them.

Oberon became impatient. The longer this took, the more time the Polly being had to get away or, worse, call in help herself. As much as it pained him, Oberon knew that his fellow Hywardathians did not have a great track record in the field of competence. They were no less intelligent on the whole than any other branch of the human family, but the planet's collective stubbornness and arrogance had held them back. Most of their contemporary member planets already had supervisor status on three or more planets, but all Hywardath had was Earth and until they could prove worthy wardens, they were unlikely to progress to full member status. *If I ruled* Hywardath, decided Oberon with absolute confidence, *things would be very different.*

Finally, the green men stood up, shakily, now in the guise of Gwen, Maddy and Helen. They were dressed in expanded Fleet uniforms, their weapons now looking tiny in their much bigger hands. Oberon thought they looked like henchwomen from a James Bond movie and suspected they were just as incompetent. He would have to keep them in close control.

They moved to the window, but he told them to wait while he found the right nerve in each of the sleeping girls' necks and pressed. That would put them out for at least another six hours. He looked across at Floothil and the two other 'girls'. Oberon had travelled vast tracts of the universe in his time and seen many things, but he was hard pressed to recall anything more ridiculous than these three. A very worrying thought, given the next few hours could well define his future and, perhaps, he thought importantly, Hywardath's place in the universe.

"Let's go," he said, suddenly filled with excitement.

Thirt turned back to the sleeping girls as he climbed through the window, his voice still deep and male, as they were not able to reproduce the girls' voices without hearing them. "Sure you don't want me to waste 'em?"

THIRTEEN

"Kylie could not have chosen a worse place to visit."

"Why?" asked Polly.

Gemma turned her fuzzy head. "Oberon."

Polly stood with Gemma and Clive and watched through the gigantic transparent walls of the spaceship as they slowly approached Earth. *Relatively slowly, that is*, thought Polly, *as they must be travelling at thousands of miles an hour.*

The moon was to their right and the earth grew larger ahead. Polly still could not get her head around this feeling of movement. Or non-movement. It was as though they were stationary in space and the Earth was flying towards them.

She had been relieved when Clive told her they were going back, but there was also a sense of disappointment. Even if she survived this adventure, there was no chance she could return to space. She would have to live out a mundane life on Earth knowing all this is out here, yet unable to experience it. There was so much she wanted – needed – to know. It was overwhelming, as was the premature feeling of loss. *Oh, well, maybe I'll be vaporised and not have to worry about it.* The thought sent a chill through her.

She turned to look at Kylie's parents. They were still, gazing at the blue planet, but their fuzzy outlines swirled tightly. Polly couldn't see their expressions, but she was starting to understand their moods; the angry storm-like volatility of their outlines, the placid layer of fog when they were calm and now, woven strings of, she imagined, pensive mist rippling all over their bodies. Tension.

"Oberon?" she asked.

Gemma's outline became more animated. "He was a senior observer with the on-ground first wave, just after your World War II."

"The nuclear bombs triggered intervention," added Clive. "Most human populations go through a nuclear stage. It's a phase, like when children discover matches. Most worlds get through it OK, but some manage to destroy their civilisations or sometimes all biological life on their planet."

"Anyway," said Gemma, "it was decided a couple of thousand years ago, that whenever a planet split the atom it provided automatic permission for an on-ground assessment by the presiding area power. In the case of Earth, that's us. With Hywardath as our proxy."

Polly felt powerless on a cosmic scale.

Clive continued. "Our council was undecided. Earth is pretty remote and away from the main trade routes and the consensus was, why bother? The humans there would either survive or not, regress or advance. It wasn't as though the survival of other humans would be affected. And samples of any unique species could easily be removed if things nose-dived."

Polly was sure they didn't mean it, but she felt offended and outraged. "It's important to us!"

Clive and Gemma turned to her. "It's not personal, Polly," said Gemma, not at all sympathetic. "All planets are self-centred, pre-membership. They imagine they are the only human planet, alone in the cosmos, that life is precious and rare, yada yada yada. They're not and it's not. A million worlds could spontaneously explode today and half the known universe wouldn't hear about it and the other half wouldn't care. We've got galaxies to spare."

Gemma paused for a moment. "Does that sound harsh?"

"Yes," said Polly. "And insensitive."

"It is what it is," said Clive, with a blurred shrug. "Tell me, have you ever stepped on an ant?"

"Yes. But not deliberately."

"Did you experience any remorse?"

"I was sorry I did it, but there are so many…" Polly suddenly stopped herself.

"Aha!" exclaimed Clive, with more triumph than Polly thought appropriate. "That's the universal authority attitude in a nutshell. They will avoid destroying a planet and even protect it if they can, but if someone 'steps on it'," – he used blurry air quotes – "or it blows itself up; oh, well, there are plenty more."

The words hung in the air. Polly's understanding of the word 'expendable' had never expanded to a planetary scale before. Had she been drunk, it would have been a sobering thought. "That's depressing," said Polly.

"No, it's not," countered Gemma. "It's life. A gigantic number of organisms milling around a random universe. But it doesn't mean you or I are unimportant."

"It just means," added Clive, "that the universe doesn't give a shit about us."

Polly laughed. "So, it's just business?"

"The natural order of things." Clive turned back to the approaching Earth. "It also means we are on our own."

"You were telling me about Oberon."

Gemma took over. "Yes, he was with the first wave, co-ordinating the watchers assigned to the White House, Kremlin and other government hotspots and information hubs."

"Did you know," said Clive, "that there have been two Hywardathian Popes so far?"

"What?" *So far?*

"I haven't finished," said Gemma, irritated. "Oberon and his crew did a good job for first timers. He had to report back to us, of course, which he and his fellow Hywardathians hated, and his agents managed to infiltrate the very highest seats of government."

"Did you know…," began Clive, but Gemma gave him such a sharp though fuzzy look he shut up immediately.

"The result was that we knew exactly what was going on and were able to avert the many occasions when World War III appeared certain."

Polly's brows knitted in puzzlement. "I thought the Cuban missile crisis was the only time a nuclear war almost happened."

"That didn't make it to the top ten," said Gemma. "I wouldn't say the history you learned is false, but let's just say the people writing it didn't have all the facts."

"But…" began Polly, but she stopped herself. Earth was growing closer and this stuff was messing with her head. She took a breath. "Why is Mr Oberon a teacher at my school? It doesn't sound much like a senior position."

"It's not," said Clive. "He was shafted."

Gemma raised a hand. "The Hywardathian government didn't like playing second fiddle to our planet and felt that we were taking credit for their success."

"Why did they think that?" asked Polly.

"Because it was true," replied Gemma. "It's very human. Most subordinate planets do the right thing and suck it up until they have planets under them and they can do the same."

"It seems very childish."

"Very human," repeated Gemma. "But Hywardath didn't suck it up. They hated playing second fiddle and decided to undermine us. They went through the regulations and discovered we had not performed a required task on the New Planet Evaluation Report."

Clive made a noise that Polly thought sounded like a snort.

Gemma turned to him for a moment before continuing. "They could have reported us, which would have meant nothing – I mean, really, who would care? – but instead they decided to perform the task themselves."

Clive laughed. "Bunch of idiots!"

"What was the task?" asked Polly.

"Sampling," said Gemma. "We were supposed to profile humans from various areas of the planet as part of the Universal Micro-Genome Project. Human and animal genetic material is thought to have originated in the Plosarchian Chamber Implosion in the Plos Tandrum, an elongated White Hole that pretty much turned a hundred stars inside out before blasting the remains into space like a shotgun. It must have been pretty spectacular."

Polly's imagination drifted into space, too, as Gemma and Clive fell into pensive silence. They were much closer to earth now. *Concentrate*, she told herself. "What do you mean by sampling?"

"Well," replied Gemma, "if we had stuck to the letter of the law, we would have removed a number of humans for testing..."

"Abduction!"

"Not abduction. We would have put them back and they wouldn't have remembered anything. But no one does that these days. Thousands of planets have been tested in this region, so there's no point."

"But it's still in the regulations," said Clive. "And the Hywardathians love regulations. They planned to use this breach as a lever to have us removed as guardians and have themselves appointed. They did this by conspiring with some like-minded allies and performing the sampling themselves."

It was Gemma's turn to laugh. "They were hopeless, picking people up in those ridiculous flying saucers, even though they hadn't perfected the cloaking mechanism. They eventually fixed that, but they still use those antiques to get around. And, worst of all, they couldn't wipe the memories of the humans they picked up and that's why all those alien abduction stories took off."

"And Oberon was behind all that?"

"He was against it, but he was put in command and, therefore, under traditional Hywardathian blame-culture, he carried the can. Hywardath became a laughing stock and their leaders claimed Oberon was solely responsible. That was accepted to allow them to save a little face, but their entire planet has been seething ever since."

And," added Clive, "no doubt Oberon has been the same, languishing in a school at the ends of the Earth."

"England is not the ends of the Earth!" protested Polly. It came out half-hearted, though. It often felt like the ends of the Earth.

"Maybe not," allowed Clive, but it's not the pointy end of interplanetary politics, either."

"You think Oberon sees me and Kylie as a chance to claw his way back to the top?"

"Yep," said Clive. "There are a very large number of very angry Hywardathians down there..." – he pointed to Earth, which was now close to filling the view – "... and the destruction of the two of you is their primary goal."

Thanks. I feel much better now, thought Polly. "I do have one more question," said Polly. "Maybe it's just me, but given what you just said, is it wise to openly travel to Earth?"

EXTRACT FROM VRYL'S GALMANAC

Cortex Implant

The Cortal Integrated External Drive Manipulation Device, commonly known as the Cortex Implant, was invented four thousand years ago after a 275 year joint research project by the University of Myrsdab and The Confederation Central Research Facility on Cvaszop (see notes for the names of the 854 scientists credited with the invention).

Granted approval after a 500 year live test study, the Implant is now the most effective and accepted means of communication in the Universe and is used by over 80% of Confederation member planets.

The Implant is combined with a small amount of stem cell tissue taken from every newborn baby, incubated for seven days and inserted into the baby's brain, where the device, by now already changing into an organic structure, attaches itself to the Dffutly Cortal muscle, where it grows with the child.

The Implant is activated after five years and children learn how to operate the device by mind manipulation in much the same way as they were taught in the distant past to use a keyboard.

Everyone with an implant has access to the base level Confederation Knowledge and Entertainment Data Base and increased access evolves over time, depending on education levels, employment needs and specialist requirements. The Implant allows for communication in real time, regardless of location, tapping directly into The Source.

The device has allowed user planets to completely eradicate written material, imaging devices such as cameras and terrestrial and space vehicles no longer require control equipment. Everything can be accessed, viewed and controlled by thought and the user has the option to switch the device off at will.

The benefits are obvious, but there is still significant

resistance and suspicion of the Cortex Implant. New Confederation members are understandably concerned and often suspect mind control as the reason the Confederation is so eager to quickly introduce the device. However, it is more than 1500 years since the Duwqirlob Incident resulted in several hundred so-called 'Zombie Planets', which forced the correction of a small design issue, so there are no concerns about the device today. Not many, anyway.

New member planets are usually quickly reassured after being issued with external headset versions of the device and most quickly switch to newborn implants within a few years.

However, approximately one percent of planets do not trust the device or the Confederation and limit themselves by going without, or using a generic inferior headset version. Most of these planets are excluded from Supervisory roles until they accept the Implant. They are officially referred to as Non-CI Users, but are more commonly known as 'Idiot Worlds'.

FOURTEEN

Kylie pushed open the door and was relieved that Polly's parents were not home. Things could turn ugly – uglier – at any moment. She didn't intend to hang around, but she needed to find Josh's address. Kate, being Polly's best friend, was too obvious and she didn't want to put her in danger. Josh, on the other hand, was a less likely choice. It was clear he liked Polly, even if Polly didn't realise it, and maybe he had a garden shed she could hide in until her parents rescued her.

Polly's room was a mess, due to Kylie emptying her cupboards and drawers for something to do earlier. She had intended to tidy up, honest, but now it would have to wait. *Hopefully not forever.*

She had Josh's phone number from Polly's phone, but thought it was too dangerous to call in case the phone was being monitored. She finally found Josh's address in a small notebook and Kylie worked out it was twenty minutes away if she walked briskly at Earth human pace. It was too risky to go there faster. She had uploaded to her memory the map of the town, one of Ugflac Krdoglen's famous handy interstellar travel tips, which had stuck with her. Unlike one of her other tips: *Never visit a planet without permission.*

She ran back down the stairs and waited a moment by the front door. It was all quiet, so she slipped outside and hurried away down the dark street. *Am I being watched. And, if yes, who by? But no sense worrying about it,* she thought with an impending sense of disaster. *But I never have an impending sense of disaster!* she thought, even more concerned.

Kylie wondered if Oberon had recovered consciousness yet. And if he had alerted the authorities before she knocked him out. That was a pretty smart piece of work, she decided. Oberon was no pushover, even if he was old and slow. It was lucky she was in such a backwater and the local watcher was a minor functionary. She wouldn't be able to surprise him again, though. *And he's going to be soooooo pissed off.*

The streets were completely deserted, but it couldn't be too late. There might be life on Earth, but there certainly wasn't much of it around here. Kylie weighed her options and found they hardly weighed anything at all. If Oberon called in security then everyone she came in contact with would be in deadly danger. It sounded dramatic, but planetary security squads were known as *Cleaners* for a reason. They were famous for their ability to render any problem obsolete. Hence their unofficial motto: *Evidence? What Evidence?*

But on the bright side… OK, there was no bright side. Kylie was beginning to think this entire episode was something of a mistake. She had made mistakes before – once or twice – but the actions involved had been calculated risks with relatively benign consequences. Not instant death. It was bad enough she had put herself in danger, but to think that Polly could suffer the same fate was, well, unthinkable. Kylie was not used to having a conscience and she didn't like it.

Self-pity was a very short distance ahead, and Kylie decided not to pay it a visit. She was still alive in the short term, at least, and decided it was in her interest to concentrate on making it the long term. She was not going to go down without a fight.

She looked up and saw with some surprise that it was a clear night. Millions of stars twinkled. Her parents and Polly were up there somewhere and so were Oberon's colleagues, many of whom were probably intent on her destruction. They could be trailing her now, she thought, spinning around. It was quiet, but she couldn't be sure. She wore a diffuser as a matter of course, which meant she was invisible to any tracking or detection device owned by the Hywardathians, but it was a small town and they could be following her, hoping she would lead them to Polly.

She stopped suddenly and ran back at speed the way she had come for fifty yards and stopped. Nothing moved and all was still quiet. She sighed in relief, but then jumped, hearts in mouth, as a cat leapt to the ground from the wall next to her and looked up into her eyes. It circled her and rubbed against her leg before wandering away. Kylie wondered briefly if it really was a cat, but then decided she was being paranoid. Maybe. She turned and walked briskly towards Josh's street.

Kylie was all alone, but instead of the usual thrill she felt when pushing boundaries, her skin, under her Polly suit, tingled with fear.

FIFTEEN

Oberon brought his car to a halt outside Polly's house. It was the last place he expected her to be, which is why he came here first. He was conscious of the fact he was on very thin ice and one single mistake on this mission and he could be shovelling Gfathol dung on Thirvia 4 for the rest of his career.

"This it?" asked Floothil, his deep voice extremely odd coming from Gwen's face. He brushed hair from his eyes and shook his head, rather too similar to Gwen for Oberon's liking.

"Let's waste 'em," said Thirt from the back, where he sat with Muoth, in their respective Maddy and Helen guises.

Oberon's active eye was almost uncontrollable as it flicked from Floothil to the other two squad members in the rear view mirror. "Yes, this is Polly's house."

Floothil pushed open the door. "Leave this to us."

"Stop!" demanded Oberon, in the voice that used to silence the deck of a spaceship. He was satisfied it was still there and even more satisfied when he saw that it still worked.

Floothil pulled the door closed.

"Now listen," said Oberon, trying very hard to concentrate with three schoolgirl faces staring back at him. "I don't want anyone 'wasted' unless I say so. We don't know if Polly and her parents are being held hostage or if they are in on this. No one gets harmed without my OK. OK?" All three stupid faces nodded.

"It's your call," conceded Floothil, brushing away another strand of hair.

My call, thought Oberon ruefully. While he didn't mind if this was his last night on Earth – *good riddance!* – he didn't like the uncertainty surrounding his next destination. He felt a surge of anger as he thought about Polly and her impersonator.

He opened his door and climbed out. "Flexers on stun and follow me."

The three squad members jumped out and followed Oberon

to the door. There were lights on inside, so he rang the bell and heard the hum of flexers behind him. He heard nothing from inside, nor could he see any furtive movement behind the frosted glass of the front door. "Open it," he said and stepped aside.

Muoth reversed his flexer and pressed the butt against the lock, which shattered into very small pieces.

Oberon bustled past him and pushed open the door. He stopped and listened again, his arm raised to keep the others still. He had downloaded a plan of the house as they drove and knew there were four main rooms, a bathroom and utility room downstairs and three bedrooms, one with en suite, and a family bathroom upstairs. Because the mother ship sent him a newspaper advertisement instead of the actual plans, he also knew the house was a 'desirable residence with woodland glimpses'. *Get me off this planet!*

"Check the house, but don't shoot unless I give the OK."

The squad set off at speed through the rooms, Oberon following. He looked at the furniture, the paintings, the carpet; the suburbia. A feeling of envy began to grow. The Harts had lived happily here, enjoying their lives, while Oberon skulked away in this backwater, hoping to climb back to his former position. All those wasted years, waiting, waiting. Envy became anger. He went through the living room, overturning tables, knocking over lamps and then he wrenched the TV from the wall, causing a shower of sparks. They quickly spluttered out, but he would not have cared if the entire house went up in flames. He raised the TV high above his head and brought it crashing down on the upturned coffee table.

Floothil appeared at the door, closely followed by his two companions, and brushed his hair from Gwen's face. "It's all clear."

Oberon turned to him, almost blind with fury. "Destroy everything!" he screamed.

The three schoolgirl faces stared back in surprise for an instant, then Floothil flicked a switch on his Flexer and swept the weapon across the room. WHUMP! All the furniture was vaporised in a rapid series of shots which did not even leave any dust.

Muoth and Thirt backed away and took out the rest of the

house contents. Oberon followed and only when the house was completely empty, except for random papers drifting to the floor, was he satisfied. "In the car," he ordered.

At the door, Oberon turned back to look inside. He felt nothing. He walked back to the car, but as he entered he received a message that sent him back into a rage: *THEY HAVE ARRIVED.*

EXTRACT FROM VRYL'S GALMANAC

The Source

Strangely, while The Source is the greatest energy discovery in the history of the universe, no one knows for certain what it is or where it comes from. It was recognised as an entity millions of years ago and inspired many religious and other legends and myths. It was, for a long time, believed to be an intelligent entity – a God, if you like – perhaps the source of all life and the reason we are here. Some planets still worship The Source and in many instances it was considered an active participant in wars and other historic events, none more so than the so-called Sun Wars of pre-confederation days. Though it is hard to separate fact from fiction after so much time, it does seem plausible that the ancient monastic order, the Knights of Jeldoy, who assisted the victors of that war were able to tap into The Source in some way, particularly as it is more powerful in that part of the universe. "Use the Source" is still a common piece of advice (only half jokingly) given to someone in a seemingly impossible situation.

Larbro Morphuw is the scientist credited with first harnessing the power of The Source. He spent years studying the Jeldoys and discovered they had a unique receptor in their brains, which allowed them to tap into The Source and use it for small scale tasks. This gave the group enormous prestige over many thousands of years in their local sector, although attempts by various grand masters to extend their influence failed as The Source became weaker the further they travelled.

Morphuw decided that if he could build an engine based on the same principles as the Jeldoy Receptor and somehow tap into The Source, it could potentially replace StarDrive as the main fuel for interstellar travel.

The first four attempts succeeded, but as their outcome was unknown for fifty years, they were considered failures at the time. The craft and crews were eventually found hundreds of light years away. In the meantime, Morphuw, thanks to measuring the power exerted on the earlier missions, was able to control the vast power resource with an improved engine and his next attempt resulted in him halting the ship after it travelled in an instant to the next galaxy. It was a massive break-through.

Theories abound as to what generates the seemingly unlimited power of The Source. The most popular theory is that another, undetected, universe is rubbing against ours, which would support the ongoing Dual or Multiverse hypothesis. There is a focal point in the Jeldoy region where the power is the strongest, suggesting perhaps that the pointy end of another universe is 'jabbing' ours, but The Source is readily accessible everywhere, so the two dimension theorists may be correct. But while extensive research and investigation is ongoing, the Confederation is believed to have an unofficial policy of not looking a gift sholuch in the grysac and the rumour persists that they have suppressed a large amount of information from general consumption. Evidently, knowing too much is considered more dangerous than knowing too little.

SIXTEEN

Earth filled the entire view through the transparent spaceship. The vessel was in orbit above South Africa. To Polly, it seemed like weeks since she had floated out there with Rafael watching the planet literally beneath her feet. But that was only hours ago. When she still had a future.

Kylie's parents stood beside her, apparently looking at the same view. There didn't seem to be much urgency, though she felt a sudden sense of tension when Gemma pointed away to their left. She followed her fuzzy finger and saw a pinprick of light growing larger above the eastern horizon.

"Here come the others," said Clive, turning to the north.

Other lights were moving towards them and as they grew closer, Polly could see they were spaceships. Not shiny, new looking craft like the one she was in, but dirty, battered vessels. Old-fashioned, even, despite them being far in advance of anything the Earth could manufacture.

"Hywardathians," announced Clive, unable or unwilling to hide the distaste in his voice.

Soon, they were surrounded by eight vessels, one 'parked' close by between them and the Earth, spoiling the view, and the others further out, but seemingly poised for action.

The closest spaceship was little more than a long cylinder which looked like an elongated rusty barrel. "How big is that?" she asked. She could not judge distance or size.

"It's a Clursbac #8, roughly four miles long and half a mile wide. OK for orbit patrols, but there wouldn't be more than a hundred of those antiques still in service in the universe. This is like visiting a museum."

Ironically, as Kylie's parents explained to Polly, the Hywardath Earth Command was compelled to report any incidents of importance to their leaders, Kylie's planet. And as the nearest starship, Clive and Gemma's vessel was well positioned to respond. "Well," Clive had told Polly, "it takes care of how we get back!"

But the surrounding spaceships made it very clear that Hywardath considered itself very much in charge.

What happens now?" Polly became nervous. "Will your captain speak to them?"

"We don't have a captain," said Gemma, fuzzily scanning the ships.

"What? Sorry, pardon?"

"Everyone aboard is equally qualified," Gemma continued. "The ship runs itself via an inbuilt SmartBrain. But if we come under attack, individual command is necessary, so SmartBrain instantly hands over control to the most qualified person. For all other missions and non-deadly situations, we can bid personally or collectively for command and SmartBrain will choose the winners.

Polly thought for a moment. "Am I right in thinking that you are both effectively captains for this situation?'

"That's right," said Clive, pride in his voice.

"You won the bid, then?"

"In a way," admitted Clive.

"In a way?"

"There were no other bidders for this one," said Gemma.

Great! thought Polly.

A high pitched whistle caused everyone to be still and Polly had to cover her ears. As the sound faded, the view of Earth was replaced by an image of an angry green person's face. "An alien?" she whispered.

"He's human, too," Gemma replied quietly. "Lugy Jwerqep. Head of the Hywardath Earth Command."

"The Gal told me about Hywardathians. Are they really as grumpy as that."

"Not all of them," said Clive. "This one's grumpier."

"But don't worry," added Gemma. "We've blurred your image, so he can't recognise you."

Despite this, Polly could feel Jwerqep's eyes boring into her and felt uneasy. She noticed the fuzzy outlines of Gemma and Clive were in turmoil, swirling in tight miniature whirlwinds. Angry or scared?

It turned out to be angry.

The silence dragged on as Jwerqep's fury grew. Finally, he had to speak. "You were summoned to…"

"Summoned!" barked Gemma.

Jwerqep flinched. Polly guessed he was not used to being spoken to without respect, but she saw his eyes adjust to the new circumstances. It wasn't that he was unused to contempt, it was more a case of forgetting what it was like. His face became greener as he tried to control his rage.

"There is a situation," he said, with some difficulty.

"We are aware of that," said Clive. "Earth's security has been breached and we are here for your report as to why you allowed it to happen."

No love lost here, thought Polly. Her temperature controlled suit suddenly felt colder.

Jwerqep's face was twitching now. "We believe one or more intruders are currently on Earth and we are close to capturing them. I stressed in my message it was not necessary to return and…"

"That is not your decision to make," said Gemma. "And given your track record, we want to make sure you are capable of resolving the matter."

Polly thought Jwerqep's head was going to explode.

Clive weighed in. "We will be monitoring you closely and will step in if we consider you not up to the task. You were warned that your refusal to employ more sophisticated equipment could result in a situation like this. Let's hope we do not have to refer this matter to a higher authority. It would not be a good look, would it?"

The Hywardathian squirmed so much Polly began to feel sorry for him. At least until he responded.

"We will track down the criminals and destroy them on sight according to Protocol sixty-three, sub-paragraph three hundred and eighty-six: Infringement Policy for Unauthorised Incursion. You may rest assured of that."

"Well," said Gemma, "I trust you will contact us before we contact you."

Jwerquep disappeared and the Earth was again visible. The eight Hywardathian spacecraft dispersed. Polly squinted at Kylie's parents and saw their cloudy outlines swirled even more violently. "Why did you have to make him even more angry than he was? Now it's going to be even more dangerous down there."

Clive's voice was tight. "We had to make sure he knows who's boss."

"Who cares?"

"It's OK," said Gemma. "We now have a couple of

advantages. He's too shitty with us to suspect our involvement. We behaved exactly the way we needed to. Hywardath managed to railroad us into appointing them to Earth, so the consistent line is to treat them like minor underlings. They hate it, but they are so rule-bound, they have no choice but to put up with it."

"The other advantage?" prompted Polly.

"Their equipment. Weapons, communication, transport. All of it is outdated. Extremely advanced by your standards, but not by ours."

Rub it in, thought Polly. "Is there a downside?"

Clive and Gemma glanced at each other, before Gemma responded. "Only if you get caught."

SEVENTEEN

Kate Andrews woke from a dream – she was sitting having tea in the middle of a hockey pitch with her friend Polly and Stephen Hawking during a game – to the sound of voices outside. Male voices, urgent and angry. She jumped out of bed and peeked through the curtains to the back garden below. There were four of them in the shadows next to the hedge. One was a big man whose silhouette looked vaguely familiar and the other three were a little shorter, each identically dressed in the same odd looking overalls and carrying short sticks – *or guns!* – like villainous painters and decorators. Then they turned and Kate gasped.

The three were 'Evil' Gwen Hooper and her groupies, Helen Kerslake and Maddy Summers. But when Gwen turned back to the shadowy man, her voice was deep and masculine. "Are you sure," said Gwen, but not in Gwen's voice. The big man must have nodded because the trio approached the back of the house.

Kate frowned, but then she realised it was a prank. Uncharacteristically elaborate, certainly, but Gwen was not going to let the events in the playground the other day stand as the last word.

Right, thought Kate. She went out into the hall and tip-toed to the stairs. She was not going to wake her parents for those idiots and would soon put them in their place. She took the first two stairs quickly, then stopped on the third as a wave of common sense and practicality enveloped her. On second thoughts, *this was a job for mum and dad!*

She turned, but at that moment the front door flew open and she looked back down the stairs. Gwen stood in the opening, but there was something different about her. There was intelligence in her eyes and her face wore a very business-like expression as she pointed her weapon at Kate. *Nothing personal.*

Helen and Maddy bustled in and stood next to Gwen, the three of them now aiming up the stairs. Kate heard her parents come out of their bedroom behind her but she couldn't take her eyes off her schoolmates. There really was something odd about them.

"What's going on?" shouted Kate's dad

"Oh!" exclaimed her mum, in her familiar understated manner. Dirt on the carpet or schoolgirl hit squad. It was all the same to her.

They didn't get the chance to say anything else, because Gwen, Helen and Maddy all fired their weapons almost silently up the stairs.

Death felt like a short blast of cold air followed by a muffled 'whump' noise. Not at all unpleasant, thought Kate, and a very interesting experience. Shame she would not be able to tell Polly about it. *Being dead and all.*

Except that she was not dead. She was frozen. One foot was still in the air, her hand on the banister rail and her body slightly twisted in mid-movement. It wasn't a restrained feeling and there was no sense of claustrophobia. The only frustration was that she could not ask the girls about their weapons and discover the paralysis mechanism.

The girls. She began to suspect they were not the actual girls. They looked like the girls, certainly, but there was something else going on. And instinctively she knew it was something to do with Polly, another girl with something going on.

Anyway, food for thought, decided Kate, but this little episode was yet to play out. She was a fully conscious observer – hopefully her parents were in the same state behind her – and the three girls stood at the foot of the stairs. Waiting.

"Why can't we waste 'em," said Helen, in a deep baritone. The accent was an odd mix, but Kate couldn't place it.

"Because," said Gwen, in an even deeper voice than Helen's.

Another figure entered the house behind them. Kate was too high up the stairs to see his face at first, but she knew those clothes and the large shape, so the wide face and twitching eye came as no surprise when he walked to the foot of the stairs. But she was surprised that she wasn't surprised. Mr Oberon!

"Search everywhere," ordered Mr Oberon.

Gwen and Helen ran up the stairs past Kate, while Maddy disappeared into the living room. Oberon stood still, staring directly into Kate's eyes the whole time.

Kate knew what it meant. She knew too much. Oberon's next command would be to have her 'wasted'. Strangely, in this frozen state, she didn't mind. But she was filled with frustrated curiosity and it seemed a shame to die not knowing what was going on.

She heard the girls rummaging around the house, opening cupboards and shifting furniture. Looking for something. Maddy crossed the hall behind Oberon into the kitchen and Gwen and Helen came back down the stairs, not so urgent this time.

"She's not here," said Gwen.

She? They must mean Polly, thought Kate. It sounded like an adventure, but sadly one she was not going to be a part of.

"No surprise," said Oberon, resigned. Kate thought he looked worried, but it was hard to tell with so much going on all round his face. With his twitching eye and scowl, it looked like someone was behind there trying to get out.

"Now can we waste 'em?" pleaded Helen.

"Shut up," barked Oberon. "Let's go to the boy's house."

Oberon turned and clumped out of the house.

They must mean Josh, decided Kate. *I have to help them! Once I'm unfrozen, that is.*

Gwen and Maddy followed Oberon, but Helen took a last look at Kate and raised her weapon. "Whoosh!" she shouted, then ran after the others and the door slammed.

Kate almost fell down the stairs, only just catching the rail. She had to jump a couple of steps to steady herself and ended up looking back up the stairs at her surprised parents.

"What are you doing?" said her dad.

Her mum turned to her dad and raised her eyebrows. "What are *we* doing?" she added. Kate's dad clearly had no idea.

Kate smiled at the funny scene, but then realised she was halfway down the stairs clinging to the stair rail and had no idea why she was there.

The three of them looked at each other until they all became embarrassed. "I think we should all go back to bed," announced Kate's mum. "It's gone a bit nippy."

Her dad looked like he was going to say something, but her mum pulled his arm and they went back inside their bedroom.

Kate didn't move for a moment. She had never sleepwalked before, as far as she knew, so something must have made her get up and head downstairs. She had a vague recollection of a dream involving school, but the details were just out of reach.

She shrugged and climbed the stairs back to her room. Mum was right, it had become cold. Her arms were covered in goosebumps.

EIGHTEEN

Josh's house was an end terrace at the edge of a large wooded area. All the lights were out and there was no sign of Oberon or a team of Hywardathian planet police. It didn't mean they weren't there, thought Kylie as she waited, hidden behind a bush across the street. It could be a trap. Unfortunately, she wouldn't know until she sprang it.

She was scared, a very odd and disconcerting feeling. She had never truly been alone, thanks to her Cortex Implant, and her only 'offline' time had been by choice. But now the device was dead. Not only was she cut off from her parents and Polly, she couldn't even tune into the Hywardathians communications. It was as though the Implant had been removed. *OK*, she thought, *now you can add panic to the list.*

It was still there of course; she could feel it when she pushed against it with her node muscle. She could only assume her parents had turned it off to protect her. Assumption in this case was better than hope.

She had thought she could hide at Josh's house, but now it seemed very exposed in the lightly populated outskirts of town. But the woods looked promising. Perhaps Josh had a secret hiding place in there where she could hold up until the rescue party arrived. She had a couple of gadgets at her disposal, but no weapons, so hiding appealed to her. Her knowledge of Earth literature and movies told her woods were always filled with either kids' hidey holes, cannibalistic witches or serial killers, all of which offered a more promising alternative to Oberon and his fellow Hywardathians.

Kylie edged out into the street, skirting around the halo cast by the lone street light at this end. She stopped frequently and waited, but nothing happened. She was reasonably certain they would have checked out Kate's house first. Unlikely though it was, Oberon couldn't take a chance in case she had performed a double bluff and actually gone to the most obvious hiding place. Planet guardians were not allowed to harm natives unless threatened with harm, so she was reasonably sure Kate and her family were safe. She hoped this time, rather than assumed. Oberon must be very angry, but surely he wouldn't... She stopped herself from thinking about that and jumped the low wall around Josh's house and flattened herself against the building next to the front door.

Assuming she was right, there wasn't much time if Oberon picked Josh's house as the next target, which was likely in the circumstances. The front doorbell was out of the question and she didn't want everyone to wake up and see the house lit up like Gerillion festerbush. The bedroom upstairs at the front was most likely Josh's parents' bedroom, so Kylie skirted around to the side of the house. There was a high fence set about twenty feet from the house, separating the garden from the woods. She crossed the lawn and leant against it while she looked up at the house. A single window upstairs faced the side garden, and she saw that it was open with the frame resting on a half-squashed football. *Bingo!*

She found a few small stones in a garden bed and threw a couple up to rap against the window pane. *I am a good shot*, she thought, then paused to listen. It was still quiet. "Josh," she called in a loud whisper.

Silence. Now she was getting annoyed. "Josh!"

She picked out the two biggest stones and tossed one, then the other through the open gap. The first thudded against something solid. The response to the second was a loud "Ouch!"

The window slid fully open and Josh's head came into view, one hand holding the window open the other rubbing his forehead. He squinted into the garden and Kylie moved from shadow into the dim light.

"Polly!" exclaimed Josh, letting go of the window, which slid down and cracked him on the back of the head. "Ouch!"

Kylie rolled her eyes. "Open the front door."

"What?" Josh nursed his head.

Kylie pointed to the front of the house. "Be quiet and go to the door."

Josh nodded and winced. Kylie returned to the front of the house.

First she went to the gate and looked down the street. Her hearts sank when she saw headlights at the end. The car was moving very slowly, but it must be them.

The front door of the house opened and Josh stood there in his striped pyjamas and with a nasty bruise forming on his forehead. *That really was a good shot.*

"Polly, what…"

Kylie ran to him, making a shushing sign with a finger against her lips. She would have to make this fast. "I'm not Polly, Josh." His eyes widened and his mouth opened, but Kylie gave him a look which said he would be dead if he made a sound. His mouth snapped shut.

"I'm from another planet and I'm called Kylie. Polly and I swapped places – call it a school exchange if you like – but the whole thing has gone arse-up. I'm not supposed to be here and Mister Oberon turns out to be from the planet Hywardath, which is supervising Earth until it is accepted into the Confederation. Hywardath was appointed by my planet, but that's another story. My parents and Polly are in space somewhere and hopefully planning to get me back and return Polly, but I've lost contact. Anyway, Oberon knows I'm not Polly and is searching for me, probably with a squad of security enforcers. Now, the thing is, by coming here I broke a few laws, rules, whatever, and if I'm caught both Polly and I will be vaporised instantly."

Josh blinked. "You'd better come in, then."

"No. It's too late. I think they're at the end of your street."

A look of panic crossed Josh's face. At least he believes some of it, thought Kylie.

"Get inside," he demanded with almost enough force for Kylie to obey, "I'll protect you."

Kylie grabbed him by the shoulders.

"Ouch!"

"No. They'll find me here and who knows what they'll do to you. Tell me about the woods over there. Where can I hide until I'm rescued?"

Josh quickly got with the program, now he had a practical problem. "Head in a straight line over there." He pointed. "About a hundred and fifty yards away is a jagged stump about four feet high – the tree came down in a storm – hang a hard left there and weave through the trees. About half a mile away is a dry stream bed – should be dry, anyway – follow it to the right and there's a huge tangle of trees and roots. It's easy to hide yourself in there."

"Great. Got it."

"I'll come with you."

"No way. There's a good chance this will end badly, so go back to bed. And close your window."

Josh didn't move and Kylie decided, judging by the tortured look on his face, that he must be thinking. "Get back inside. Go!"

He reluctantly obeyed and closed the door, much to Kylie's relief. She had more than enough to worry about. She could hear the soft purr of the car and edged to the front garden wall. The car was halfway down the street and had thankfully dimmed its lights. Scanner rays shone on either side and slightly in front of the vehicle and they were painstakingly checking every garden on the approach. All she had to do was hop over the wall and run into the woods. She would be well away by the time they reached Josh's house.

Kylie straddled the wall, careful to move slowly and was lifting the other leg when everything changed.

"Kylie! Don't speak." Gemma's voice.

Mum!

The voice provided so much relief that Kylie almost burst into tears. But the shock made her catch her foot on the wall and she tumbled to the footpath on the other side of the wall.

"We're coming down, so stay hidden until we contact you. Ta ta for now."

Light exploded all around her and Kylie found herself lit up by the car's headlights, full beam. The car's engine roared and the vehicle surged towards her.

NINETEEN

"Don't you think we should tell Kylie?" Polly couldn't help thinking this could be a mistake. There was something about Kylie's parents that didn't inspire confidence.

"No," said Clive. "Too risky. We'll let her know when we get down there."

Polly and Kylie's parents looked out over the Earth, looking very beautiful from their vantage point. *So near and yet so far.*

When Gemma and Clive told Polly they had a 'window of opportunity' to send a pod down to Earth, she was very happy. *Send me down in the pod. I jump out, Kylie jumps in and Bob's your uncle.*

But no. Gemma and Clive were coming, too, much to Polly's surprise. "But if we're caught, you will both be blasted as well!"

"Not necessarily," replied Gemma, although she didn't sound very convincing.

Clive jumped in. "Now we've made contact with the buffoons, we have every right to check on progress."

"That's not what you said earlier," Polly reminded him. "You still need their permission to go down there." There seemed to be a demarcation dispute as to who were the actual buffoons. *Both parties, probably.*

"We'll work it out," said Gemma.

"Can I contact my parents to say goodbye?" asked Polly. She was serious.

Gemma sighed. "It won't come to that, Polly. We know what we are doing is dangerous, but we can't let you go down alone. It's too dangerous for you and Kylie. If you were caught, that would be it."

Polly winced at the 'it'.

"If we're with you," added Clive, "and we are all caught, at least we can pull rank and perhaps get a stay of…"

No use pussyfooting around, thought Polly. "Execution."

"That's not so bad," said Gemma enthusiastically. "We'll go to appeal and it will be decades after you died of old age when the ruling comes through."

Great! "That sounds a bit better than death, I suppose. But am I right in thinking I won't be able to live on Earth again?"

Clive nodded fuzzily and his edges swirled dramatically. "Probably. Well, yes, that's a distinct possibility."

"So I'll have to live on your planet?" All Polly could think about was her eyesight being ruined by squinting.

"Oh, no," said Gemma, making the question sound ridiculous. She stopped herself from saying more, but her smoky outline raged.

Polly felt her stomach lurch. "Go on."

Gemma hesitated and her head turned towards Clive, who didn't seem inclined to help. "You would have to stay in space, as visiting any planet would allow the Hywardathians to claim you. And once in their hands..."

Polly thought about this and decided to be philosophical. This was a very small drama in a huge universe and really a couple of lives in the scheme of things was insignificant. *On the other hand, one of them is mine!* "Space sounds fine to me."

"It won't come to that," said Clive. "We'll have you swapped over in no time and it will be as if none of this ever happened."

I wish! "Well, let's get going then."

"OK," said Gemma.

A pod was already behind her. *I must find out how they do that*, thought Polly.

The three of them walked into the vehicle and, instantly, the vast spaceship was racing away from them as they dropped towards Earth. "They won't see us?" asked Polly, suddenly worried.

Clive replied. "We're in a protective corridor, something like a tube, from the ship to the destination. We're completely invisible to them."

Polly sensed tension and noticed that Gemma and Clive's fuzzy outlines were swirling violently. "What haven't you told me?"

They were silent for a moment, then Gemma spoke. "Kylie is in great danger. Oberon has been to your house – don't worry, your parents weren't home – and to your friend's house. Kate?"

Polly's stomach lurched. "Is she OK?"

"She doesn't even know. Any idea where Kylie would go if

not either of those places?"

"You can't track her?"

"Not without alerting Oberon," said Clive. "Once we're on the ground I'll get a reading."

Polly thought. "Probably to Josh's house. Another friend. He's the only other person she knows."

"Not good," said Gemma, real worry in her voice. "That's where Oberon and his team are headed.

"Team?"

"You might as well know, Polly. His team is a hit squad."

Polly looked through the invisible exterior of the pod as night-time southern England rose up to meet them. It was no longer a magical view.

The pod dropped into her garden and Polly jumped out and ran into the house. She froze in the open doorway. She could see into the living room and kitchen and all the furniture was gone. She ran from room to room. There was nothing left. Her computer, her dad's. Disbelieving, she dashed up the stairs. It was the same. Her room was completely empty. Her stuff, all gone! She burst into tears.

Gemma entered the room behind her and gave her a hug. "They're not nice people, but it's only stuff, Polly."

Polly sniffed. Gemma was right. There were bigger fish to fry if she was to live and replace all her stuff.

They went back downstairs, where Clive waited in the kitchen. The family photo Josh had dropped was sitting in the square of dust on the floor where the fridge had been. Polly picked it up.

"I know where Kylie is," announced Clive.

A map appeared on the empty wall. "That's where Josh lives!" exclaimed Polly.

Gemma turned to Clive. "We have to speak to her."

"It's risky," said Clive, "but OK. Make it quick."

Gemma took a breath. "Kylie! Don't speak. We're coming down, so stay hidden until we contact you. Ta ta for now." She looked at Clive. "Did that sound OK?"

"What now?" asked Polly.

"Now we go get her," said Clive as he turned for the door.

"Wait a minute." Gemma called him back. "We can't go like this."

"Like what?"

"In this form. We might get spotted."

"There's no time," said Clive, frustrated. "And we can't take Polly's form. Triplets would be just as conspicuous."

Gemma took the photo from Polly's hand. "Your parents."

"Yes."

"Perfect."

Resigned, Clive grabbed a corner of the photo and Polly watched, fascinated as they both became mini-whirlwinds. *This is going to be weird.*

Gemma and Clive stopped spinning and Polly found herself looking at perfect replicas of her parents wearing the same clothes as in the photograph.

"How do we look?" asked Gemma.

"Weird," said Polly. They would probably fool most people, but there was something odd about them. Mum's hair colour wasn't quite right and the tufts of hair over dad's ears looked fake. And their smiles. There was something creepy going on there, as though the expression placed a little too much pressure on their faces. It reminded her of when Polly used to sulk and her real mum snapped her out of it by using reverse psychology, saying, 'don't smile or your face will crack!' It always made her laugh, but it was an alarming image now.

"Maybe don't smile," Polly advised.

"Just as well," agreed Clive. "Not much to smile about here." He hurried out of the door with a walk most un-dadlike. Polly and Gemma followed, but Clive had stopped outside the front door next to Polly's dad's car. "We need a vehicle. Who does this one belong to?"

"That's my dad's," said Polly, "but I don't think we should…"

"I command an interstellar spaceship. How hard can this be?"

The engine roared into life before they all jumped in, – *how do they do that?* – Gemma and Clive in the front, Polly in the back. Polly noticed Clive seemed a little lost. "You're in the passenger seat," she informed him.

Clive sighed and opened his door. "Stay there," ordered Gemma. She quickly looked at the controls and backed out into the street, crunched the automatic gears by changing them while still going backwards and shot forward down the road. Polly grimaced, but accepted that there were a variety of ways to die. "Turn left at the end of the street."

NOW

TWENTY

Kylie rested behind another tree. The hologram projection refractor used a lot of energy and the images faded almost as quickly as they generated, so she had to stop frequently to recharge by tapping The Source.

A glance back showed more empty fields where once was heavily-treed woods and Oberon and his team moved steadily towards her. She had been shocked to see that the three person team comprised Gwen and her cronies, but quickly realised the hit squad were just using their form to blend in with Earth humans. Well, given their penchant for destroying everything around them with weapons unknown on Earth, blending in might not be the right term.

It was amazing she had survived this far, Kylie mused, after stumbling and being caught in the car headlights outside Josh's house. She had quickly jumped back to her feet and gritted her teeth in expectation of the vaporon blast, but the occupants of the car had become excited and somehow decided to all try to get out of the same door, resulting in them tumbling into the road accompanied by some very impressive Hywardathian swearing. Swearing was one of Kylie's interests and at last count she knew the three worst words in four hundred and eighty-three languages. She had chosen to switch off 'profanity' on her translator so she could enjoy the words in all their original glory.

The jumble of bodies gave Kylie a chance to dash into the woods and by the time they opened up with their weapons, she was a good distance away. From the sound, there was a lot of disintegrating going on and she hoped they had not destroyed Josh's house.

That was only ten minutes ago and they were gaining on her fast. It was hard to concentrate with the earth-shattering whumps and the stop-start nature of her getaway. And the internal argument she was conducting with herself. Her mother's words kept returning. "One day there will be serious consequences for one of your escapades." "Yeah, yeah," she had replied. Kylie didn't know what was worse, being vaporised or her mother being right.

She stole another look around the tree. The quartet was moving slightly further away across the field they created, which presented the possibility of moving without using the holograms. She moved around the tree trunk and then quietly walked away, keeping a tree between her and Oberon's team.

The large shadowy figure hurtling at her from the right caught her completely by surprise. She had the impression, just before impact, that it was human shaped and it left the ground at speed to perform a flying rugby tackle. It crashed into her with great force, but of course she didn't feel a thing and the figure bounced off and ended up a tangle of groaning limbs at her feet.

"Arrrrghhh," gasped Josh, fortunately very quietly as he was seriously winded.

"Josh!" Kylie bent down to sit him up. "What the…"

Josh looked up at her and tried to explain. "Arrrrghhh," he said, with more pain this time as the shock wore off.

"You already said that," Kylie replied, anxiously looking back to the field. "What are you doing here?"

"I…" he blew out his cheeks. "…came to save you."

"Good plan," said Kylie, "except you've now probably killed us both." She looked at him. "And Polly," she added, just to make him feel worse.

"Oh no!" said Josh, breathless. "But it can't be that bad."

Really! thought Kylie. From her point of view the only positive was that Josh had changed out of those awful pyjamas into jeans, shirt and sneakers. Not exactly a life-saving observation.

Time to take charge. "OK, Josh. We may be able to get out of this, but you have to do what I say, OK?"

"Hmm," said Josh.

"I'm serious. This is life or death. You see those trees behind us?"

"There are no trees."

"My point exactly. There'll be no us, either, if we're caught in those rays. So do as I say, or you can find your own way out."

"OK."

Kylie helped him to his feet. "Where does it hurt? Can you walk."

"I think so," said Josh, his breath returning. "My shoulder is killing me and my head hurts."

Kylie pushed him ahead of her further into the woods. "Why are you limping?"

The limping stopped. *What is it with guys?* thought Kylie.

Another WHUMP! and a grove of trees disappeared only a hundred yards away. "We have to move. Let's get to that stream bed you told me about. It'll give us some cover."

"That's why I followed you. You're going the wrong way. Follow me."

Kylie was irritated. She wasn't going the wrong way, because if she had gone the right way, she would be dead. She knew exactly where to go from here, but stayed silent because Josh led her in a different direction.

They soon put more distance between themselves and Oberon, but the squad were methodically destroying the woods and reducing potential cover. Josh picked up the speed, though he still clutched his shoulder. But then he disappeared and Kylie heard a splash. "Arrrgghhh!" he exclaimed. Then, "I found it."

Kylie stopped and looked down. The earthen bank had collapsed and Josh lay in a shallow stream about ten feet below. *So much for a dry creek bed.* She jumped down and helped him up. This time he had a real limp, but Kylie was very happy they were out of the line of sight at last.

"Kylie!" It was Polly's voice.

Kylie felt a wave of relief.

"I'm with your parents and we're nearby and we've got a car. We know you are in Martin's Woods, but we can't get an accurate fix without alerting Oberon's people. Where can we pick you up?"

"Josh. Where does this come out. I've got Polly online. She's nearby with a car."

"Why the hell is Josh with you?" yelled Polly.

"Because he's an idiot," replied Kylie.

Josh had stopped and looked back at her, puzzled. *Idiot!*

He shook his head to clear it. *Probably very easy*, thought Kylie. "The closest street is Hastings Road. We'll come out on the hill behind the phone booth. In about ten minutes."

"We heard that," said Gemma. "On the way." Kylie heard screeching and her dad yelling, "Watch out for that bin!"

followed by a loud crash.

"What's happening?" asked Josh.

"You don't want to know. Let's keep moving."

Josh followed the stream, which was slow going due to the darkness and the tangle of roots. Soil erupted around them with every explosive WHUMP!

"This is where we get out," said Josh. He scrambled up the bank and turned back to look at Kylie, a very worried expression on his face.

She joined him and saw why. There was an open stretch of grass, maybe seventy yards wide, between them and the hill running down to the road. The town rooftops and streetlights were beyond, oblivious to the drama in the soon-to-be-gone woods. The top of the hill was fringed by a line of trees, so it was a simple matter of getting past them, down the hill and into the waiting car. *If it hasn't been wrecked.*

But Kylie's hearts sank when she looked behind them over the lip of the gully. Oberon and the three girls could be seen through the trees walking steadily in a line and heading directly towards them. Josh was looking the same way and he exchanged glances with Kylie. She was sure her face had the same grim expression as his.

The ground shook as more trees disappeared and the quartet was even more visible. Another blast and there would be no cover at all.

"That's not good, is it?" stated Josh.

Normally, Kylie would have snapped back, but… "No."

It was now or never. "When I say go, we have to get to that hill fast. I mean Olympic record fast. Can you do it?"

A very determined look came across Josh's face, much to Kylie's relief, and he grinned tightly. "You bet."

Kylie turned back to the pursuers and activated her refractor. A hundred Kylie holograms filled the ditch like soldiers in a trench ready to go over the top. It was all or nothing. The hologram Kylies vaulted out of the trench and hurled themselves at Oberon and into the fields and remaining trees at either side of the group.

"Go!" yelled Kylie, her hand under Josh's bum pushing him over the top. He scrambled to his feet and took off at speed. Kylie was much faster, so she gathered up the back of his shirt in her fist and propelled him with her, his feet barely touching the ground.

Oberon's team opened up, full blast and the earth shook around them as they finished off the remaining trees by firing at the holograms.

Kylie and Josh were getting closer to the hill, but time seemed to slow and she thought they could not possibly make it. She clenched her teeth and increased speed as they approached the trees. A massive WHUMP! Almost knocked them off their feet and she knew they were seconds from death. There was only one thing to do. Kylie flipped Josh over and hurled him the last twenty yards cartwheeling through the air between two of the trees and over the lip of the hill.

She surged after him and as the earth shook around her she threw herself after Josh, turning in the air as she went over the hill to see all the trees at the top vanish instantly. Then she hit the hillside and tumbled all the way down with Josh in a tangle of arms and legs. They crashed into the back of the phone booth, which was just as well because the car came to a screeching halt in front of the booth and would have run them over.

The back door of the car flew open and Polly leant out. "Get in!"

Poor Josh was a battered mess, so Kylie picked him up and chucked him into the car next to Polly, followed him in and slammed the door behind her.

Her relieved parents – their appearance didn't fool Kylie – turned and smiled. Josh stared at them, open mouthed, turned to Polly, then looked at Kylie and shook his head, completely confused. Kylie almost felt sorry for him. Polly looked very concerned and grabbed his hand. He looked like crap, but Kylie had to concede he had a nice smile.

"Can we go before we are vaporised?"

Gemma slammed her foot down and the car surged forward. Kylie twisted in her seat and a second before they turned the corner, the phone booth disintegrated with a WHUMP! that shook the neighbourhood.

TWENTY-ONE

Oberon released a cry of rage followed by a barked sentence containing every crude word in Hywardathian and a choice selection of universal profanity. So foul, in fact, that Floothil, Muoth and Thirt, disguised as the three schoolgirls, appeared embarrassed.

They were looking down on the empty street from the top of the hill, the WHUMP! from the disappeared phone box still ringing in their ears.

Oberon turned and glared at the trio, the former woods behind them now a large expanse of fields. "You let them escape!" he said, quietly but with venom.

Floothil was ready. "You are in command, remember? You insisted on being in charge and doing things your way. I have two witnesses."

They both looked at Muoth and Thirt, who, despite not being the brightest stars in the universe, were experienced enough to stay silent. It doesn't matter which planet you are on, when in deep shit the best thing to do is to stop digging. "You will all be lucky to get work on a Fuopian space dredger after this," added Oberon, bitterly, though he knew that particular fate was his, too.

Deep down, he conceded it was his fault the Polly impersonator got away, though he would publicly deny it until his dying breath and do everything Hywardathianly possible to shift the blame to Floothil and his men. Floothil had questioned his order to restrict the firing distance, which would no doubt come back to haunt him, but the risk of exposure was too great. The problem had to be contained, although that was a moot point after the woods had been destroyed.

The only consolation was that no Hywardathian on Earth would escape blame for this incident and as much effort would be placed on covering arses as the continued hunt.

"Let's get back to the car," said Oberon.

"No need," said Floothil, shaking Gwen's long locks away from his face with a toss of his head and pointing to his earpiece. "We're getting a lift."

Oberon looked back across the fields and his face hardened. Two small craft were coming in low to the ground. He felt a familiar ping of embarrassment at the saucer shapes, taken instantly back to the debacle of decades ago. The saucer of his misfortune.

The craft came to a halt a few yards back from the hill and Floothil led the group to them. Spinning rapidly, the three squad members returned to their normal small, green bodies.

The craft were three-seaters, so Floothil and Muoth jumped into one – they were built for Hywardathian sized people – while Oberon and Thirt squeezed into the other. Oberon was almost bent double and the pilot had trouble closing the door. "You need to lose some weight, old man," he said angrily.

"Shut up!" growled Oberon. He considered cuffing the man round the back of the head, but he was too cramped to move. They glared at each other for a moment and then the pilot turned back to his controls and they rose into the sky.

"You should have let me waste 'em," said Thirt.

"You can shut up, too."

The journey was short, so Oberon went over all of his excuses. The Polly-person should have been stopped by security, he was not warned she had penetrated earth defences, he had no support and when he did, the squad sent to him were useless and incompetent and disputed his orders. And, in summary, *it's not my fault!*

It was unlikely to do him any good, as everyone else would be doing the same thing. However, if he kicked up enough of a stink, he might be able to bring others down with him or perhaps enlist allies who might have more to gain for themselves by supporting him.

For a Hywardathian, a fall from grace is almost inevitable. Success is resented and any promotion brings a new collection of enemies trying to bring you down. This results in the best and most able people ruining each other's careers and the mediocre and incompetent rising through the ranks to the top by default. Oberon had been naïve all those years ago, but now he had little to lose.

He felt a strange tugging sensation at the corners of his mouth. It was so long since he had left Earth, he thought it must be the gravitational pull, but then he saw his distorted reflection in the back of the pilot's helmet. To his surprise, he detected the beginnings of a smile. And his eye, which had been performing gymnastics since the crisis began, stared calmly back. His anger and resentment began to wane, only a little, though – he was a Hywardathian, after all – and a strange feeling crept over his body. Altitude sickness? No, that wasn't it. Had he been drugged? No, the commander would want him fully conscious when he berated him publicly. What then?

He knew the answer, even though he had never been happy in his life. It was a feeling of well-being and, dare he say it, positivity. He turned to Thirt, who was staring at him strangely, his green face only inches away. Oberon increased his grin, feeling his skin creak, and Thirt shrank back against the outer shell of the craft, alarmed by the change.

Ahead was the Hywardathian mother ship, far away from its permanent geostationary orbit above Antarctica. Only an order from off-world could authorise such a move. The idea forming in Oberon's mind took on new possibilities.

He was surprised at the condition of the craft as they got closer. It was a vast, neglected rust-bucket, much worse than his last visit in 1951. Oberon had monitored some of the communications traffic over the years and knew Hywardath High Command would not authorise the purchase of a new ship until this one actually began to fall apart. And they were too proud to accept a second hand, reconditioned confederation fleet vessel. He had agreed, but now, seeing this… Things might have to change. *Don't get ahead of yourself*, he cautioned.

Scores of saucers were buzzing around the mother ship like angry insects, a reflection of the unofficial Hywardathian mantra, *if you don't know what to do, look busy.*

Oberon shook his head. Nothing had changed.

The vast hangar door began to open as they approached. He couldn't be sure, but it seemed to stutter and, if sound could travel in space, no doubt it would creak loudly. *What a sad state of affairs*, thought Oberon happily, gathering yet more ammunition.

Inside the hanger there were no saucers, all the craft pointlessly deployed around the planet, no doubt. Not pointlessly, really; to make it look like 'something' was being done.

But if the hangar was devoid of flying saucers, there was no shortage of military personnel. Hundreds of angry faces surrounded their landing spot. Oberon felt Thirt's tension next to him. The trooper knew he was guilty by association and therefore likely to spend years performing some terrible task at the ends of the universe. The pilot twisted to look at them after landing the craft. "I'd say good luck, but I'd be wasting my breath." He nodded outside to the restless crowd of troops, who had no doubt been whipped into even more hostility by their commanders. They knew as well as Thirt that associating, sympathising with or exhibiting any familiarity with someone who has fallen from favour, or, as is inevitable, *will* fall from favour, is a recipe for disaster. As a result, everyone on Hywardath hates everyone else in advance. Oberon often thought it amazing his race had not become extinct.

He awkwardly exited the saucer backwards and stood up. He was glad he had kept his earth form; it meant he towered over the assembled sea of green faces. He would need every advantage possible in the coming minutes. The men pressed in, each trying to outdo his or her companion in the facial expression of anger, though he was amused to see a glint of fear whenever he caught an eye. "Tough crowd," said Oberon under his breath.

A feeling of calm enveloped him. This was precisely where his disgrace in 1951 took place. It was lower-key back then. Hywardath was only a new player in the planet supervision game and although the consequences were devastating for Oberon, only embarrassment was caused to his planet and the entire incident was put down to teething troubles.

But now, with Hywardathian High Command actively undermining its planetary superior and pushing for more planets to supervise, this crisis was very serious indeed, as were the consequences; even though in the grand scheme of things one intruder, as this appeared to be, would hardly raise an eyebrow anywhere else. But this was Hywardath and there was no such thing as a minor incident. Everything has to escalate, heads have to roll and faces must be saved. Who better, then, than a tried and true scapegoat from the past to be the perfect scapegoat now. A man with an unenviable and conveniently renewable track record. What were the odds of a Polly impersonator landing in his neck of the woods? *Well, fields now*. The irony was not lost on Oberon.

The other saucer landed nearby and Floothil and Muoth were jostled through the crowd to join Thirt behind Oberon, who twisted round to give them a *you're-going-down-too* look. The three green men wouldn't meet his eye, but they looked grim.

The assembly pushed in closer now and a narrow corridor opened up leading to the bridge of the ship. *Don't these people have something better to do?* thought Oberon. Evidently not. There was something wonderfully Hywardathian about the grand spectacle of someone falling from grace. He felt the strange sensation again, warmth and well-being. He was not sure he liked it – he was much more comfortable with anger and resentment – but it did provide an unusual and unfamiliar clarity of thought. He looked at the angry mob all around him, driving him forward. *If it's a spectacle they want, then a spectacle they shall have!*

Oberon was forced through a small door into a corridor between the hanger and the formal bridge. The real bridge was what you would expect, a medium sized control room appropriate to such a vessel. The formal bridge, however, designed to impress visitors was completely over the top. Oberon cringed as he entered. The room was enormous, ornate in the Hywardathian classical style – which, to be honest, was never anything to write home about – filled with columns and garish images showcasing the best of Hywardath. Sad, really, and more likely to inspire visitors to declare war than put them in awe. In his decades on Earth, a planet renowned throughout the universe as having the largest collection of structures built in the worse of taste, Oberon had never seen anything to match the formal bridge of this ship.

The space comfortably held one thousand people on the tiered stands circling most of the room, but there were double that number in attendance. The atmosphere – as in any gathering of more than one Hywardathian – was extremely hostile. Oberon and his three companions were led into the middle of the room, where they were hastily abandoned by their guards lest they be contaminated by disgrace.

Ahead of the four was a giant image, beamed live from Hywardath, of the members of the Grand Interplanetary Supervisory Control Committee, a rather inaccurate name for a body designed to oversee one planet. So far, anyway. Oberon stared up at the twelve angry green men.

Sitting below the image in the centre of the room, his chair raised on a step and resplendent in his robes, was the Supreme Commander of Earth Operations, Lugy Jwerquep. Oberon hated this man more than any other Hywardathian, which was a very impressive level of hostility. His actions had resulted in almost seventy years in the wilderness for Oberon, and there he sat, his small green face looking like death, the veins on his neck and forehead pulsing with animosity, waiting to explode.

It was all an act of self-preservation, of course, and, Oberon had to admit, very effective. The crowd was openly hostile now and yelling abuse at Oberon and his companions. Jwerquep allowed them to do so for another moment, as indeed Oberon would have done. Then he stood, descended the step and raised a hand. The room fell silent, though not as instantly as he had intended, so some of the drama was wasted. He glared at them for a moment, before turning his venomous attention back to Oberon.

Jerquep's raised hand extended out in front of him until his outstretched finger was pointing directly at Oberon, shaking slightly with fury. *A nice touch*, thought Oberon. "You have failed!" screamed Jerquep.

Oberon sighed as this set off another wave of yelling from the assembly and this time Jerquep had to wait until the furore subsided. Oberon was impressed with himself. The normal reaction would be to hurl abuse back at the crowd, as Floothil and his companions were doing. But Oberon felt calm and merely stared back at Jerquep, who was starting to look concerned. His was a position demanding total control, but Oberon had thrown him. His decades on earth were proving very useful and at that moment he realised – knew – he had already won.

"YOU!" screamed Oberon, instantly silencing the crowd. He jabbed a large finger back at Jerquep. "YOU DARE CONDEMN ME?"

Taken by surprise, Jerquep edged back, tripped on the step and sat heavily on the edge of his chair, only just managing to stay upright.

Oberon walked forward until he towered over the

commander, still pointing. "You, the man responsible for this debacle? The man responsible for allowing an incursion into Hywardathian airspace? The man who has brought shame upon himself and every Hywardathian in the universe?"

Oberon was satisfied by the look of realisation that crossed Jerquep's face. The commander was no fool, though, and could recover at any moment in the now silent auditorium. *Time to finish him off.* "You fool! Your actions have condemned every man and woman here to possible exile. You have led them to the edge of disaster."

The crowd didn't like that and Oberon saw their eyes and hostility shift from him to Jerquep. But he had not finished. He looked up to the bemused committee. "And these august men. Your actions will reflect very poorly upon them. The very men who trusted you to perform one simple task are now under threat due to your actions." The collective look of alarm on the faces of the twelve was everything Oberon could have hoped for.

He raised his arms towards the ceiling and released in a forlorn voice the words they were all thinking. "Oh, what will become of us all?"

There was no point saying more, as the room erupted in abuse, all of it directed at Jerquep, who was in a state of confusion.

The committee was in uproar and the picture disappeared for more than a minute. It returned and the men were composed, but nervous, now, their leader standing. "Silence!" he said and the room obeyed.

He pointed at Jerquep, who must by now be regretting raising his own finger and starting this trend. "Lugy Jwerquep, you are hereby relieved of command. You will be replaced by Kurf Obserl." Oberon had not heard his real name spoken for many years, so it took him a moment to realise the extent of his victory. As commander, Jerquep's fate was now in his hands.

The committee leader's finger traced a line to Oberon. "Do not fail." And then they were gone.

The crowd now cheered, a rare occurrence in Hywardathian circles, though everyone was keen to confirm their allegiance before getting back to their usual backbiting and undermining.

The four senior officers present approached Oberon and he looked down on them. But first he indicated for Flothill, Thirt and Muoth to approach. They did so hesitantly. "Take Jerquep to his quarters and see he does not leave." He turned to look at the vanquished leader. "Until I decide what to do with him."

He addressed the officers. "What is the latest news?"

The senior officer, Commander Grtyu Rewsz, replied. "A distorter beam was detected, which we believe was activated to disguise the extraction of the intruder, which must be imminent. We can't get an accurate reading," she added, "but we believe it is in the vicinity of your search."

Oberon thought for a moment. "I agree. I want every detector trained on the area. How many sauc… shuttles do we have?"

"Eight thousand across the planet."

"I want them all deployed. Half within and half outside the atmosphere."

The woman's expression showed she approved. Her green eyebrows asked a further silent question.

Oberon was suddenly reminded of the last few hours and his face grew dark with anger and he felt his eye begin to twitch. "Find and destroy."

EXTRACT FROM VRYL'S GALMANAC

Revelation

The reactions of planets when they discover they are not alone in the universe are often hilarious. Initial contact is rarely taken seriously, although when it is, it is usually considered to be a threat and has inspired many a war.

The favoured method, after thousands of years of trial and error, is for the Induction Committee to 'hijack' a meeting of world leaders and inform them of their invitation to join the Confederation. It is fairly easy to convince these people, but when they try to convince the people of their planet, the fun and games really start. Many have been assassinated or removed from office in less radical ways and the news generally sends everyone (except the die-hard "I-told-you-so" crowd) into denial.

Religious authorities tend to take the news the hardest, as the sudden realisation that their world is just another planet – and not particularly special – calls for a rapid and often forlorn revision of doctrine.

The news can also prompt panic, though this generally occurs much later. By the time they are contacted, planets are often well advanced in media and entertainment technology and are very sceptical when shown images of the wider universe. For instance, on Earth, there is a significant portion of the population who believe the moon landings were faked. These people are going to have serious coping issues when the induction process begins.

Many planets have actually declared war on the confederation, mobilising troops and weapons across the planet in preparation for the invasion. The confederation withdraws in these cases and leaves them to it for a generation, leaving the inhabitants in a very long state of anti-climax and, often, financially bankrupt (see the entry for **Resisting Planets**, the hilarious Cortex Implant reality show now in its four hundred and sixty-third season).

Eventually, the Confederation will stage something

spectacular outside the atmosphere if necessary, which usually inspires the planet to fall over the line into acceptance. It can take generations to fully believe what is happening, but the benefits of having a single world government and, for individuals, being a citizen of their world, rather than a country, is a very positive and stabilising development in all aspects of life.

TWENTY-TWO

This is completely nuts. Polly looked at her four companions as they sat in the darkened car which was parked in the shadows under the canopy of a large tree at the end of Suakin Close.

In front, Kylie's parents sat staring out of the window, as did Kylie on the back seat. Josh stared at Polly, his expression a mix of awe, excitement and sheer terror.

This is completely nuts, she thought. *You already thought that*, she thought, accusingly. *Maybe I'm nuts*, she then thought, unhelpfully. *I'd better stop thinking.*

"Why have we stopped?" she asked.

Kylie turned to her, annoyed. "We're communicating with base."

Gemma shook her head. "The reason we are parked here is to give our colleagues time to counter the Quakers – I'll explain later – and the escape plan is almost ready."

"Good," said Polly, silently busting to ask if this meant the Baxters, the Quaker family who lived on the corner, were actually aliens. "Hopefully there's intelligent life up there."

Kylie gave her a nasty look, but Polly didn't care. She was growing more and more angry with these, these… She wanted to call them aliens, but they were actually human and, though she had hoped for more, they were proving to be just as dumb as the people of this planet. Dumber, even. *How did that work?*

They *seemed* intelligent, she thought, but there was an awful lot they didn't know and, from the extracts from Vryl's Galmanac, there was a lot of stuff happening in the universe that 'people' generally didn't understand or had no explanation for. Like the Source nonsense. Surely, for something that pretty much drives the universe, someone must have worked out what it is?

It was all academic, really, she decided. They were all doomed and she would never get to explore the universe and all its wonders.

"Where there's life, there's hope," said Josh suddenly and

quietly, as though he'd read her mind.

Polly looked at him, more closely this time. He was very cute, she noticed with some surprise, battered and bruised, his face heroically fighting through the obvious pain at whatever Kylie had put him through. How and why had he got involved in all this? It would be easy to blame Kylie for getting him added to the death list, but knowing Josh, he just couldn't help himself. She had no doubt at all that he was a willing participant in this, their final adventure.

He was still staring at her, his big eyes filled with… something… as he tried to smile through his pain.

"Oh, shut up," she snapped.

She tapped Clive and Gemma on the shoulders, causing them to turn. "Right!" said Polly. "What the hell is going on? If Josh and I are going to die, we're entitled to information."

Kylie didn't like this and glared at Polly.

Polly glared back and pointed at Kylie's face. "Don't you dare say anything. This is all your fault and if you screw up anything else I'll kill you myself before these Haywirewhatsits get anywhere near you!"

Between them, Josh shrank back into his seat.

"Don't you dare speak to me like that!" yelled Kylie, clearly unused to being spoken to like that.

"Or what?" snapped Polly.

Out of the corner of her eye, Polly saw that Josh was preparing to sit up and intervene. The guy has a death wish, thought Polly. She shook her head at him slightly and he got the hint.

"Well?" asked Polly, noting with satisfaction the uncertainty on Kylie's face. It might not have been obvious to everyone, but Kylie was wearing Polly's face and she recognised the look from her mirror.

Gemma and Clive were also staring at Kylie. If she thought she was going to get any sympathy from that quarter, she was sadly mistaken. "Haven't you done enough?" asked Gemma.

Kylie's face sank into a full-on sulk and Polly made a mental note never to sulk again. She looked so ugly! She smiled slightly at Kylie to rub it in, then turned to Gemma and Clive, feeling very powerful.

"Don't get any ideas," snapped Gemma. "You are as bad as each other, as far as we're concerned." She slightly turned to

Clive, who nodded his agreement. It was obviously risky not to.

Polly had to bite her tongue, but she nodded reluctantly.

"Good," said Gemma, now totally in control. It was a moment, thought Polly, that Gemma the space human and Marianne Hart became one. Both reassuring and scary.

Gemma began. "We're in deep shit."

Polly was hoping for a more reassuring opening statement, but beggars can't be choosers. She held up a hand. "Before you go on, how about we let Josh go home. He's not part of this."

Josh looked relieved, but then his face hardened. "No chance. I'm not leaving you alone to…"

"Don't worry. There's two of me, remember," she said nodding at Kylie, who looked away and folded her arms. "And my parents are here!"

"They're not your parents."

Polly almost replied that they know what they are doing, but managed to choke back the lie. "No, but they are Kylie's parents and they'll make sure I'm OK." Lying was becoming easier.

Gemma shook her head. "If Oberon recognised Josh, they will vaporise him on sight."

"Vaporise!" said Josh in a tiny voice.

Kylie turned to him. "Remember in the Star Trek movies when they transport people? They go all fuzzy and disintegrate. Then they get put back together at the other end of the journey?"

Josh nodded.

"Well, vaporisation is the first part without the second."

"That's not helpful!" snapped Gemma.

Kylie turned back to the window.

Polly squeezed Josh's arm and smiled. "Ouch," he said.

"Get on with it, Gemma," said Clive. "We only have a few minutes before we have to go."

"If everyone stops interrupting, I will," she replied, testily.

Polly didn't mind being nervous, but when the only people who can save you are so jumpy, it's a bit of a worry.

Gemma twisted in her seat until she looked at the three of them in the back. "As a result of Kylie's incredible stupidity, there has now been a change in the leadership of

Hywardathian Earth Command." She looked at Polly. "Your Mr Oberon is now in charge."

"Oberon!" exclaimed Polly and Josh together.

"We don't have full details," added Clive, excited, "but it sounds like he defeated Jwerqep in an absolutely brilliant political coup."

Gemma glared at him. "Whose side are you on?"

Clive smiled and turned back to the front windscreen. "Credit where it's due."

"It caught us by surprise," continued Gemma. "Oberon has been given more power than his predecessor, and he's treating Kylie's incursion like a full scale invasion of the planet."

Polly didn't understand interplanetary politics, but this didn't sound good. "But surely this is a minor incident. How can he justify…"

"Well, he can, because of all those old rules that have never been revised. He has declared martial law over the entire planet under an ordinance that hasn't been used in centuries. It allows Hywardath to temporarily displace our command and be in full control of Earth in a dictatorial capacity."

"How temporarily," asked Polly, knowing full well she would regret the reply.

"Up to twenty-five years."

"I'll be forty!" exclaimed Josh.

"None of us will make it to forty," said Kylie. "We're all toast."

"I know things look bad," conceded Gemma, "but we're still alive and everything is going to be fine. It has to be." She pointed a finger at Kylie. "You are responsible for this mess, so start thinking about how you can help instead of wallowing in self-pity."

Polly grinned, but Gemma's finger traced an arc until it pointed at her nose. "I hold you equally responsible for not recognising what a stupid and irresponsible idea this was. What if Kylie had been a hostile alien? You could have destroyed your planet. It's happened before, you know."

Thanks for the pep talk, 'mum', thought Polly. But she did have a point.

Gemma looked back and forth at Polly and Kylie, waiting for a response. "Nothing to say?"

Silence.

"Good. At this moment we are the most wanted people on this planet, possibly the universe, and Oberon is leaving no stone unturned. This operation makes the hunt for bin Laden look like a search for a missing cat."

"He's thrown a cordon around Europe in case we managed to get away from this area. He doesn't know who we are, so he's taking no chances. And if we're caught he's not going to bother taking us into custody to find out."

"Toast?" asked Polly.

"Burnt toast," said Clive.

Gemma frowned at her husband. "Let's not be under any illusions about what can happen."

Polly was puzzled. "You said he's thrown a cordon around Europe. What does that mean?"

"The Hywardathians have a series of what we call Quaker Craft stationed in orbit around the Earth. They are old technology, but still quite effective. They bathe the planet in a magnetic energy beam. It's designed to filter out normal earth technology and alert them to anything out of the ordinary or of concern, such as unauthorised use of nuclear weapons or use of The Source. Stuff like that."

Stuff!

"For example, every time terrorists or other undesirables get their hands on a nuclear weapon, the Hywardathians neutralise the problem."

"Every time?" exclaimed Josh.

"It's pretty common, but nothing to be concerned about."

Polly wondered why she still felt concerned. "Europe," she said. "The matter at hand."

Gemma nodded. "Oberon has redeployed his Quakers, so that three quarters of them are now over this hemisphere. Their settings have been narrowed to detect any non-Earth power source."

"Like the pod," asked Polly.

"Not just the pod. Us. Our survival suits are powered by the Source, too."

Polly sighed. "Is there any good news?"

"We're not dead yet," replied Kylie.

Josh leant forward. "Maybe I should take my chances on my own. I think I'm in more danger staying with you."

"No," said Clive. "Your house is red-lit. You go anywhere near home, you are gone and your family are in danger. Some of your stuff has been seized and currently your genetic profile is being extracted, analysed and profiled for a separate targeted mission to locate you."

Josh blinked. "OK, I'll hang around a bit longer." He sat back in his seat.

"All is not lost," said Gemma.

"I know," said Polly. "We're not dead yet," she repeated.

Polly saw Gemma was staring at her, as she must have rolled her eyes. "Sorry," she said.

Gemma sighed. "You're right. It's a mess. But we all need to be together on this. It's the only chance we have."

Polly felt tears well in her eyes. She wasn't normally sentimental and didn't even cry when both of her parents blubbered during the wedding scene in The Sound of Music, but the look on Gemma's face suddenly brought home how fragile they all were. She made a fist and extended her arm in front of her. "All for one."

Josh placed his hand over her fist, which gave Polly a strange, warm feeling, and the others quickly understood. Kylie added her hand, followed by Gemma, who elbowed Clive lightly in the side of the head. He twisted around and added his hand to the bunch. Polly felt tingly and energised and as she looked around at the other four faces, like hers they were all grinning.

"And all for one" shouted Josh.

Polly didn't bother suppressing an eye roll this time. "It's *one for all*. Everyone knows that!"

EXTRACT FROM VRYL'S GALMANAC

SourceStopper™

Incursions onto supervisory planets have been rare in the last one thousand years, although in days gone by, when there was no formalised supervisory system, planets used to compete and claim authority over new member planets. At first this led to wars being fought on these planets and in some cases – about four thousand – the planet concerned was destroyed in the conflict.

This did not affect the warring parties, who could retreat to their own planets, but for the hapless world hosting the hostilities, it meant annihilation.

After many centuries, the current rules were drafted, allowing only one authorised planet to be responsible for a new member. This put a stop to major conflicts, but on many occasions, disgruntled losers would disrupt worlds by guerrilla means, infiltrating planets and causing havoc to the supervisors and even starting surface wars among the natives.*

For this reason the Gauntlet Defence was developed initially controlled by a series of Celstquaclt Orbiters,

---

* A more serious ongoing incursion issue existed for almost fifteen hundred years, after the displaced population of Dpojly, a persistently offending warlike planet which had to be destroyed by the authorities, decided to go 'rogue'. They roamed the universe, disrupting trade routes and planetary operations at random, a cross between interplanetary terrorists and space pirates.

They even reached Earth, where a small band of Dpojlyans infiltrated a remote tribe and turned them into a huge warrior army. Their leader, Tmojyin, who became known locally as the Genghis Kahn, had a huge impact on Earth's history before order was restored.

An expedition led by the great Ollyu Trasgatin eventually killed the Dpojly leaders and captured four million survivors. All attempts to rehabilitate them failed and the entire population is now housed on the prison planet, Gaolos 6375.

commonly known as Quaker Craft, positioned around the planet. These vehicles formed a force field often set to detect any Source-powered vehicles entering the local solar system. They were not infallible, however, and scientific advances gradually found chinks in the Quaker armour and incursions were possible. And although the Quakers could be rotated to scan areas of the planet, it was a case of too little too late.

Quakers are now old technology and most supervisor planets outsource defence to the Akmoft Defender Group, which developed the SourceStopper™, which carries a one thousand year guarantee.

There was some suspicion regarding this product for many decades, but it has gradually replaced Quakers in all but a few hundred recalcitrant planetary supervisors. The Central Authority recently mandated use of the new device and it is gradually being shipped to all supervisor planets which have not purchased it.

TWENTY-THREE

The doors creaked open, causing Oberon to wince. Everywhere he went on this ship he saw only decay and disrepair. It was so bad, he now had the repair crew foreman trail behind him everywhere he went. "Door," he said, pointing, and the man grumbled into his comm-band.

The room was ill lit and dank, smelling of old socks, but it was a huge improvement on the formal bridge. This room was better, more suited to a command post, compact and efficient. Control modules were still being set up by a group of cursing technicians, but that didn't matter. Power was at his fingertips and it felt good.

He marched past a group of angrily squabbling officers and knew all was well. It was time to worry when officers were not squabbling. The window stretching across the entire hull wall of the bridge beckoned, so he walked up to it. It was caked in dirt. "Window," he said, not pointing this time, and the repair foreman barked an order. The view of the Earth was expansive. *Mine*, he thought. It was not safe to say it out loud. Attaining this position meant the countdown to his fall had begun. He was a realist, but he was determined to stretch it out for as long as he could. And he knew he could last for a very long time. After all, that fool Jwerqep had been in charge for decades. But Oberon also knew Jwerqep had not faced a crisis like this one. This was make or break.

A shuttle flew past and Oberon saw his reflection in the window against the dark hull of the craft. It was hard to get used to his real appearance after more than sixty years in the guise of an earth schoolteacher. He was still handsome, he decided, his features sharp and his eyes bright. The dodgy one still tended to do its own thing, but he thought that was just habit and it would correct itself. But really, it felt good to be green again. All he missed was his Earth height. Here he was just average at a little under four feet, but he still had a very large and forceful personality and people feared him. As they should. He now had all the power he could have wished for. He could banish and, even worse, send people home in disgrace and humiliation. And, if he was particularly vindictive, as he was with Jerquep's right hand general, he could demote them to be assistant to the repair crew's lowest apprentice.

He turned and glared at his officers, who immediately approached. "News?"

"None, sir," replied Commander Grtyu Rewsz. Oberon didn't like her. She looked intelligent.

"Why not?"

"We have detected no movement."

Oberon frowned. There was no surprise at this news, of course, but a leader should always look displeased. "Are you sure you have not allowed them to escape?" He emphasised the 'you'. He used this 'you' in all conversations with officers to reinforce the fact that with responsibility came the certainty they would join him if he fell.

"Yes, sir."

Oberon turned away from them and back to the window and the officers moved back across the room and continued squabbling. It was like music.

The ship was in a geostationary orbit above Europe and Oberon gazed down at southern England – or at least where he thought it was beneath the huge grey cloud mass covering the British Isles – and shuddered at the thought of returning to that backwater.

Oberon paused. Something didn't add up. On the surface, it appeared that someone had stolen or assumed Polly's identity and maybe she had been kidnapped or killed. Same for Josh, if that was him or his double in the woods with the Polly-impersonator. The real Josh was certainly missing now, which in itself was of little concern. The main problem was, who had helped them escape?

There was evidence that a shuttle pod or similar craft had visited Polly's garden, but the residue had not been identified. *No wonder*, thought Oberon. Everything Hywardathian was so outdated. The ship, the weapons, the uniforms. Everything was antique. It was like being in charge of a museum. What he would give for modern equipment.

Something else didn't add up. Oberon had reviewed the exchange between Jwerqep and the arrogant Syssine commanders. They had easily outwitted the former commander, but as he watched and listened again and again to those fuzzy freaks, he had heard something in their voices. Fear? Excitement? Anger, certainly, but was it really directed at Jerquep, or was there something else? Their explanation made sense if taken on blurred face value – they were always trying to interfere – yet…

Oberon ran his hands over his bumpy green head. He was Hywardathian and therefore naturally suspicious of everything. Paranoia was unknown on Hywardath because everyone actually *was* out to get you. And this highly developed sense of suspicion and heightened sensitivity meant his people could read other humans very well, even ones with a blurry outer shell.

They knew something! He was certain of it. Were they involved? Or worse, were they helping the intruders? He felt a surge of almost uncontrollable anger. *YOU CANNOT BREAK THE RULES!*

He spun away from the window and glared at the assembled crew, the veins on his face pulsating painfully. All became silent as they stared back at him with a mixture of fear and resentment.

They must be in on it! He felt certain. Besides, he had nothing else. *So, if I'm right*, he thought, *what would they do? We're all human, but they are not as devious or suspicious as me. They would do something logical and obvious, without fear of reprisal.* Oberon felt his head throb as he tried to think like a normal human. He considered himself far more intelligent than non-Hywardathian humans, so it wasn't easy. But he would do his best.

Suddenly, Oberon smiled. The crowd around him shrank further away and glances were exchanged. He quickly replaced the expression with anger and looks of relief appeared on the faces around him. "Commander Rewsz!"

She hurried over to him. "Sir."

"I want all communications ready to be switched to Hy-Code Z when I give the order."

"But we're not allowed to…"

"We are under invasion. I can do what I like under emergency provision TRDS-12954. Do it!"

"Yes, sir." She barked the orders angrily.

Oberon was briefly troubled as to whether the exception

was 54 or 56, but it was certainly one of them. "Get me the Cargo Superintendent."

Several officers gave the order and Oberon performed the Earth human habit of crossing his fingers.

"Gather," he said and the officers crowded around him. "It's too quiet down there, so I believe the invaders are hiding somewhere very close to where they went missing. I also believe they have been monitoring us and know we have the bulk of our Quakers trained on Europe. If this is the case, then they may have superior technology available to escape undetected."

"They may be gone already, then," said Rewsz.

Oberon snarled at her. "Not if they are waiting for assistance. Quakers are not completely reliable, but the concentration we have on the area would make it difficult for them to move. They are waiting until we broaden the search and hoping to slip away then."

Oberon knew he had made a lot of assumptions and his commanders would memorise them all to throw back in his face if he was wrong. They all looked less miserable, so he knew he was right about that at least. But was he right about the invaders?

"Are the comms changes ready?"

Rewsz nodded. "Yes."

A man approached nervously. He was shorter than Oberon, but much wider, with enough fabric in his uniform to clothe two normal sized men. The officers opened a path and the Cargo Officer came to attention in front of Oberon.

The plan hinged on what this man was about to tell him.

"A shipment arrived almost a year ago from the Central Authorities."

The man's eyes opened wide and he broke out in a sweat.

"What was in that shipment?"

"Er, Commander Jerquep swore me to secrecy."

"Jerquep has gone. Do you want to join him?"

"No, sir!" He was now shifting from foot to foot.

"TELL ME!"

"The, er, shipment was two hundred SourceStopper devices, sir."

Bingo! Thought Oberon, trying to suppress a smile. The officers were in shock and clearly didn't know about the shipment. Oberon had suspected after seeing a coded exchange between Jerquep and the Committee. He had persuaded them that Earth's defences were more than adequate and 'any new equipment' was not required. Knowing his government's reluctance to admit their technology was in any way deficient, and knowing Jerquep's personality and also knowing that there was a vibrant black market among criminals for SourceStoppers, Oberon put two and two together.

"How many are left?"

The man turned a deeper shade of green and appeared ready to faint. He looked frantically around at the officers who were grimly enjoying his discomfort while they could. He swallowed. "One hundred and seventy-eight, sir. But Commander Jerquep ordered me not to acknowledge receipt, so, officially, no one knows we have them."

Interesting. And more than Oberon had expected. "How quickly can you make them operational?"

Now he looked ready to cry. "At least six months, sir. There's a lot of work involved."

Oberon felt his world caving in. *So close!* His mind whirled. He knew the SourceStoppers must be here, but he needed them now. "Huystrfghsov!" he bellowed, which caused everyone to step back. It was a word used infrequently and only when something very bad was imminent. Oberon had shown that it was in everyone's interests that he succeed, at least in the short term, or he would take every high ranking officer with him. Everyone glared at the hapless cargo man, who wilted further.

But Oberon saw something in the man's face. "What is it?"

The man hesitated.

Oberon pushed his face close to the man's. "Understand this. You cannot possibly make your situation any worse."

"Well," squeaked the man. "There is one, sir. A SourceStopper. Me and some of the boys got it going. Bit of unofficial practice, sir."

Oberon felt hope surge and his expression frightened the man further. "In our own time, sir," the man added hastily.

"How quickly can I use it?'

"It's ready, sir. I can have it pointed at any area on Earth and operational within minutes."

"Then go and stand by!" yelled Oberon, not unkindly. His spirits soared. The man waddled away at tremendous speed.

Oberon turned to his officers. "When the SourceStopper is trained on southern England, I want an open communication sent to all operatives telling them that the fugitives have not been found and the search area is being increased to cover the entire planet. As soon as that message has been broadcast, redeploy all the Quakers to support that statement, then switch to code and order half the shuttles back here."

Oberon thought while his officers relayed the instructions. Then they turned back to him. This time he did not hide his smile and it clearly frightened the assembly. He was beginning to enjoy himself.

"Anything else, sir?" asked Commander Rewsz.

"No. The next move will be dictated by our illegal visitors down there."

TWENTY-FOUR

"Where are we going?"

The car rolled slowly along Oudenarde Avenue and Polly knew where they were headed, even if Kylie didn't.

"We're going to Kate's house."

Clive turned from the driver's seat. "How did you know that?"

Because it's obvious, thought Polly, irritated. And if it was obvious to her, then perhaps it was also obvious to Oberon.

"You said you had a pod hidden somewhere else in town and Kate's house is the logical choice. They know we didn't go there."

Clive turned back to the road, a concerned look on his face. It was a worry that the plan hadn't even fooled a teenage girl.

Polly looked across at Josh and Kylie. They were tense, like her, and Kylie's parents sat silently in the front. Gemma had told them that the pod they arrived in had been destroyed and disguised back at Polly's house to throw the Hywardathians off the scent. Any movement at the moment was fraught with risk, but the opportunity had arrived and they had no choice but to go.

On the plus side, the news received by Gemma and Clive was positive. They had hoped the Hywardathian's impatience – they were known for it – would force them into doing something, even if that something turned out to be a mistake. And they had. They were taking the heat off by redeploying their Quakers around the planet, leaving holes in their cordon like an Earth-sized Swiss cheese.

"But what if it's a trick?" Josh had asked, echoing what everyone was thinking.

"They can't disguise moving the Quakers," Gemma reassured them, "and even if it's a trick to get us into the open, there will still be huge holes in their defence we can exploit. Our pods are way ahead of their clunky flying saucers and we'll be safe before they can react."

Polly thought Gemma was convincing, and the words certainly calmed Josh and Kylie, but… But what? Of course!

Everything she had heard about the Hywardathians pointed to them screwing up and allowing the group to escape. They were incompetent, arrogant, delusional, vindictive and complacent. And those were their good qualities. But Oberon was different. In many ways he fitted those stereotypes, but he also had a sharp intelligence which belied his origins, perhaps a result of being on earth for so long, which would be ironic if true. She sensed a very dangerous cunning in her former teacher.

"Don't underestimate Oberon," she said.

Gemma didn't seem surprised and since then they had driven silently through the wet, darkened streets, their inhabitants sleeping quietly and completely unaware of the drama being played out. Polly had wanted adventure, but now a boring life in a boring town was very inviting.

Clive killed the car's lights as they turned the corner into Kate's street. They slowly drove past. "There it is," said Clive, relieved.

"There what is?" asked Josh.

"The pod," replied Kylie. "It's on the front lawn."

Polly recognised the slight shimmering and distortion of the bricks in the wall of the house.

"I can't see anything," said Josh.

"Good," said Gemma.

Clive turned at the end of the street and cruised past the house again.

Gemma turned to Polly, Kylie and Josh. "OK, the Quakers are dispersing. Here's the plan. When I say go, we pile out of the car and into the pod."

Polly waited, but Gemma turned back to the road. Polly turned to Josh. "See what I have to put up with!"

She tapped Gemma on the shoulder. "Then what?"

"We go back to the ship."

Polly looked across Josh to Kylie, but she shrugged. *Do I really look like that when I shrug?* she thought. It made her look stupid. "Just like that? Straight up and bingo, we're there."

"Something like that," said Clive.

Polly decided to stay quiet. It was all too frustrating. She turned to Josh. "You know when you get too close and it annoys me?"

Josh nodded, embarrassed, and Polly wondered why he did it when he knew it annoyed her. But she would save that question for another time. "I want you to stick that close to me when we get out of the car, OK?"

That cheered him up and a big smile spread across his face. Kylie grinned at Polly. Polly wondered if she would die in a space battle or of embarrassment.

"Here we go," said Clive. He performed a three point turn – actually, four points as he was not a very good driver – and headed back to Kate's house. He swung the car into the driveway and slammed on the brakes next to the front lawn.

"Odd," said Gemma, in reaction to something she picked up from base.

An icy finger of fear tickled the back of Polly's neck, but Gemma quickly recovered and jumped out of the car. She flung open the back door and pulled Kylie out. Josh and Polly piled out after her as Clive ran around from the other side of the car.

Gemma ran up the invisible ramp to the invisible pod, closely followed by Kylie. Polly pushed Josh ahead, but he stumbled and Polly had to almost drag him into the vehicle. "You will get used to it," she promised as Josh was enveloped by the unseen force and moved into a sitting position. The look on his face was almost comical, but then he grinned again and Polly felt reassured. They had made it.

The pod lifted off, or, rather, the ground seemed to drop away beneath them and they hovered at the height of the upstairs bedrooms. All five of them floated, in a sitting position and in a circle, their knees almost touching. "Isn't this cozy?" said Kylie, as Polly and Josh joined her in relieved laughter. But Clive and Gemma looked grim.

Josh gripped Kylie's arm, realised she was not Polly and grabbed Polly's as well.

"It's weird, but just enjoy it," advised Polly.

The pod felt completed stationary, but the houses around them moved and weaved around the vehicle. Polly knew they were zig-zagging through the housing estate, but it was like watching an iMax movie. Alarm bells rang in her head. "Why aren't we going up?"

I thought you might ask that," said Gemma. "There's been a slight complication."

Here we go again, thought Polly. "Slight, as in a short delay? Or slight, as in we're all going to die?"

"Don't be so negative," replied Kylie. "We're trying to save you."

Josh started laughing and couldn't stop. The others all stared at him as the houses sped by around them. "Apart," he began, finally, "from being in a spaceship with aliens, this is just like a road trip with my parents and sister."

"We're not aliens," said Kylie. "We're human, just like you."

Josh shrugged and grinned. Polly smiled at him and squeezed his hand. She turned to Gemma. "So, what's this complication?"

"Straight after the Hywardathians moved their Quakers, they switched to a code for all communications. It's not permitted, although I'm sure they'll find a supporting rule, and we haven't been able to break it yet."

Clive chipped in. "It probably means nothing, but we're not taking chances. We're cloaked, so they can't detect us unless they accidentally get a direct fix. However, we're more exposed to visual surveillance in the air, particularly here over the town, so we are staying low to the ground until we cross the coastline. Our crew can then make sure all is clear before we get off the planet."

It sounded reasonable to Polly, although the possibility of Oberon getting a direct fix on them despite the cloaking device was a worry. She could see it in Clive and Gemma's faces, too. It was weird staring at replicas of her own parents. They looked identical, but their expressions were subtly different, in the same way as Kylie's Polly face was a variation and not a copy.

Polly turned to look ahead. The houses were becoming sparse as they whizzed past. They were at the edge of town now, weaving their way between trees and hedgerows. It was close to daybreak and they were heading west with the growing light behind them. It was quite beautiful.

Josh stared ahead, his eyes wide, just as Polly's had been when she first experienced the pod. The day before yesterday! Since then she'd spacewalked, travelled throughout the solar system and, through Kylie and her parents, and Vryl's Galmanac, learned a little about the vast human-filled universe completely unknown to anyone else on earth. Except for Josh. If they survived, at least she could talk about the experience with him. Gazing at him now, she thought that was a nice prospect, as annoying as he was.

The sun was higher behind them now and a bigger town was racing towards them, the early morning sunlight playing on the tops of the tallest buildings. "Where are we," asked Josh.

"That's Bristol," replied Clive. "Once through, we'll follow the Welsh coast to Saint David's, cross the Irish Sea to Rosslare, right round to Dingle on the west coast, then out into the Atlantic."

Polly knew her geography. *They are even more worried than I thought.*

TWENTY-FIVE

Captain Yulgi Floothil fought his growing fear as he trudged along the Hywardathian mother ship's corridors. He was surrounded by ten armed troopers, five on each side as they, leading the even more frightened Muoth and Thirt, escorted the trio to their fate.

It had been incredible to witness Oberon turn the tables on ex-Commander Jerquep after they arrived from Earth and Floothil's admiration was mixed with trepidation. He knew Oberon hated him; it was obvious from their exchanges during the chase. And Floothil had not endeared himself to his new commander, assuming that the man was of no importance and treating him as such. Had he suspected this would happen he would have grovelled and sucked-up to Oberon in the time-honoured Hywardathian tradition. At least until it was time to abandon or shaft him.

But it was too late now. After escorting Jwerqep to his cell following the amazing events on the ceremonial bridge and assuming – hoping – he had been forgotten, Floothil had slipped away and effectively hidden in his quarters. However, a few moments ago he was ordered to appear – that was the word used – before Oberon. It sounded very much like a sentence would be announced. Floothil, of course, would do all he could to blame Muoth and Thirt for all their problems and was amending his main 'pass the buck' speech (all Hywardathians had a selection of them) as he walked. He doubted it would make any difference, but he would make sure these two fools went down with him.

Floothil was the first of his line to qualify for off-planet duties. It had been a triumphant, but dirty business and like all members of his rank, he had left a huge number of enemies in his wake. At best he would be demoted, allowing many of them to rise above him, where they would take great pleasure in making his life miserable. As if being Hywardathian was not miserable enough.

At worst? There were rumours that Jwerqep was to be exiled on Earth by Oberon. That was better than being sent back to Hywardath in disgrace, but there wasn't much in it. Oberon himself had suffered decades living in that awful Earth town. However, neither of those fates were likely for Floothil. Most likely, Oberon would have found out who was his greatest enemy and he would be consigned to his command. His career was over.

The group stopped outside the new bridge. Floothil turned back to look at Thirt and Muoth, who were quaking with fear. He gave them a dirty look to ensure they knew they would get no support from him, then turned back as the doors were thrown open. The troopers marched them inside and Floothil's eyes opened wide.

The room was spotless and a hive of purposeful activity, far different to the slovenliness under Jwerqep and, indeed, the usual Hywardathian surliness appeared to be absent from the faces of the crew in the room. They looked determined and, though he could be mistaken, efficient.

The troopers stopped in the centre of the room and their leader walked across to the giant window overlooking the Earth. A man wearing the ceremonial Supreme Commander's robes stood looking out. Even though no longer disguised as a human, Floothil recognised Oberon from his stance. He raised his head as the trooper captain spoke then nodded. The captain walked back and ordered his men to leave. He followed them out, leaving Floothil, Thirt and Muoth standing alone and ignored.

Oberon dealt with other business, listening to, then dismissing, several crew members with a flick of the hand. Then he turned and faced Floothil. He still looked like the earth Oberon, even though he was much smaller and green. The same hard face and twitching eye – though it had improved – and that horrible grin he had been using since leaving Earth. That was easily the scariest thing about him. Hywardathians NEVER smiled.

Oberon beckoned. "Come on, you idiots," said Floothil, and Muoth and Thirt followed reluctantly.

They stood before Oberon and Floothil opened his mouth to recite all the reasons he was not to blame for anything that happened. Ever. But Oberon raised a hand. "I have a mission for you."

Inside, Floothil had never felt so relieved. But, remaining

Hywardathian, he scowled resentfully.

"Look at this," continued Oberon, turning back to the window. The view of Europe zoomed in until the window was filled by southern England. The most striking feature, aside from the lack of clouds, was a red dot moving east over the westernmost reaches of the Thames.

"Our intruders are aboard that pod," said Oberon, turning to look at Floothil, that horrible smile playing on his thin lips. "They believe we have broadened our search and given them the opportunity to escape. However…"

Oberon swept his arm across the window and the image returned to the actual view of the Earth from the ship, although the planet was almost obscured by a fleet of small craft streaming away. It was a hugely impressive sight and as they moved further away Floothil noticed all of England was actually under cloud, so the close-up had been enhanced.

"As soon as they clear the Irish coast, five hundred of my craft will meet them. And destroy them."

It sounded like a plan, thought Floothil. "And our mission?" he asked, feeling a little better now he knew it couldn't be anything important.

Oberon looked at him for a moment before speaking. "Jerquep ran a very loose ship, Floothil. Everything I've seen since coming aboard has been sub-standard, from the state of the ship to the slovenliness of the crew. And your actions when you joined me on Earth did little to prove otherwise."

Floothil winced.

"You were clearly not briefed about my authority and, even worse, assumed you were in control of the search. I hold you personally responsible for the failure to capture the criminals down there. You should not assume because I have not yet dealt with that particular issue that it is resolved."

This was standard practice, thought Floothil, even more relieved. They were off the hook, unless everything went arse-up. In which case, Oberon was making it clear he would drag them down to hell with him. Perfectly reasonable. Anything less would be an insult to any Hywardathian.

"Now," said Oberon, seeing on Floothil's face that he had made himself clear, "in view of my mistrust of those five hundred pilots out there, I want you three in the air in case anything goes wrong. I am not convinced you are any less incompetent, but this is your chance to impress me."

This was sounding better all the time, decided Floothil. Sheer weight of numbers should ensure success. The odds were on his side, five hundred-to-one. The only worry was the 'should'.

"This time I'll get them!" roared Oberon, causing everyone to jump.

Floothil, though usually suspicious of everyone and everything, believed him. A very odd feeling. He couldn't remember having confidence in a leader before, but as they say on Hywardath, *there's a last time for everything*.

Floothil saluted and turned, almost crashing in Muoth and Thirt, who were cowering in terror behind him. *Idiots!* He pushed them towards the door, but Oberon called them back.

"Wait," he said. "What's your name?" He pointed at Thirt.

The man looked like he was about to give a false name, but thought better of it. "Er…Thirt, sir."

Oberon nodded and smiled, which sent shivers down both of Floothil's spines. "Well, er-Thirt," mocked the Commander, "this time you *can* waste 'em."

TWENTY-SIX

The expressions on Clive and Gemma's faces were what worried Josh the most. They didn't know how to disguise what they were thinking on their Earth human faces. Polly's real parents would have looked completely blank. That wouldn't have fooled him either, but he would have appreciated the effort.

The Welsh coast was speeding past the pod and they were about to head out across the Irish sea. There wasn't much conversation, with Kylie sulking and Polly with that cute, preoccupied look on her face as she bit into her lower lip. Josh sat between the two girls, tongue-tied. He wanted to speak – ask questions, lots of questions – but he didn't know where to start. Or probably stop, once he started.

Gemma and Clive were presumably in communication with their colleagues and – *call it a hunch* – the news wasn't good. In fact, since Polly, no, Kylie, threw those stones at his window, the news had been steadily spiralling downwards.

Josh didn't want to complain. He often thought his life was completely boring and a galactic adventure should be just the ticket to relieve that boredom, but he had mixed thoughts about the reality. The danger part was actually quite exciting, despite the likelihood of violent death at any second. However, the attendance of three aliens disguised as Polly and her parents added a level of the mundane. The effect gave him the sense that this was all part of a very weird dream.

The pod suddenly increased speed and Josh was disconcerted when he actually felt movement for the first time. It was only slight, like when dad put his foot down on the accelerator, but he had the feeling that the pod was being pushed beyond its usual limits. The look of alarm on his companions' faces confirmed his suspicion and he gritted his teeth.

Gemma spoke. "We've been spotted," she said, unprompted.

That got Kylie's attention. "Spotted! But they moved their Quakers away."

"True," said Clive. "But we just heard that the Central authorities sent them a shipment of SourceStoppers a year ago. There was no official acknowledgement of receipt, so we weren't notified. They must be using them."

"They outfoxed you," said Polly. "The Hywardathians."

"Well," replied Gemma defensively, "let's see who has the last laugh."

Josh bristled at the word 'last'. There was so much he didn't know, but Polly seemed to be clued up on everything and she was anything but a passenger. Josh felt very small and insignificant and homesick.

The pod crossed the Irish Sea in a flash and traced its way around the Irish coast, even faster now. The stabilisers were straining and Josh and the others were now swaying as the pod performed frequent adjustments to its flight path before sweeping away from the coast and out to sea.

All five of them were scanning the skies now. Josh wondered what they were looking for.

"What are we looking for?" he asked.

"Flying saucers," said Polly.

Josh stared at her and laughed nervously.

"I'm serious."

Heavy, low grey clouds filled the morning sky. Josh studied them carefully. He wanted to believe Polly was messing with his head, but he searched intently for flying saucers. Then he laughed again, a very quick burst of hysteria, before going quiet. Everyone stared at him and then Polly squeezed his hand. "It's a bit like that, isn't it?" He smiled back gratefully.

"Polly's got a boyfriend," sang Kylie.

"Shut up!" snapped her mother.

Josh didn't mind, though Polly snatched her hand away.

Over Gemma's shoulder, Josh saw a patch of blue sky, a strangely symmetrical round hole in the dark clouds. "Look, the weather's improve..."

"Here we go," said Gemma quietly. "You ready?"

"Yes," said Clive.

They all turned to where Josh was looking. The cloud swirled all around the opening, which increased in size until sunlight flowed through to spotlight the sea ahead.

A black speck dropped through the hole and hovered above

the sea – Josh thought it was a large bird – but then another joined it. And another.

His mouth dry, Josh swallowed and noticed goosebumps up and down his arms. Polly grabbed his hand again.

"Expect turbulence," warned Gemma, in what turned out to be a gross understatement. Josh smiled tightly, remembering his father's favourite – both regular and ominous – announcement, "Expect flatulence."

The pod veered to the right, away from the flying saucers. Josh twisted round to watch them. More and more were dropping from the hole in the clouds. There must be hundreds, but still they came, forming a cloud of their own, like a tightly packed flock of birds. The first of them came closer, until Josh could indeed see they were flying saucers, just like the ones he'd seen in pictures on the internet. He had no idea how big they were, so the distance was impossible to estimate and he didn't want to ask.

Gemma and Clive were concentrating hard and looking at each other, while Polly, Kylie and Josh watched the growing spectacle.

The forerunner saucers had stopped while the others caught up and now they were building a giant grid in the sky. Josh tried to count the craft, but there were too many as this saucer wall grew. It didn't change, though, so it must be keeping pace.

"What are they going to do," asked Polly, nervously.

Gemma and Clive appeared not to hear, but Kylie knew. "They are going to fire at us."

Gemma looked sharply at Kylie and then turned to Josh and Polly. "The first blast is a range finder and will fall well clear. We've worked it out."

Josh glanced sideways at Polly, whose expression said, *you have got to be kidding me*. Josh swallowed. Tried to swallow.

Clive turned to the wall of saucers. "Cover your eyes."

Polly withdrew her hand and Josh used his to cover his eyes. Almost immediately there was a massive flash, so bright he could see his bones through his hands, followed by a huge WHUMP! sound that popped his ears.

The flash dwindled, but when Josh dropped his hands the wall of saucers looked like it was on fire and Gemma and Clive, highlighted in the brightness, looked like they were wearing halos. But what took Josh's breath away was the giant trench in the water almost beneath them, a huge black gap hundreds of yards long and at least a hundred wide. A hole in the water!

Instantly, the saucers scattered their formation and formed a new one, a giant shape in the sky parallel to the ocean around them. "It's been nice knowing you all," said Kylie.

"Ha!" said Gemma, which Josh thought was as good a last word as any.

The pod shunted sideways and then dropped like a stone into the hole in the ocean, just as the sea, presumably now over the shock of being breached, erupted, sending massive waves pouring into the gap.

The pod was pummelled like a sock in a washing machine and Josh and the others lurched from side to side, his stomach performing summersaults. *Don't let me throw up in front of Polly!* he thought as they were pushed deeper and deeper under the sea.

Perhaps we might survive, he thought, suddenly hopeful. But then a large drop of water splattered against his forehead.

TWENTY-SEVEN

There was much to admire about the Jkoyian Grid. First employed in the decisive Battle of Nifsu that ended the Eighteenth Core Nebula War, it was a tried and true tactic. The concentrated fire of four million fighters was seen by some as overkill, but after a conflict lasting two and a half thousand years, something had to be done.

Oberon watched, astounded, as the attack over the sea unfolded. He could feel his anger build, but for the moment he was still in shock. Admittedly, his pep talk to Commander Hrsuth may have contained the words 'at war' and 'all weapons at your disposal', but surely the man could distinguish a small pod containing five individuals from a fleet of two million Scrili Hunterships? Apparently not.

So intent had Hrsuth been in getting the formation perfect, he had neglected to notice that the pod had altered its trajectory to place it slightly out of range. It would be a small matter to have a junior officer testify that he had warned Hrsuth and therefore exonerate Oberon of the blame, but the pod had escaped. How infuriating!

Oberon watched the image filling his vision. Saucers buzzed over the ocean as water poured into the gap after the pod. The saucers could not follow, thanks to their outdated design, but with any luck, the pod would be crushed by the weight of water. He doubted this, but stranger things had happened.

The SourceStopper signal now displayed a circle a mile in diameter over the ocean surface, distorted by the currents beneath the waves.

"Hrsuth!" he barked.

The nervous voice of the Commander replied immediately. "Sir!"

"You idiot!" said Oberon. "You are relieved of command. Get back here and report to the Latrine Squad. I will decide what to do with you later."

"Floothil!"

"Sir!"

"You are now Fleet Commander. You know what you must do."

"Yes, sir!" replied Floothil, his voice an equal combination of excitement and fear.

Oberon was deliberately vague in case this enterprise failed. He had been thrown in at the deep end at short notice and would maximise this excuse and blame the poor quality of officers he had inherited.

But now, as he watched, Floothil organised the saucers into circular bombing squads a mile wide and prepared them to fly over the red highlighted SourceStopper zone. It was clearly a very smart move and Oberon made a mental note to claim full credit if it worked.

It would work, he decided. How could it not? The pod was being tracked and he had hundreds of saucers at his command, with enough combined firepower to change the orbit of the Earth. Not a bad thing, in his opinion, but outside his authority.

Yet one thing still niggled. The Syssine spaceship was still in orbit. Unable to interfere, certainly, now he had declared a state of emergency, but irritatingly close by. Those fuzz-heads were up to something. The feeling coursed through all three of his bloodstreams, making his extremities tingle. The ship was over Africa now and although the pod was still heading west, he could not discount interference.

Floothil now had his first 'saucer of saucers' poised over the sea, ready to move over the SourceStopper red zone. In a moment, Syssine would be rendered irrelevant by the destruction of the pod.

TWENTY-EIGHT

The pod was battered as the crashing water plunged it tumbling deeper and deeper into the ocean. Polly felt the pod shudder under the force, but her 'suit' made her feel as though she was upright, and her companions in place, as they flipped and spun.

Next to her Josh looked scared, but he managed a grin when he caught her eye. "You OK?" he shouted over the din.

She nodded. "Yes. Apart from a sinking feeling."

Kylie groaned.

Gemma and Clive didn't appear too concerned. "We'll let the water take us to the bottom," said Gemma, as though it was deliberate.

"We have a choice?" said Polly.

Clive grinned. "Not exactly, but if we did we would go the same way."

Josh spoke, but it came out as a croak. He coughed and started again. "Are we going to drown?"

Polly noticed what he meant. The previously invisible casing of the pod was now visible due to rivulets of water flowing from several breaches in the hull.

"No," said Gemma. "We won't drown."

Polly turned to Josh. "You can't tell, but you are wearing a protective suit supplying oxygen and everything else you need."

Josh felt his arms and face and didn't seem very reassured.

"You'll be fine," said Kylie, punching him on the shoulder.

"Ouch."

"What now?" asked Polly to no one in particular.

"The saucers are forming a grid structure above the sea," Clive seemed to be enjoying this, Polly realised.

"They can't follow?"

"No. Well, they can, but they are pretty useless under water. Too buoyant. We tried to get them to update to these pods, but they wouldn't listen."

"Just as well!" said Polly. "So, what will they do?"

"They will track us, assuming they have SourceStoppers,"

continued Clive. "The good thing is that accuracy falls away the deeper we go underwater…"

Polly waited, but Clive hesitated. "The bad thing?"

"Well, we have to get much further out into the ocean. The depth here off Ireland is less than six hundred feet."

Polly looked outside. The water was murky, due to being completely churned up, but they had steadied a little. A large fish bounced off the pod. Given all fish looked stunned to begin with, she wondered what it thought, crashing into something it couldn't see.

"How deep do we have to be to be safe?" asked Josh.

"Over ten thousand feet, ideally," said Clive. "If we can get to that depth, we'll head south, staying this side of the Mid-Atlantic Ridge until we cross it through a deep channel near the equator, and weave our way through deep water down to Cape Horn. There's some shallow water to negotiate down there, but hopefully we will have shaken them off by then and make it into the Pacific."

Polly listened to this, incredulous. There were hundreds of saucers. Surely Oberon would have the whole world covered. The thought of her teacher effectively ruling the world was extremely bizarre and she imagined him sitting on a throne, his eye spinning…

"What are you laughing at?" asked Kylie.

"This whole thing," said Polly. "It's completely nuts. We're in an invisible pod deep under water trying to escape from flying saucers."

"That is pretty funny," admitted Kylie.

"And Mr Oberon is in charge of the planet."

Josh grimaced. "That is not funny."

Gemma raised a hand. "OK, brace yourselves. More turbulence is on the way."

Polly gritted her teeth. Gemma was very good at understating things that turned out to be very bad indeed.

She did not disappoint on this occasion, either.

The murky water beyond Gemma disappeared, replaced by a gigantic hole in the water. Light flooded the well. The blast must have missed them by inches and Polly could see a wall of ocean a hundred yards away across the void, frozen for a second, as though in shock, before the whole thing collapsed. The delayed WHUMP! followed a split second later and reverberated through her brain as the pod tumbled down with the water.

All five of them were now floating within the pod, as whatever gravitational force had been holding them steady failed.

The noise of the violently churning water was tremendous and Clive had to yell. "Stay calm!" Followed by the ridiculous, "We're all safe."

"You could have fooled me," shouted Kylie.

"I'm going to flood the pod," Gemma yelled.

"We'll all drown!" Josh looked panicked.

Polly hugged him to her. "I told you, we all have protective suits. You can't feel it, but it was kind of sprayed on when you stepped aboard. You will still be able to breathe."

Josh didn't look convinced and as the water rose around them she felt her own panic rise. Another gigantic WHUMP! nearby did not make her feel any better.

"That was further away." The water was settling, though still in uproar, and Clive didn't have to speak so loud.

The water reached Polly's neck and the panic threatened to join it in overwhelming her, but she suddenly relaxed. Josh's face reflected the same calm and she turned to Gemma, puzzled.

"Drugs."

The water enveloped them all and the pod sank deeper.

These suits are amazing! thought Polly. Things looked dire with the sea erupting all around them, blasts from the saucers instantly evaporating huge slices of water either side of the pod. It seemed only a matter of time before they were hit and… nothing. They wouldn't know anything. They would simply cease to exist. Normally, she would have been worried by such a prospect – Kylie, Clive and Gemma clearly were – but Polly and Josh were enjoying the wild ride.

"Fun, eh?" said Polly to Kylie, who returned daggers. Polly laughed, making her double even more angry.

The pod hit the seabed and rolled, bumping over rocks as the churning water forced them one way then another. The force – the Source – holding the five of them roughly in place completely failed now and they all floated weightless around the inside of the pod, a jumble of tangled limbs. Polly and Josh burst out laughing every time they came face to face, or, more often, face to someone's bottom.

A sudden thought struck Polly, cutting through the drugs and sobering her up in an instant. "That grid thing the saucers did…"

A look flashed between Clive and Gemma.

"…what happens if they do that now? Above us, I mean."

From the silence that followed, Polly received a very eloquent answer. They were cactus.

"What are you going to do about it?" chipped in Josh.

"Yeah," said Polly. "If we are going to be reduced to nothing, let's go down swinging!"

Gemma and Clive were looking very embarrassed and even Kylie was staring at them.

"We're taking evasive action," said Gemma.

"You are certainly evading giving us an answer," said Polly. She was not going to defer to adults in her last seconds and had a fair bit to say. "All I've heard is how hopeless and pathetic these Hyawa-whatsits are, with their arrogance and antiquated equipment. How they can't be taken seriously. Figures of ridicule. Yet Oberon appears to have outwitted all of you. He almost caught us and now he's going to finish us off. What happened to your superior technology? Your authority? Who is in charge?"

Clive and Gemma didn't reply and Polly felt a wave of anger surge up inside her. Josh recognised it and shifted away from her. "I can now see why Kylie is such an idiot. It's bloody hereditary!"

She glared at Gemma and Clive and resisted the urge to bang their heads together. They turned to Kylie and glared at her.

The pod lurched alarmingly, presumably taking 'evasive action'.

Clive turned back to Polly. If he was angry at the way she had spoken, he didn't show it. "Here's what's happening up there."

The murky water disappeared and they were looking at the view of the ocean from several thousand feet in the sky, as though the pod was flying instead of swimming. Beneath, thousands of flying saucers milled about like a spooked flock of birds, although unlike birds they did not fly in unison. Yet.

"This is three hundred miles ahead of us," said Gemma.

That explains the relative calm of the last few moments, thought Polly.

"Look over there," said Clive.

Polly followed his pointed finger into the distance, where a hundred or so saucers had formed a small grid over the sea. And it was growing. The milling saucers were not milling, they were positioning themselves to join the grid.

Polly's anger drained away, replaced by cold fingers of fear. "How big will that be?"

"It depends on the structure, but our estimate is that they will be able to take anything out in one hundred square miles."

Josh screwed up his face. "Just a minute. If they take out that much sea, it'll cause a huge tsunami."

"They won't do that," replied Gemma. "They will use drillshot, which will be like millions of individual bullet holes, if you like, being drilled through the water only inches apart. The water will be severely disrupted but won't cause a tsunami, even though everything in the water that isn't a tiny fish will be destroyed. And earth instruments will record a minor earthquake.

Well, that's reassuring, thought Polly. "You are remarkably calm," she said.

"We do have a plan," said Gemma.

"Then why did you let me carry on like that?" asked Polly, embarrassed.

"Because you are right." Gemma looked embarrassed, too. "Kylie is stupid and so are we. We underestimated Oberon." Kylie was still sulking, a look Polly was swiftly coming to hate seeing on her own, albeit, replica face. *I'm smiling from now on,* she decided. *If I survive.*

Polly could only agree as she watched the flying saucer grid fill the sky. "Well," Polly conceded, "no one's perfect." It sounded pathetic to her, but it was all she could come up with by way of apology.

Josh was getting excited. "What's the plan? It looks like it will be easier to evade something that big."

"Actually, no," said Clive. "The odd thing about their saucers is that in grid formation they become faster and more manoeuvrable than an individual vehicle. Once they lock into place, the grid is effectively a giant single craft. That's the original design. The saucers were only supposed to be a means of turning a battle when in danger of defeat. They would disperse and reform into a new grid. Or multiple grids. Pretty clever, but in peace this is no longer necessary. The Hywardathians should have ditched them and moved to pods for Earth duties, but they didn't want to spend the money. This is the first time in centuries they have formed a grid, so I am sure there's a huge amount of excitement in their little green world."

"Enough to cloud their judgement, I hope," added Gemma.

If they were trying to make her feel better, thought Polly, this was a major fail. "The plan?" she prompted.

The water around the pod was relatively calm and the vehicle moved much slower than before. Polly thought they must look very much like they were inside a fish bowl, a curiosity to passing fish.

"Oh, yes. The plan," said Gemma, with a rather unsettling degree of casualness.

A map of the Atlantic appeared, showing the Mid-Atlantic Ridge weaving from north to south, evenly dividing Europe and Africa from the Americas. "We are here." She pointed to a red dot to the west of the Canary Islands off the African coast. Polly gasped. They had been travelling much faster than she thought.

"The plan requires us to be here." The dot sprouted a line of dashes, like footprints, tracing a line south east of the ridge, then cutting west through a deep trench in the narrow part of the ocean between east Africa and Brazil. The dotted line then turned south for a short distance and stopped, very close to the centre of the outline of a square, which appeared to be growing bigger as Polly watched. "That's close to Ascension Island. Rather appropriate, don't you think?"

"That square," said Polly – not knowing why she bothered to ask – "It's the Hywardathian saucer grid, isn't it?"

"It is."

"So I assume we will be out of range deep in that trench?"

"Not exactly." Gemma remained curiously upbeat. "The grid is far more powerful than individual saucers, so they can penetrate any trench in the Atlantic."

Polly opened her mouth to continue with the ritual questioning, but Josh beat her to it. "Then why are we going there? Aren't you trying to escape?"

Clive shook his head. "The pod isn't in great shape and we can't outrun them. There's a slight risk the plan won't work, but we need their power."

Everyone was quiet for a moment, until Polly couldn't stand it any longer. "How slight?"

Clive glanced at Gemma. "Fifty-fifty."

TWENTY-NINE

The grid was almost complete. Thousands of saucers were locked into position, the rest in an orderly queue ready to join the giant, perfectly geometric jigsaw ten thousand feet above the ocean.

Oberon reclined on his command chair in the bridge, looking up at the image, but down on the action. Every few minutes a commercial earth airliner flew over the grid, completely oblivious to the titanic operation beneath them. He winced a little as an image of another Titanic in the Atlantic popped into his head, but nothing could spoil this moment.

His rehabilitation was almost complete. Jwerqep's downfall had been the cake and this was the icing. Jwerqep, once his assistant, was the man who had kidnapped the technician sent to install the new saucer cloaking technology all those years ago. This treachery, which meant Oberon could not meet his deadline, led to his fall and exile, and to Jwerquep's rise. He had been outsmarted by that fool, but revenge was indeed sweet and the destruction of the invaders would close the circle and he could begin his career again.

He opened the image further so that the grid and ocean filled his vision, as though he was really there, over the ocean. The progress of the pod was marked by a red dot moving westwards across the ocean near the eastern horizon. It had slowed, yet it was heading directly towards where the grid hovered over the sea. Oberon wondered why the pod had not tried to change direction, but if, as he suspected, they knew the grid was forming, they also knew there was no escape. His guess was that they would try to surrender before they reached the point of no return.

Oberon grinned. That point was way behind them already.

The final one hundred or so saucers clicked into place and the grid was complete. Only Floothil's and one other command vehicle remained isolated, both viewing the formation from high above the grid. It really is a magnificent sight, thought Oberon. Thousands of craft formed into a single machine of destruction. Overkill, perhaps, but that really was the Hywardathian way. And, he decided, if Syssine had anything to do with this criminal incursion, better to ensure there are no survivors to avoid any subsequent embarrassment or diplomatic consequences.

"You are ready." It was not a question.

Floothil's voice was strong, confident. "Yes. Contact will occur in three-point-five minutes."

"Ignore any contact from the pod," ordered Oberon, "and destroy them."

"It will be done."

THIRTY

"Three minutes," said Clive.

To death, thought Polly. She hoped she was wrong, but the vision of that gigantic grid forming over the ocean some, well, three minutes away, didn't fill her with confidence regardless of any plan in the works.

She squeezed Josh's hand and was surprised to see Kylie do the same with his other hand. Josh looked incredibly pleased and embarrassed at the same time. Clive and Gemma also held hands, which was cute, but worrying.

The churlish look had disappeared from Kylie's face and she was, for the first time, visibly scared. Polly thought the consequences of her actions had finally hit home. Her anger dissipated as she realised she could have said no and none of this would have happened.

But then Polly would have missed the adventure of a lifetime. Travelling through space, meeting alien – OK, human – lifeforms, learning about a universe incredibly different from the one she imagined. The universe wasn't a void, it was more like a crowded shopping centre on Saturday morning.

And she couldn't possibly have missed all this, she knew. It was worth the risk. And the look on Josh's face, a mix of awe, fear and excitement, told her he was the same. He caught her eye and on impulse she leant across and kissed him hard on the lips. The pod was buffeted and they clashed teeth and both recoiled holding their mouths and laughing through the pain.

"I'm glad someone's having fun," said Kylie.

Clive raised a hand. "Less than a minute."

Polly looked up to see that the view above the water had widened. The vast grid was complete. Waiting for the pod. Then a beam of light descended from the sky above to pierce the centre of the square and drilled into the ocean below.

Gritting her teeth, Polly anticipated an explosion, but nothing happened. "What is it?" asked Josh.

"It's from our ship." Clive didn't take his eyes from the scene

"But it didn't work!" Polly was tingling all over.

"That's only part one," said Gemma, equally transfixed. "The beam is focussed on the point where the grid will fire on us. We just have to hope they won't shoot early."

Great! thought Polly. Her fate was again – still – in the hands of hope and wishful thinking.

"Ten, nine, eight..." began Clive, but Gemma stopped him.

"Don't you think this is dramatic enough?" she snapped.

But it was too late. Polly – and she was sure the others – continued a silent countdown as the pod cruised smoothly through the water and underneath the giant shadow cast over the ocean by thousands of flying saucers. The visual display switched off and they were alone in the murky depths for one, seemingly very long second before all hell broke loose.

"Cover your eyes!" Gemma yelled.

The fact that Polly noticed all hell breaking loose was strangely reassuring, given she expected the zero to be the last thought she would ever have.

She registered a super bright light hitting the pod which hurt her eyes, and which she found out later was the beam from Kylie's spaceship. This was followed instantly by an even brighter flash, the concentrated fire from the grid. The WHUMP! was like someone heavily slapping her eyes simultaneously and the pod was instantly rammed into the seabed, then forced violently up, down and sideways like a pinball. The sea around them turned to froth and Polly had no idea which way up they were. But the outer skin of the pod was no long invisible; it was covered in cracks. At least Polly now knew they were upside down.

She looked around at her companions, who were all grim-faced and gritting their teeth, as she was. But they were still in one piece and, to her surprise, all holding hands in a circle.

"Look!" Josh let go of Polly's hand and pointed.

A saucer drifted by in the churning water, three small shocked green faces staring at them from their bubble cockpit as they disappeared into the murky depths below.

Then another bounced off the pod and more came drifting by, some with shocked occupants, others with angry faces and shaking fists. They came like rain, hundreds of them, sinking as the pod weaved among them.

"What happened?" Polly stared at the incredible sight.

Clive looked very pleased with himself, but could not hide

his relief. "The beam from our ship turned us into a Source refraction inhibitor. By calculating the power frequency of the saucers' weapon systems, we were able to turn all that power back onto the entire grid, effectively shorting, for want of a better term, all their power systems."

"Cool," said Josh.

It was cool, Polly had to admit, but she was alarmed by the sheer volume of saucers sinking to the bottom of the sea. "Will they all die?"

"No," said Gemma, "but the rescue operation is going to keep the Hywardathians extremely busy for a while."

"Not to mention the breach in the concealment regulations. That blast was detected by earthquake monitoring equipment around the world and a tsunami warning just went out to all countries with Atlantic coasts. Our people have hit Oberon with a very high level 'please explain' notice.

The pod continued to weave through the powerless saucers until the water finally calmed and there were no more to be seen.

The relief was enormous and even Kylie had a huge grin on her face. Polly let go of Josh's hand and was surprised that her finger joints ached.

The murkiness outside began to clear, although the pod was almost completely filled with seawater. Their 'suits' kept them all alive, but Polly thought it was a very weird feeling. "What now?" she asked. "Can we go home?" She wasn't quite sure if she wanted a yes or a no.

"I doubt we'll be able to clear the atmosphere as the pod is in pretty bad shape," said Gemma. "We'll get clear of this area and head for the nearest coast. The ship will pick us up and we can consider what we are going to do with you two."

Polly glanced at Josh. "We could be stuck in space forever."

Josh grinned and shrugged. "Oh, well."

"Where is the nearest coast?" asked Kylie.

"Brazil," replied Clive.

"I've always wanted to go there," said Polly.

"I'm not sure we'll have time to sightsee," said Gemma, "but we should be able to enjoy a little time on a nice quiet beach."

Nice and quiet sounds good, thought Polly. A pleasant end to their adventure.

THIRTY-ONE

Oberon tried very hard to keep his temper in check as the senior Syssinian ambassador lectured him, waving a condescending fuzzy finger via an image from his opulent residence. The man was a blur, but his surroundings were very much at odds with the Hywardathian spartan style of living and Oberon hated him for it.

Another image showed the subservient Hywardathian committee, their heads bowed as they also listened to this lecture, which pointed out all the failings of their planet and the administration of Earth. But it was just noise to Oberon. His head was filled with another image; the destruction of the grid at the very moment – the very second – of his victory. A victory that never was. That never would be.

Maybe.

Oberon had little interest in the formal proceedings, as he was also watching two other images. The first showed the churning ocean into which all the saucers from the grid had submerged. He would have liked to leave them all there to teach them a lesson, but now that power was lost they were vulnerable to any earth humans who came across the site. And that would not do.

A fleet of dredge shuttles descended into the atmosphere and would soon drag the waterlogged saucers out and return them to the mother ship. The pilots, of course, were not at fault, but Oberon would ensure they were all punished for the failure. For Hywardathians, responsibility was always a two way street.

The other image tracked the fugitive craft, which had now emerged from the ocean and was flying close to the surface towards South America. It was obviously in distress, as it had trouble maintaining a straight line of flight. The cloaking device was clearly damaged also, as it flickered in and out of sight. Perhaps it wouldn't make it – wherever it was going – and fall into the sea. There would be no shuttle rescue then, Oberon decided.

He still suspected Syssine was somehow involved, but

proving it would be difficult unless they were captured.

"Do you have them?" Oberon asked quietly.

Floothil's voice was scratchy. The Source had been severely disrupted. "Yes, we're tracking them."

Oberon expanded the image until, some miles behind the mystery craft, two saucers, Floothil's vehicle and the grid supervisor's craft, were slowly gaining on the fugitives.

"You know what will happen if you fail."

Floothil's voice was tight. "I prefer to think of what will happen if I succeed."

When all is lost, Oberon mused, someone has to win.

THIRTY-TWO

Most of the water had drained now that the pod was above the sea, but it still came up to their shins. The pod was rocking and making strange sounds as the invisible skin sometimes became visible and flickered in and out of view like a faulty television.

Polly could hardly believe they had survived and while she still worried about what would happen, as she was now presumably an intergalactic criminal, it didn't seem as bad as the alternative.

Gemma must have guessed her thoughts. Kylie's mum and dad had Polly's parent's faces, but their expressions, even the way they smiled, were completely different. "We should be able to work everything out now and get you both home."

Home. Mum and dad. *My real mum and dad.* Polly suddenly had a pang of homesickness so strong her stomach lurched. She couldn't speak, but Gemma squeezed her knee and smiled.

Josh was also grinning, the danger of a few minutes ago seemingly forgotten. At least they would be able to discuss what happened afterwards, which was something. But how could Polly live a life on earth after seeing and experiencing all this? She had been excited by the world and her future, but now life on earth felt small and limited.

A heavy thump shook the pod, which began to jerk from side to side. Clive and Gemma looked at each other. "We need a new landing spot," he said.

Gemma was thoughtful, presumably conferring with the mother ship. She nodded.

"Good news?" asked Polly.

Gemma smiled. "We will rendezvous on a beach in a few minutes. The ship will arrive soon after and fetch us."

Polly looked ahead and saw land in the distance. She glanced at Kylie, who had become more withdrawn again. "You OK?"

Kylie looked away.

"She's not OK," said Clive, "because she was counting on

being killed. It was preferable to her fate after we get her back home."

"It was her fault, too," said Kylie, pointing a finger at Polly.

Polly felt annoyed, then angry, but before she could answer, another feeling came over her. "She's right," she said, looking at Gemma and Clive. "I wasn't forced into any of this. Kylie gave me a choice and I made it. And even if I had known I was committing a crime punishable by death, I would still have said yes."

This was news to Josh, who became worried.

Kylie had a stunned look on her face and then she looked at her mother. "It's true," she said, quietly and hopefully.

"But don't let that stop you punishing her," added Polly. "It was her suggestion."

Kylie's expression turned foul yet again, which made Polly grin. *Kylie was such a spoiled brat.*

"Let's come back to this later," said Gemma urgently. "Brace yourselves for a forced landing."

Brace ourselves against what? wondered Polly. *We're in an invisible pod with nothing to hold onto!*

The pod hurtled towards a long, narrow beach which was fringed by palm trees and jungle, like a photo from a travel brochure. Polly was alarmed by the speed, which would send them ploughing through the trees like a bowling ball, but the pod lurched to the left and came around in a stuttering arc until it was lined up along the length of the beach. Then it dropped like a stone.

They hit the sand heavily and bounced into the air, the five of them all flailing limbs, grunts, groans and cries of pain. Another shuddering impact and then the pod seemed to roll for a very long time until everything was still and they lay in a tangled heap.

"Let's get out of here," said Clive, his voice muffled from the bottom of the heap.

The pod fell apart or rather, Polly thought, dissolved, as suddenly they were all rolling down a pile of sand.

Polly stood up and helped Josh to his feet. He spat out a mouthful of sand and tried to clear the rest with his fingers. "It's stuck in my teeth," he complained. "Yuck it's..." He broke off when he followed Polly's gaze down the beach.

There were two large round holes in the distance where the pod had bounced and a long, deep furrow, more than four hundred yards long which ended in their heap of sand. A mouthful of sand didn't seem important any more.

Clive looked into the sky directly above. "They'll be here any minute."

"Is that them?" asked Polly, pointing to two low flying objects rapidly approaching from the ocean.

The look on Clive's face said, 'no way!'

"Should we run?" asked Josh, sliding down the mound to the beach proper.

"No point," said Gemma, resigned. Polly didn't like the resigned tone. They had been so close!

The objects were two flying saucers, coming in so close together they seemed to be touching. They hurtled towards the pod at incredible speed, but stopped abruptly, some two hundred feet in the air, descended slowly, then dropped the last twenty feet to the beach, sending two small explosions of sand into the air. The ground shook and then the saucers were motionless, thirty yards away.

They had looked shiny and new in the grid, but closer Polly saw they were old and battered, with dents and scorch marks and the cockpits, beyond which she could see movement, were opaque with dirt.

Polly swallowed nervously and looked around. Josh was transfixed, Gemma and Kylie were scared and Clive searched the heavens frantically. *So much for reassurance.*

The top of each saucer lifted and peeled back with ear-piercing creaks and the occupants climbed out and slid down to the sand, their rifle-like weapons held in front of them. But Polly only noticed the weapons in passing as her jaw dropped open. She had seen angry green faces as the saucers dropped beneath the waves, but here they were in the flesh and she was shocked. The green-skinned people were dressed in overalls, some greener than others. And they were bald and small, none of them over four feet. They were literally little green men. Maybe some little green women, too, for all she knew. And they were all very angry.

"No one move," said Gemma, quietly. She walked a little way toward them, holding her arms open and smiling. Clive moved to her side, flashing his teeth. Neither smile extended to Kylie's parents' eyes, and Clive took another glance to the sky. Polly's heart was pounding.

The green people, seven of them, fanned out in a line, the middle one – their leader – slightly ahead.

"Hello!" shouted Gemma over the sound of the surf pounding the beach.

It was very clear to Polly that they were not here to talk and that Gemma was trying merely to stall them. It didn't work.

The green leader raised his weapon to his shoulder, the signal for the others to do the same, and yelled, "Fire!"

Yet as he said the word, the seven men flickered strangely. Polly thought it must have been the effect of their guns, but then they fired, an eruption of light pouring from the barrels. But instead of instantly vaporising Polly and her companions, the rays smashed against some unseen barrier, filling Polly's vision with a wall of light that slowly faded.

As the green men came back into view, they looked even angrier. Polly recognised the barrier as the curtain-like cloaking device she saw first with the satellite image and later when Kylie visited in the pod. The green men shimmered beyond the curtain, while inside Gemma sagged in relief.

"Suck on that!" yelled Kylie, holding her hands in an odd shape that presumably enhanced the insult.

"Shut up!" ordered Clive. "That barrier only protects us from weapons."

Polly's eyes widened as the green men dropped their guns and ran at them, straight through the barrier. "That's not good," said Josh.

The seven green men raced at them. "Jab them under the left ear! It knocks them…!"

Clive was silenced by two green men who crash tackled him and started to drag him back towards their saucers. Two more barrelled into Gemma, though she got in a punch on the first which lifted him high into the air.

That left one apiece for Polly, Josh and Kylie. Polly's arrived too quickly and head butted her in the stomach – he was only half her height – driving the air from her lungs and propelling her onto her back. He leapt after her and straddled her, raining down a couple of hard punches before she managed to grab his wrists. He was incredibly heavy and strong and seriously pissed off. She saw he had very fine features and neat little white teeth as he strained to loosen her grip. His face came close as he pushed her down into the sand and Polly noted his breath smelled, not unpleasantly, of liquorice.

He pushed harder, trying to force at least one of her arms to the side so he could press down on her neck with his forearm. She strained and head-butted him, but he merely grunted and Polly winced from pain.

He was too strong and her arms began to weaken, but suddenly the green man rolled away, unconscious. Josh grabbed Polly's hand and pulled her to her feet, proudly holding up an index finger. "Worked like a charm!"

Polly looked down at her attacker, who was sleeping like a baby. Just like the green man who attacked Josh a few feet away. Polly quickly looked around. Kylie had overpowered her guy. She had him in an arm-lock face down in the sand while she tried to find the pressure point under the guy's ear. Josh ran over to help, but, angrily waving him away with a shake of the head, Kylie found the spot and the man rolled over into a foetal position.

Polly saw Gemma had overpowered one of her assailants, but the other was putting up a strong fight. The remaining two green men almost had Clive out of the safe zone. "Go and help your dad," said Polly. Kylie raced away as Polly ran towards Gemma, closely followed by Josh.

The green man was on Gemma's back, as though she was giving a child a piggy-back, and she couldn't shake him off. Polly and Josh grabbed a leg each, causing the man to kick out ferociously as he clung to Gemma's neck. All of them crashed to the sand, where Josh sent the green man sprawling with a punch to the jaw. Gemma reacted quickly and put him to sleep with a hard prod. They all ran to help Kylie and Clive.

Kylie had dislodged one of them, allowing Clive to knock the other one out, but the last man, the leader, was laying into Kylie. Josh, clearly enjoying himself, launched a flying rugby tackle and the man landed head first in the sand. Clive and Gemma pinned him there. An angry Kylie lined up a kick to the head, but Gemma stopped her. "Don't you dare!"

"Oh, can I do this one?" asked Polly.

"Go ahead," said Clive.

Polly knelt in the sand and started prodding the struggling little man.

"It's under the left ear!"

"Sorry." Polly found the spot and the man turned jelly-like and slid to the sand, his thumb sliding gently into his mouth.

They all stood and shook off sand. Clive looked up. "Better late than never."

A dozen pods slowly descended towards them, dropping through the tunnel formed by the translucent curtain walls.

Polly looked at the seven still shapes of the green men. "Are you going to take them?"

"Not our problem," said Gemma. "Oberon will have them collected."

Polly winced at the name. What would happen now?

She looked at her companions. Gemma and Clive were exhausted, but relieved. Kylie looked confused, presumably wondering if she was better off dead compared to the punishment her parents were likely to inflict. Josh grinned happily. He stood too close again, but oddly, Polly didn't mind.

And Polly? *How do I feel?* She had a sense of things coming to an end, but also that perhaps they were just beginning. She – they – had been through a lot and as she looked at their faces, she felt a very warm mushy feeling and tears formed in her eyes. She smiled because the tears made everyone look blurred.

Everyone was looking at her.

"Group hug?" she suggested with considerable success.

THE NEXT DAY

AFTERMATH
(or, in this case, before maths)

Polly stopped on the corner a block away from school. She could see kids milling around the playground as though nothing had happened. Which, for them, was fair enough. Nothing had actually happened as far as they were concerned. Well, almost.

Polly and Josh had only spent a few hours aboard Kylie's spaceship. Not long enough for Josh, but enough time for him to get an idea of what Polly had experienced. Gemma and Clive had conferred with their peers after changing back to their normal blurry appearance – the look on Josh's face had been priceless – and the consensus had been that she and Josh should go back and pretend they had no memory of anything that happened.

Oberon's failure to capture them had been turned against him and the Hywardathian high command by the Syssine authorities, who had now launched a full enquiry. Syssine could veto any request from Hywardath to question Polly and Josh, particularly as Oberon had no evidence of their involvement in the incident so, despite his suspicions, he was powerless to pursue them.

She did, however, worry about the school teacher's anger. They had all watched when Oberon accompanied the recovery party to the beach. The leader, lying peacefully sleeping in the sand, sucking his thumb, had sent Oberon into a frenzy. He had applied a number of heavy kicks to the man's backside before regaining control of himself.

Oberon's hold on power, Gemma told her, would probably continue, mainly because the short time in charge meant he could offset most of the blame for the failure to others. Also, unofficially, they had heard that he had threatened his superior committee and vowed to take down half the senior command if they moved against him.

The upshot was that Oberon and the Hywardathians had enough of a power struggle on their plate to be too concerned about a couple of schoolkids who may or may not have broken the rules.

Gemma and Clive would run the Syssine investigation to ensure the enquiry went nowhere, which meant their ship would be in Earth's orbit for some time, something Polly found reassuring. Kylie was also happy, too, as it meant a stay of execution, so to speak. Her parents had enrolled her in a new school that, from what she had heard, apparently made Polly's look exciting. *It must be really bad*, thought Polly, gazing at the uninspiring buildings.

"What are you waiting for?" Kylie spoke in her ear.

"I'm meeting Josh. We'll go in together."

"I see."

"What does that mean," asked Polly, defensively.

"Nothing. Oh, here he comes."

Josh arrived, grinning. Polly couldn't help but grin back. "Did you sleep?" he asked.

"Not much." She had tried to sleep on the floor, because there was no furniture. Her parents were due home today and she had left them a note saying she would explain why there was no furniture after school. She hadn't figured out what to say, so it would be an interesting conversation.

"I didn't get a wink. It was..." He looked at her closely. "That must hurt."

Polly had a black eye and a bruise in the middle of her forehead. "It's a bit sore, but..." She shrugged. "Shall we go in?"

She had a strong urge to grab Josh's hand, but resisted it. He was walking very close and that was enough for now.

They walked through the gate into the normal world, but Polly and Josh were no longer normal. They never would be again.

A figure raced across the playground and grabbed Polly by the shoulder. It was Kate, almost beside herself. "Oh my God, did you hear what happened?"

Polly shook her head.

"Gwen and her stupid friends broke into a classroom last night and trashed it before passing out. They must have been on drugs or something. You should see it! And what about Martins Woods near your house, Josh? They've gone! It's all over breakfast TV. They think it was a meteor, but there's no impact crater. I reckon it must have exploded in the atmosphere like the Tunguska event in Russia in 1908.

There's no other explanation, although there was no explosion either. What a thing to happen! Here! And... what happened to your face?"

Polly smiled. "I was beaten up by an alien."

"That's funny. I also had a weird dream where Gwen was dressed in overalls and froze me with a ray gun. The world has gone mad!" Kate was loving it, Polly realised.

"I'm going to be late for maths, so let's talk at lunchtime, eh?"

"OK," said Kate. Polly walked away, but Kate tugged at her arm. "And Oberon has gone. Bit sudden, don't you think? The new science teacher is over there. He's really weird."

Polly saw the man talking to Mrs Elswick, the headmistress. He was strange, dressed in a very long coat and huge boots. His face was very pale and he looked angrier than Oberon.

"What's his name?

"Jwerkevski or something," said Kate.

Polly glanced at Josh. "I think we'll stay away from him."

They resumed their walk to the school building. "That's Jwerqep, alright," said Kylie's voice in Polly's ear. "Maybe Oberon has a sense of humour after all."

"Do you think he knows," asked Josh.

"Suspects, probably," said Kylie. "But mum and dad reckon he can't prove anything.

Mrs Elswick had disappeared inside the building and Jwerqep eyed them with some hostility as Polly and Josh walked past him and went up the stairs. "Not a happy chappie, is he?" said Polly.

They had almost reached the door when the headmistress barrelled back out through it and confronted Polly, waving a piece of paper.

"Miss Hart," she announced, in her official voice, "I have the results of your urine test. Come with me." She turned on her heel and went back inside.

Kylie muttered something in Polly's ear which sounded like, "Oh, shit!"

Polly followed Mrs Elswick down the corridor, puzzled. "What happened, Kylie?" she whispered.

Silence.

"Kylie! Kylie! Kylie..."

THE END

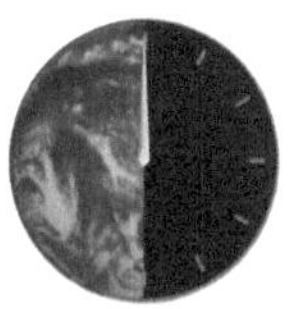

Elsewhen Press

delivering outstanding new talents in speculative fiction

Visit the Elsewhen Press website at elsewhen.press for the latest information on all of our titles, authors and events; to read our blog; find out where to buy our books and ebooks; or to place an order.

Sign up for the Elsewhen Press InFlight Newsletter at elsewhen.press/newsletter

TimeStorm
Steve Harrison

In 1795 a convict ship leaves England for New South Wales in Australia. Nearing its destination, it encounters a savage storm but, miraculously, the battered ship stays afloat and limps into Sydney Harbour. The convicts rebel, overpower the crew and make their escape, destroying the ship in the process. Fleeing the sinking vessel with only the clothes on their backs, the survivors struggle ashore.

Among the escaped convicts, seething resentments fuel an appetite for brutal revenge against their former captors, while the crew attempts to track down and kill or recapture the escapees. However, it soon becomes apparent that both convicts and crew have more to concern them than shipwreck and a ruthless fight for survival; they have arrived in Sydney in 2017.

TimeStorm is a thrilling epic adventure story of revenge, survival and honour. In the literary footsteps of Hornblower, comes Lieutenant Christopher 'Kit' Blaney, an old-fashioned hero, a man of honour, duty and principle. But dragged into the 21st century… literally.

A great fan of the grand seafaring adventure fiction of CS Forester, Patrick O'Brien and Alexander Kent and modern action thriller writers like Lee Child, Steve Harrison combines several genres in his fast-paced debut novel as a group of desperate men from the 1700s clash in modern-day Sydney.

ISBN: 9781908168542 (epub, kindle) / 9781908168443 (368pp paperback)

Visit bit.ly/TimeStorm

Existence is Elsewhen

Twenty stories from twenty great authors including

John Gribbin
Steve Harrison
Christopher Nuttall
Douglas Thompson

The title *Existence is Elsewhen* paraphrases the last sentence of André Breton's 1924 *Manifesto of Surrealism*, perfectly summing up the intent behind this anthology of stories from a wonderful collection of authors. Different worlds... different times. It's what Elsewhen Press has been about since we launched our first title in 2011.

Here, we present twenty science fiction stories for you to enjoy. We are delighted that headlining this collection is the fantastic **John Gribbin,** with a worrying vision of medical research in the near future. Future global healthcare is the theme of **J A Christy's** story; while the ultimate in spare part surgery is where **Dave Weaver** takes us. **Edwin Hayward's** search for a renewable protein source turns out to be digital; and **Tanya Reimer's** story with characters we think we know gives us pause for thought about another food we take for granted. Evolution is examined too, with **Andy McKell's** chilling tale of what states could become if genetics are used to drive policy. Similarly, **Robin Moran's** story explores the societal impact of an undesirable evolutionary trend; while **Douglas Thompson** provides a truly surreal warning of an impending disaster that will reverse evolution, with dire consequences.

On a lighter note, we have satire from **Steve Harrison** discovering who really owns the Earth (and why); and **Ira Nayman,** who uses the surreal alternative realities of his *Transdimensional Authority* series as the setting for a detective story mash-up of Agatha Christie and Dashiel Hammett. Pursuing the crime-solving theme, **Peter Wolfe** explores life, and death, on a space station; while **Stefan Jackson** follows a police investigation into some bizarre cold-blooded murders in a cyberpunk future. Going into the past, albeit an 1831 set in the alternate Britain of his *Royal Sorceress* series, **Christopher Nuttall** reports on an investigation into a girl with strange powers.

Strange powers in the present-day is the theme for **Tej Turner**, who tells a poignant tale of how extra-sensory perception makes it easier for a husband to bear his dying wife's last few days. Difficult decisions are the theme of **Chloe Skye's** heart-rending story exploring personal sacrifice. Relationships aren't always so close, as **Susan Oke's** tale demonstrates, when sibling rivalry is taken to the limit. Relationships are the backdrop to **Peter R. Ellis's** story where a spectacular mid-winter event on a newly-colonised distant planet involves a Madonna and Child. Coming right back to Earth and in what feels like an almost imminent future, **Siobhan McVeigh** tells a cautionary tale for anyone thinking of using technology to deflect the blame for their actions. Building on the remarkable setting of Pera from her *LiGa* series, and developing Pera's legendary *Book of Shadow*, **Sanem Ozdural** spins the creation myth of the first light tree in a lyrical and poetic song. Also exploring language, the master of fantastika and absurdism, **Rhys Hughes,** extrapolates the way in which language changes over time, with an entertaining result.

ISBN: 9781908168955 (epub, kindle) / ISBN: 9781908168856 (320pp paperback)

About Steve Harrison

Steve Harrison was born in Yorkshire, England, grew up in Lancashire, migrated to New Zealand and eventually settled in Sydney, Australia, where he lives with his wife.

As he juggled careers in shipping, insurance, online gardening and the postal service, Steve wrote short stories, sports articles and a long running newspaper humour column called *HARRISCOPE: a mix of ancient wisdom and modern nonsense*.

His first novel *TimeStorm*, published by Elsewhen Press, was Highly Commended in the Fellowship of Australian Writers (FAW) National Literary Awards, Jim Hamilton Award in the fantasy/science fiction category, for an unpublished novel of sustained quality and distinction by an Australian author.

www.ingramcontent.com/pod-product-compliance
Lightning Source LLC
Chambersburg PA
CBHW030747190726
48285CB00003B/740
9781911409465